The Governess Tales

Sweeping romances with fairy-tale endings!

Meet Joanna Radcliff, Rachel Talbot,
Isabel Morton and Grace Bertram.

These four friends grew up together in
Madame Dubois's school for young ladies, where
they indulged in midnight feasts, broke the rules
and shared their innermost secrets!

But now they are thrust into the real world and
each must adapt to their new life as a governess.

One will rise, one will travel, one will run
and one will find her real home...

And each will meet their soul mate,
who'll give them the happy-ever-after
they've always dreamed of!

Read Joanna's story in
The Cinderella Governess

Read Rachel's story in
Governess to the Sheikh

Read Isabel's story in
The Runaway Governess

All available now!

And look for Grace's story in
The Governess's Secret Baby

Coming soon!

Author Note

When my editor suggested I write about a woman with a natural gift for song, I was deeply interested.

Having grown up in a home with very little music and a mother who was tone deaf, I am impressed by people who have musical ability and can elicit an emotional response from a listener. I once watched with amazement as people around me tried to control their emotions when a much-lauded singer performed, and I felt no response. However, the beauty of violin music has caused my tears to flow.

Stage fright is very real, though, and some people who have musical talent resist every opportunity to perform, even in front of close friends. I cannot imagine a bird who would not sing to the heavens, and it is sad when a gifted performer cannot experience the joy of sharing their good fortune with an audience. Even if stage fright prevents some people from singing or playing music in front of others, I hope they often express their musical abilities for their own enjoyment.

My mother sang to her children, though, and her voice was beautiful to us. I wish everyone who reads this story and has the ability to sing takes a moment to delight in the sound of their song.

Liz Tyner

—

The Runaway Governess

Special thanks and acknowledgment are given to Liz Tyner for her contribution to The Governess Tales series.

Recycling programs
for this product may
not exist in your area.

ISBN-13: 978-0-373-29905-8

The Runaway Governess

Copyright © 2016 by Harlequin Books S.A.

Printed in U.S.A.

www.Harlequin.com

Liz Tyner lives with her husband on an Oklahoma acreage she imagines is similar to the one in the children's book *Where the Wild Things Are*. Her lifestyle is a blend of old and new, and is sometimes comparable to how people lived long ago. Liz is a member of various writing groups and has been writing since childhood. For more about her, visit liztyner.com.

Books by Liz Tyner

Harlequin Historical

The Governess Tales
The Runaway Governess

English Rogues and Grecian Goddesses
Safe in the Earl's Arms
A Captain and a Rogue
Forbidden to the Duke

Stand-Alone Novel
The Notorious Countess

Visit the Author Profile page at Harlequin.com.

Chapter One

Isabel watched from the window as the older couple's driver stepped on to his carriage perch and called to the horses. She'd not believed her luck when she'd spotted the man and woman waiting for their carriage to be readied. It had taken her all of a minute to find out their destination and pour out her sad tale.

She didn't want to think of what might happen when the other coach arrived in Sussex without her. But the family could find another governess. This was her one chance. Her chance to soar.

Isabel turned to the man whose eyelids almost concealed his vision and the woman who matched him in age, but her eyes danced with life. Isabel clasped her hands at her chest and promised herself she would never again lie, except in extreme circumstances such as this. Taking a deep breath, she let the words rise from deep within herself. 'You have *saved* my life.'

A barmaid, hair frazzled from the August heat, stood

behind the couple. She looked up long enough to roll her eyes heavenward.

'Miss…' the wife patted Isabel's glove '…we just could not bear that your evil uncle was selling you into marriage to a man old enough to be your father—and your betrothed a murderer as well.'

'Thank you so much.' She sighed. 'If my parents were alive today…' they were, but they'd understand and forgive her once they discovered how famous she'd be '…they would fall upon their knees in gratitude for your saving my life.'

The barmaid snorted and Isabel sighed with emphasis, knowing she mustn't let the couple notice the scepticism.

'You're sure if you go to London with us, your family will give you a home?' the wife questioned.

'Oh. Yes.' The word lengthened to twice its usual length. 'Aunt Anna, my mother's sister, who has no idea of the tragedy that has befallen me as my great-uncle would not allow me paper or ink, would give me refuge in a heartbeat. I have always been her favourite niece, of course. It is just that my uncle told her I was…tragically killed in a fall from a horse, trampled by hooves and had to be immediately buried because the sight was too exceptionally hideous for anyone to see as I would not have wanted to be remembered as such.'

The woman's eyes could not have been more kind. 'Tragic.'

'Yes. Frightfully so.'

The man arched one brow, enough that Isabel could

see the scepticism. 'We will certainly deliver you to your aunt in London,' he said. 'To her doorstep.'

'I will be in your gratitude for ever.' Oh, good heavens. That might not end well as she had no aunt in London. 'It is near Charles Street—Drury Lane.' She almost shivered, just saying the words *Drury Lane*. Not that she was going to be an actress. Oh, no. Not something so disreputable as that. Her voice would be her fortune. Her very best friends, Joanna, Rachel and Grace, had told her time and time again at Madame Dubois's School for Young Ladies that she could sing better than anyone else they'd ever heard. Even the headmistress, Madame Dubois, had commented that Isabel's singing voice was bearable. Since Madame Dubois had called Grace Bertram 'passable,' whom Isabel thought favoured a painting of a heavenly angel—then to have a bearable voice was the highest praise from Madame Dubois.

She'd been so lucky Mr Thomas Wren had heard of her when he attended one of the school presentations. Now he was her patron—albeit a secret patron. She would be the lead of his new musicale. She would sing her heart out. Even though her voice was not perfection itself, something about the way she sang stirred people. When she was performing, others would listen and eyes would water. Nothing made her happier than when someone gave her that rapt attention and they were brought to tears. She *loved* making people cry in such a way.

She gathered her satchel and linked her arm around the older woman's. 'My Aunt Anna will be so grateful.'

'We must meet her and make sure she will not return

you to that dreadful man.' The woman's voice oozed concern.

Isabel leaned forward and batted her lashes. 'Of course. You simply must meet my aunt.' Easily said, albeit completely impossible.

The couple's meal was left behind, crumbs still clinging to the man's waistcoat, and they spirited her to their carriage.

When she stepped into the vehicle, she slumped a bit, keeping the man's frame between her and the windows of the coaching inn. It would not do for anyone from the other carriage to note her leaving before the end of the brief stop. She grasped her satchel and settled into the seat, ever so pleased to be leaving the governess part of her life behind. True, she had enjoyed the friendships of the school. But as she became closer and closer to graduation, she'd felt trapped. Mr Thomas Wren's notice of her was indeed fortunate. Apparently another student's father had informed him of Isabel's voice. Mr Wren had known the rules of the school and had known to be secretive in their correspondence. He'd offered her the lead in a new production he'd planned.

She could barely concentrate on the task at hand for thinking of the good fortune of her life. This change of carriage would even make a grand tale. She could imagine recounting the tale of how she stowed away, risking all to travel with a couple she could but hope was reputable, and who transported her at great personal risk to help her achieve her life's dream.

Isabel spoke as quickly as the wheels turned on the carriage, not wanting to give the couple a chance to think too much of the events of the day. She recounted honest tales of her youth at the governess school, leaving out the parts about the visits to her parents—and keeping as close to the facts as possible. She had already used her share of untruths for the year and it would not be good to blunder at this point.

When the carriage neared Drury Lane, Isabel kept one eye to the road, knowing she must make a quick decision.

A woman wearing a tattered shawl and with one strand of grey hanging from her knot of hair walked near an opening between two structures. Isabel saw the chance she had to take.

'My aunt,' she gasped, pointing. 'It's my aunt.' She turned to the man across. 'Stop the carriage.'

He raised his hand to the vehicle top, thumping.

She bolted up and tumbled out the door before the conveyance fully stopped, scurrying to the woman. 'Aunt. Aunt,' she called out. The woman must have had a niece somewhere because she paused, turning to look at Isabel.

Isabel scurried, then darted sideways behind a looming structure, running with all her might, turning right, then left. When she knew she was not being chased, she stopped, leaning against the side of a building. She gulped, and when her breathing righted she reflected.

She would become the best songstress in all London. She knew it. Mr Thomas Wren knew it. The future was hers. Now she just had to find it. She was lost beyond hope in the biggest city of the world.

Isabel tried to scrape the street refuse from her shoe without it being noticed what she was doing. She didn't know how she was going to get the muck off her dress. A stranger who wore a drooping cravat was eyeing her bosom quite openly. Only the fact that she was certain she could outrun him, even in her soiled slippers, kept her from screaming.

He tipped his hat to her and ambled into a doorway across the street.

Her dress, the only one with the entire bodice made from silk, would have to be altered now. The rip in the skirt—*thank you, dog who didn't appreciate my trespassing in his gardens*—was not something she could mend. She didn't think it could be fixed. The skirt would have to be ripped from the bodice and replaced. That would not be simple.

How? How had she got herself into this? Oh, well, she decided, she would buy all new clothing when Mr Thomas Wren gave her the funds he'd promised.

Yet, she didn't quite know where to begin in her search for him and she'd have to find him before nightfall. She would certainly ask someone as soon as she left this disreputable part of London. The dead fish head at her feet didn't give her the encouragement she needed.

But then she looked up. Straight into a ray of sunshine illuminating a placard hanging from a building. A bird on it. She didn't have to search. Providence had put out its golden torch and led her right to the very place she was searching for. This sign—well, the sign was a sign of her future. This was Mr Thomas Wren's establishment. The man with the ill-mannered eyes had gone inside but still, one did sometimes have to sing for unpleasant people and one could only hope they gleaned some lesson from the song. She had quite the repertoire of songs with lessons hidden in the words and knew when to use them.

She opened the satchel, pulled out the plume, and examined it. She straightened the unfortunate new crimp in it as best she could and put the splash of blue into the little slot she'd added to her bonnet. She picked up her satchel, realising she had got a bit of the street muck on it—and began again her new life.

Begin her new life, she repeated to herself, unmoving. She looked at the paint peeling from the exterior and watched as another man came from the doorway, waistcoat buttoned at an angle. Gripping the satchel with both hands, she locked her eyes on the wayward man.

Her stomach began a song of its own and very off-key. She couldn't turn back. She had no funds to hire a carriage. She knew no one in London but Mr Wren. And he had been so complimentary and kind to everyone at Madame Dubois's School for Young Ladies. Not just her. She could manage. She would have to. His compliments had not been idle, surely.

She held her head the way she planned to look over the audience when she first walked on stage and put one foot in front of the other, ignoring everything but the entrance in front of her.

As she walked through the doorway, head high, the first thing Isabel noticed was the stage. A woman was singing. Isabel concealed her shudder and hoped her ears would forgive her. She supposed she would be replacing the woman. The songstress's bosom was obviously well padded because it would be hard for nature to be so overzealous, but perhaps it had been to make up for the error of her voice.

A man with silver hair and a gold-tipped cane sat gaping at the stage. The woman put her arms tighter to the side of her body and bent forward to emphasise her words.

Isabel turned her head. She could not believe it. She would have to have a word with Mr Wren about this, although—

Then her eyes skipped from person to person to person. It would take more than a word. Men sat around a table playing Five Card Loo, but it seemed only pence were on the table.

The men at the game could not decide whether to watch the stage or their hand. Two women obviously championed their favourites, alternately cheering and gasping at the cards. Then the game ended. Whoops erupted. A man stood, bowed to the table, and waited. The other players reached into their purses, took out coins and handed them to the women. The winner put his arm around the women's waists and led them through a curtained hallway.

She let out a breath and all her dreams fluttered away with it.

William strode under the faded placard and stepped into Wren House, giving himself a moment to let his eyes adjust from the bright August sun to the dim light of a world only illuminated because men needed to see the cards in their hand. He'd have to go to a stable to get the scent of Wren's out of his nostrils.

If his father knew this was where Cousin Sylvester spent every Wednesday night, things might have been different. But now Sylvester had Marvel and Ivory, the two best horses in England and the only ones whose eyes flickered regard when William neared them. The beasts would always stick out their necks for a treat when William appeared. 'Spoiled,' the stable master muttered each time.

William always replied, 'And worth it.'

William surveyed the table, and spotted his cousin immediately. Sylvester mumbled a greeting and two others looked over, recognising William and giving him a grunt of their own before they returned to the cards. William jerked his head sideways, motioning for Sylvester to join him. The answer, a quick shake of Sylvester's head, and a brief upturn of the lips, didn't surprise William. He took a seat near the corner where he could watch the room. He didn't want anyone at his back. A woman on stage finished singing, thankfully.

He ordered an ale and when the barmaid brought the drink, her brows lifted in question and she looked to the curtain at the back. He shook his head, smiling to soften the refusal. His fingers clasped the mug, but as he lifted it, he paused. Sticky residue lay under his touch. Jam? He gazed into the liquid, half-expecting to see something floating, but nothing looked alive in it. Then he sat the mug back on the table.

A perfect ending to a perfect day, but Marvel and Ivory were worth it.

And having a roof over one's head did have some merit.

William's father had visited early in the morning and had pontificated well into the day. The Viscount had picked a fine time to regain an interest in life and an excellent plan to disinherit his only son. The Viscount knew the entailment laws as well as anyone. He had to leave his property to William. But he could, however, lease his nephew the estate for the next fifty years. Upon the Viscount's death, William would receive the proceeds of the lease. A bargain to Sylvester at one pound per year.

If his father had mentioned that once, he'd mentioned it one hundred times. And he'd had no smell of brandy on his breath.

The inheritance could be dealt with later. Marvel and Ivory were already gone from the stables.

Sylvester smirked at the cards, but William knew the smugness was directed his way. No hand could be that good.

William glanced around and, even though his eyes didn't stop until they returned to his mug, he noted the woman sitting on a bench at the other side of the room. She sat close to the wall, her body slanted away from the group of men. The shadowed interior hid more of her than it revealed. He was certain she had a face, but she'd pulled the bonnet off-centre and it perched askew so he couldn't see her features unless she turned his way. If not for the plume, he wouldn't have noticed her.

In one movement to relax his frame, he twisted his chair just a bit in her direction so he could stare forward, but see her from the corner of his eye.

The barmaid sauntered by him. He waved a coin her way and asked for another drink, discarding any thought of asking for a clean mug. He didn't imagine she would take kindly to that, particularly when he saw the crust at her fingernails.

He thought the lady at the bench was above the others in the room, particularly by the way her back didn't leave the wall behind her and her hands gripped the satchel as if it might protect her. He wondered why she stayed.

The barmaid plunked another mug in front of him and brushed against his side before leaving.

Nothing floated in the liquid. Nothing stuck to his hand. He would take that as an omen that the ale was— he took a drink and smothered a cough. The mug's contents could have been watered down more. He hoped his tongue hadn't blistered. The owner apparently didn't mind if his customers wobbled a bit and knew drink could loosen the ties of a purse.

The door opened and light dappled across the bonnet the miss on the bench wore. She turned towards the light. For an instant he could see wisps of her hair. Copper.

He took a small sip. The ale tasted better than it had before.

Copper. Just under the ghastly plume. His favourite colour of hair—now. He didn't think he'd ever seen a woman with just that shade of hair. A shame the bonnet covered it.

Someone from Sylvester's table belched and the woman with the falling plume stiffened even more and twisted away from them.

William noted the dress. Not quite the dash of colour his sisters insisted on. It reminded him of something he might see on a miss at a country fair, yet not a walking dress. Not a soirée dress either. He could see underskirts peeking from a tear in the skirt. All his muscles stilled. A woman would not be going about with such a rip in her skirts. Particularly not one sitting so straight and gloves locked on her satchel.

He stood, mug still in hand, planning to offer her his assistance. At his movement, her eyes darted to him. She took in a breath and the back of her head bumped against the wall.

He gave her a grim-lipped smile. The woman didn't want him to approach her, obviously. Perhaps she was at Wren's hoping to find her husband. In that case, William certainly didn't want to draw notice her way. He sat the mug at the table and moved to stand at Sylvester's side.

Putting a hand on the woollen shoulder of Sylvester's coat, William leaned forward. 'I must talk with you.'

'Anything you have to say,' Sylvester's voice boomed, 'you can say in front of my friends.'

'I'm sure I can,' William answered. 'But I thought we might step out to speak of family matters.' Sylvester had to have noticed if the Viscount was sotted when he gave the horses away.

'These men are like family,' Sylvester answered.

'Only better, because they do not gift me with horses not worth feeding.' He spoke to the man on his left. 'Did I tell you my uncle gave me two horses? Broken-down old things. I could hardly refuse them and hurt the man's feelings, particularly if his mind is clear as a cloudless day.'

Sylvester wouldn't have said the Viscount's mind was clear if it wasn't true. 'I will take them off your hands.'

'Oh, I could not do that to you.' Sylvester let out a breath. 'I'll just keep them for now, though I don't see feeding them like they're used to. A bit on the plump side. A few less rations will be good for them. Or maybe I should just put them down.'

William tightened his grip on Sylvester's coat. 'You will feed them properly and you will care for them.'

Sylvester laughed. 'Just having a jest with you, dear Cousin. I know those beasts are your favourites. Your father does as well. Can't think what he's up to.' He brushed a hand over his chin, tugging at it. 'Or maybe I can.' Sylvester spoke to the other players. 'If Cousin William doesn't get it on his mind to marry and have an heir, sadly, the title will pass to my son, should I have one, and I intend to have a full brood. I can't think if I were in his boots that would be difficult. I'd be wedded, bedded and enjoying the bondage of matrimony, although that is not how I put it to Uncle. I told him I'm deeply in love and near to proposing. And I am.' He smirked again. 'Deeply in love with William's inheritance and near to proposing to…' Looking around the table, he asked, 'Any of you have an unmarried sister who wants a husband?'

'Not that we'd let wed you,' one of the men answered. The rest laughed.

'I will have Marvel and Ivory back.' William released his cousin's shoulder.

'Well, I'm going to wager the horses if I run out of funds. Of course, with the way my luck is going tonight, I'll own everyone's livestock before I leave.'

'I'll buy them from whomever you lose them to.' William leaned forward and briefly met eyes with the others at the table. 'If any of you men win those horses from Sylvester, I'll buy them from you at double what you'd get at Tattersalls.'

The others grinned, chuckling.

'That's why Uncle is concerned about you, William.' Sylvester pulled out a card, waved it for others to see the back of and then dropped it on to the table with a flourish. 'You're planning to buy a pair of old horses not worth a pence when you might be able to win them with a single game of chance. Yet, you gambled away a carriage once. You've even lost your own boots and then threw in the stockings. It's all a game to you, but you don't care if you win or lose.' He raked in the coins. 'I play to win.'

'I enjoy the sport,' William said. He'd had enough of the night.

Turning to leave, he made it as far as the door before looking back at that feathery trimming. His youngest sister had once pulled such an adornment from his middle sister's bonnet and the roof had barely stayed on the house in the aftermath.

He retraced his steps to the sticky mug. He sat, staring straight ahead. The joy of being called a wastrel by one's father meant William could sit all night watching a plume on a bonnet. He tried to imagine the bird that lost the feather, but he could only see a caricature of a bird prancing, preening, and sprouting a blast of unnatural feathers from its head, while wobbling under the weight.

He needed to stop with the ale.

The singer returned to the stage and opened her mouth. He would not call it singing, exactly, but if one didn't care much about quality of voice, then it could pass the time. He swatted at a fly that landed on the edge of the mug. Just because he didn't want the drink didn't mean he intended to share.

The woman with the tear in her dress adjusted the bag in her lap. The singer hit a high note, or had her foot mashed by a carriage. He squeezed his eyes shut, wishing he could do the same for his ears. As the note ended, he opened his eyes while pulling the cleaner mug to his lips. His hand stopped when he caught Miss Plume watching him.

She looked away and his hand moved again. He finished the drink, not tasting it. He would wait until her husband arrived to take her home. If the husband walked in with some woman hanging on him, William would make sure to give the man a reminder of propriety. A man didn't embarrass his wife so. To let her wait alone in a place like Wren's was unforgiveable.

William looked directly at her, not able to see through the glove on her left hand, or into her mind to see what memories resided there.

He eased back in the chair. He wasn't leaving until she did.

Isabel knew the man who wanted his horses was aware of her. But he was hoping to get his stock returned and he wanted them fed properly. The other men even seemed more decent after he'd spoken with them. When she'd noted him walking to the door, leaving, fear tremored in her midsection and she'd had an urge to follow, not wanting to remain without his presence. But he'd paused and returned to his chair. He must want to be certain he received those horses.

She peered around her bonnet brim, searching for Wren.

Mr Wren should be about. Earlier she'd asked that barmaid and the woman had glared and mumbled that he'd be in when he walked in. Wren had told Isabel he would meet her. He'd said he spent each day working, except when he attended Sunday Services. She no longer believed that, unless he attended with her aunt.

The one, William they'd called him—his face had pinched when the singer got stuck on that dreadful note. Apparently he could hear quite well. And when he'd opened his eyes and caught her examining his expression, he'd looked startled.

He was rather ordinary except for those legs that didn't want to fit under the table, but yet, he made her feel safer.

Then the barmaid approached and brought him another mug. He'd not requested it, but he took it. The woman brushed a lock of his hair over his ear, which hadn't needed touching, but Isabel couldn't blame the woman. That hair did make a person curious about what it felt like.

The woman whispered something to him. He laughed, changing everything in his face, and creating the same thump in Isabel's heart that she felt when the music was perfect. His smile could carry its own tune.

He saw Isabel watching. He gave a flicker of a smile and shrugged his shoulders.

She ducked her head, pleased not to feel so alone.

The barmaid was a tart, but Isabel couldn't blame her for noticing him. He was the only man in the place who didn't make her feel like bathing.

The door opened and she saw the familiar checked waistcoat of Mr Thomas Wren, his eyebrows as light as the gold buttons on his coat. She wasn't as impressed with the fastenings as she'd been before.

He made his way to her bench, his grin almost suffocating her. She scooted away, gently wedging the soiled side of her satchel in his direction as she put it between them. Half her bottom was already off the bench, but she could not let Mr Thomas Wren's breath closer. Apparently he'd had something to do with the fish she'd seen in the street.

She forced a positive lilt to her voice. 'Mr Wren, I do believe you forgot to tell me something in your letters.'

'No.' His eyes widened. 'I can't think I did.' He put

an arm at the back of the bench. He could not possibly have eight hairy fingers on one hand, but that's what it felt like when his knuckles brushed at the top of her glove. 'You really do sing quite well, Miss Morton, and I am happy to have you on my stage.'

'You mentioned a suitable chaperon.'

'Why, yes, I believe I did. And if you look around, you'll notice there are plenty of women here to…'

She lowered her chin, but raised her brows at him. He didn't appear chagrined at all. Instead, he grinned while his eyes devoured her.

The air in the room boiled into her and she could hardly force the words past the sweltering heat. 'I fear that on the way here,' she spoke, 'I realised that I cannot forgo my duties as a governess. I will not be able to accept the position.'

She didn't know how she'd manage or what she'd do. She had hardly enough coins in her satchel to buy bread. She could only hope for another married couple to notice her and this time she would tell the truth. Some of it. She hoped she had not totally used her portion of lies for the year.

'Oh, my.' Wren's words mocked themselves. 'I seem to recall in your correspondence a distinct aversion to those duties and a sincere wish to follow your true talent. And you are quite talented, Miss…Morton.'

'I can't. I wouldn't be—'

He leaned forward, his voice covering her with fumes of the summer heat. 'I am saddened. But I admit, I considered the possibility you would not wish to continue in our bargain.' He stood, his tongue clucking as if he'd caught her doing something terribly wrong. He whisked one hand to the bottom of the satchel and the other over hers on the grip. Involuntarily, she jerked her hands from his touch.

Brows lifted, he turned, striding away. 'Come with me to my office and I will see what we must do now.'

'We can discuss it here.' She stood, running a hand down the side of her skirt, hoping to pull that rend together just a little more.

He paused, turning back. 'Will you be needing funds to return to your home?' His voice faded so low that she read the words on his lips more than heard them.

He hadn't given her money for the trip to London, saying he'd once done so and the woman he'd hired never arrived.

She couldn't answer.

'Then come with me,' he continued. 'We can discuss it in my office. The funds are in my safe.' He looked to the window. 'The hour is getting late. I hate to think of you alone on the streets, in darkness and finding your way. It's not safe at night for a woman out and about. Just last month, one of the women, Molly, went out. They found her the next morning, bruises on her neck. Blood on her hands. Buried her in a pauper's grave.'

Before she answered, he was at the curtain, her satchel clasped in his hand.

She stood, glancing around, hoping no one would see her follow. She would be ruined. If she wasn't already. But it was better to be ruined than buried in some lost grave. She didn't quite think Mr Wren would be rushing to see that a proper burial would take place.

She watched his retreating coat. She would never again complain about being a governess.

He had the only funds she had—hidden in the bag. An unmarked grave would not quite fulfil her dreams. She followed, planning to grab the satchel as soon as he released it and run.

Stepping through the curtain and into a cramped office, relief brightened her spirit. A copy of a Mrs Radcliffe novel lay on his desk. Surely a man who liked to read had some refinement.

'Please sit.' He indicated a chair, one rung missing from the back. She did, noting he sat the satchel down at his right side, his body between her and the bag. He still stood. He turned.

'I don't believe you realise what position you put me in.' He shook his head while picking up the novel. 'We can't have that.'

'I just—' She moved to rise, the fish smell wafting over her.

He crashed the novel to the wall. Before she could believe what her eyes told her had just happened, his hand clamped on her shoulder. The surprise and force thrust her on to the wooden chair seat.

'I—'

'You *wish* to hear me out.' She could feel all of the fingers again. This time they pressed. Pinched. His hand slid, not releasing, until his thumbnail rested in the soft skin at the base of her jaw. He took a step, moving his body forward, still beside her, her head held back by his thumb. Her backbone firm against the chair, him above forcing her neck back. He untied her bonnet strings and pushed it to the floor.

Her mouth dried. She could breathe—just. Her hands clasped his wrist, pushing. But she could not move him.

'Sweet, you have to understand, I looked for a long time to find just the right woman. Just the right blend of woman. Taller than most so she stood out. A haunting voice that could also trill in happiness. A look of freshness. Eyes that made a man think he could see her wanting him. Lips that he could imagine on his body.'

'No,' she gasped.

'Do not interrupt.' He put his other hand over her mouth and leaned closer. She shuddered. All of his bulk loomed over her, his cheeks ruddy. 'You understand that even the other women would increase their coin by satisfying your cast-offs. You would even be a boon to them.' He paused. 'Feel free to nod.'

He took his hand from her throat, but not her mouth. One of his legs pressed against hers.

'Nod.' His eyes glistened with an intensity that covered her like the coil of a serpent's skin against hers.

She didn't move. Her lower face was in his vice-like grasp. She could feel the pressure of his thumb. The tightness. But no pain. Nothing hurt. Nothing. Except she could not breathe.

His clothes rustled and he moved so that she could see nothing but his face.

'You understand, I have to have you. I have no choice. No choice. I've spent too much time finding you and waiting on you.' He reached to his waistcoat and a thin sliver of steel flashed in front of her. The blade pressed at her neck. 'Nod, Sweet.'

She did—the barest amount.

'You understand there are rules one must observe to work here. You will learn them in time.' The knife moved, tracing the circle of her neck. 'Nod, Sweet.' He moved her head up and down with his hand. 'Get used to that.'

She remembered how easy it had been to convince the couple of a lie. She nodded, moving her hand from his wrist. He trailed the blade in the same way of an artist's pen making swirls on a page. He slipped the tip to her shoulder. 'You don't have to worry about me hurting your face, permanently. But a man might be aroused by a gentle scar trailing away under clothing.' The blade caught her sleeve, but rested at skin, pressing. Testing. Drooling, he stared at the blade. 'He might wonder where a scar led. Where it ended.'

The blade pressed harder, and the sleeve pulled, fabric falling away—no barrier to the steel. Pressure flared at her arm.

Spit pooled at the edge of his lips. 'Scars, in their way, can be beauty marks.'

William glanced across at his cousin. Sylvester scratched his earlobe, stared at the cards, and grumbled.

Something had thumped in the back, but none of the others' attentions wavered from the cards.

Miss Plume was beyond the curtain with Wren. William tapped the side of his mug and pushed his chair back, standing. With the woman on the way to finding whatever she looked for, he had no wish to continue enjoying the smell of worn boots.

He stared at the curtain, unable to move, imagining the look on the woman's face as she'd left the room. Wren had swooped up the bag and darted to the back. Miss Plume had hesitated before moving.

He shrugged, noting the worn threads where so many had touched the curtain before him, but striding towards it.

He walked through and saw several doors. This would not be the time to open the wrong one.

Ignoring his misgivings, he pressed a hand to the first door and pushed it.

Wren stood over a woman, a blade at the woman's arm. Instantly, it moved to her throat. In seconds Wren could slice and nothing would be able to erase the moment, ever.

William's breath left his body. His mind took a moment to adjust to the sight his eyes tried to make sense of. The woman was one movement from death. Wren's face had the look of a rabid animal, all thoughts absorbed by the sickness. No way to understand reason.

William could not move forward to rescue the woman because Wren could act on impulse. The knife pressed against the slender neck. Wren could kill in the moments it would take William to close the distance. A jolt against Wren's arm would press the blade into skin. She would be dead and nothing could ever change those seconds.

Chapter Two

Wren increased the pressure of the blade. Isabel's pulse thumped against the tip.

'My pardon,' the man at the door spoke. 'I didn't realise this was a private conversation.' Nothing flickered on his face. He didn't even seem to see her.

'Get the hell out,' Wren rasped.

Isabel swallowed. Could the man not understand there was a blade at her neck?

'I certainly will,' the man at the door spoke. He leaned back a bit, turning his head.

His hand tightened on the door and he was going to leave, letting Wren do as he wished. She could tell. The stranger had not once looked at her eyes.

'But, I was thinking of making an investment.' Soft words from the man at the door. His body stilled before turning in her direction.

Finally, he noticed Isabel. His brows lifted and he wet his lips. He appraised her in the same way a butcher might decide which chicken was to be the first to the block. A nausea filled her.

'I would like to invest, Wren.' He chuckled. 'And all it would take would be a bit of pleasure to convince me.'

'I need no investors.' The knife didn't lessen. 'I own everything under this roof. Everything.'

'True enough,' the man spoke. His eyes were again on Wren. 'I hear nothing but good about this establishment. Nothing. And an investor like myself feels a bit left out.' His gaze locked on Wren's face. 'I have a good bit of coin. A good bit, and I certainly can find better ways to spend it than on gaming.'

The pressure at Isabel's throat lessened.

'A man cannot have too much coin,' Wren said. 'But he can have too many women about.' At those words, the knife jabbed forward, tapping Isabel's neck like a pointed fingernail with a razor at the end.

The stranger's eyes widened and he caught his breath, speaking as he exhaled. 'Don't damage the goods, Wren.' His voice strengthened. 'Wouldn't want to hurt an investment.'

Wren took the knife from Isabel's neck, looking at it as if he'd forgotten he had it in his hand.

In that moment, the man threw his body in front of Isabel, knocking her backwards with a crash.

For less than a second she could only see the ceiling. She pushed herself up, scrambling to her feet. Wren's back was on the desk and the stranger's right fist plunged into Wren's face.

Wren rolled, falling from the desk, kicking the man's ribs when he moved forward. But the stranger only turned with the blow. He continued forward, driving on to Wren, using his body as a battering ram. His left hand gripped Wren's neck and he rose, just enough for leverage, keeping Wren pinned to the floor.

The stranger's fist rose and hammered Wren's face, pummelling a groan from him.

She could not bear it. 'No,' she shouted, the words more a scream than a command. 'Stop. No. I beg you, please stop.' The words could have carried to the top of the Tower.

She shuddered, her voice now pleaded. 'Please stop.'

The stranger looked at her. His eyes held no recognition of the moment, but his fist stilled on the upswing. Nothing from inside him acknowledged her words, but he stopped pummelling. Again his arm moved up, ready for a downswing.

'No…' The word pulled her last thread of strength.

William stopped, pulling the world around him back into focus. The woman's body trembled in a circular motion. Another second and she would topple. Dazed eyes locked on him, but he didn't think she truly saw anything.

William lunged upwards and scooped the knife from the floor so Wren couldn't grab it. He had to get the woman away from the place. Neither she nor his family would be helped by tales of these events.

In one stride, William had a hand at her shoulder. 'Miss?' He tightened his clasp.

She blinked, but didn't speak and her glance fell to his hand.

'Miss?' he repeated. 'Where do you live?'

He released her shoulder and took her chin in his gasp, pulling her gaze to his. His heart slammed against his ribs with a stronger punch than any Wren had managed.

Seizing her around the waist, he lifted her to the door. Stopping outside, he let her feet flutter to the floor. She kept moving downwards and he pulled her up, tight against him. Her colourless face wasn't far from his own, yet she offered no resistance.

He had a knife in one hand and a woman in the other. The door still open, he led her to the taproom, trying to keep her on the side opposite the patrons.

Everyone in Wren's looked towards the curtain when he strode through. They'd heard the commotion apparently, but hadn't moved. Sylvester's cards fluttered to the table.

A customer entered at the door. Light filtered on to the woman's hair, showing the unusual colour to all in the room. The stranger stared at William, unmoving. Uncertainty stilled him as if he couldn't decide whether to enter or run for safety.

Sylvester's voice jarred the moments, reminding William of the others. 'Cousin—you must introduce us to your friend.'

'Yes, I must.' William tramped forward. 'Just not today.'

He glared at the man at the door, gesturing him aside—and then Will realised he gestured with the knife. He dropped the weapon and the man jumped backwards, pulling the door with him. William stopped the swing with his boot. The man darted away.

Sprinting the woman into the fading sunlight, William moved towards his carriage. He shouted to the driver, 'Just go. Keep us moving.' The driver stared, then his posture straightened and his chin snapped up in agreement.

Once inside the vehicle, William reached across her to lower the shade on her side. She gasped and the sound slashed into him. She pressed against her side of the carriage.

With the same control he'd used when he spoke to Wren, he turned to her.

He opened his mouth to ask her where she lived, but closed it again. He could not deliver such a bedraggled miss anywhere. She'd been so prim on the bench. And her dress had been ripped even then.

'You must stop shaking.' He spoke in the tone that could soothe two sisters trying to strangle each other over an apricot tart.

One at a time, he reached for her hands, holding tight to one when she tried to pull away, but freeing the other. He couldn't have her darting from the door of a moving carriage.

He stared at the slice on his own knuckles and then remembered her arm. If it had meant losing the horses to put himself in Wren's while she was there, then he would thank Sylvester—at least silently.

He reached into his pocket and took out a handkerchief. Even in the darkening light, he saw the moisture, but the wound on her arm only trickled blood.

He pressed and waited, making sure it wasn't serious. 'Just relax,' he spoke in the apricot-tart tone, 'you'll be all better in a minute.' If it would have been his sister, he would have started singing a nursery song, because it always worked, even if they complained about the nonsense.

'You're hurt,' she said.

Relief flooded him. She was aware of something other than the fright.

'I'm fine.' He daubed at the dried blood on her shoulder. 'My horses give me worse bruises and we call it fun.'

She looked at the handkerchief and then her shoulder. 'Oh,' she squeaked, not in pain, but surprise.

'Yes.' He pressed the cloth at her injury again, not really needing to. 'But it will mend quickly. I'm sure you've had worse.'

She reached up to relieve him of the cloth and for a moment their fingers tangled, then their eyes met, and she breathed in and pulled away.

He hated to move, but he did. He would ask her the location to deliver her and he would see that she arrived safely. Even if it was some distance away, he could direct the coachman easily enough. But his question changed before he spoke.

'Why were you in Wren's?' he asked.

She gazed at him. 'I was seeking work there.'

He'd been so wrong. His voice strengthened and the first words he thought flew from his mouth. *'In a brothel?'*

Life returned to her eyes. 'You insult me.' She

straightened. 'Do I look like someone who would—?' Her eyes opened wide. She cried out, using both hands to pull the dress over her bare shoulder, then adjusting her grasp, pulling the rip in her skirts closed. 'Do I look like a...*fallen woman*?'

'Not... No. No. Not at all.' She looked well past fallen, but he had learned as a youth that a pre-emptive reassurance was easier than stopping tears.

'I must go back,' she said. 'You must take me back to that terrible, forsaken place.' Her eyes widened. Pleading. 'I need your help.'

'No. You are not going back.'

'You don't understand. I left my satchel. All I have in the world. A dress. My funds.' She held the handkerchief at her shoulder while reaching to clasp his wrist. Her eyes searched his face and then she sighed, and relaxed.

Letting her hold him, he extended an arm around her shoulders, barely touching, but close enough that he could free her hand of the fabric and hold it in place for her.

'Is it a great sum of money?' he asked. She certainly shouldn't have been in Wren's if she had funds.

Her voice barely reached him and her head tilted so he couldn't see her expression. 'It's not truly all I have in the world,' she said. 'It is not truly all I have. It is just the rest of my things are on the way to Sussex.'

'How much did you leave in Wren's?' he pressed.

'My songs. A dress. A fan which had paste jewels on one edge. Hair ribbons. Enough to buy a bowl of soup.' She made a fist. 'I cannot believe I left the fan. The fan was a gift from three dear friends, but I'm sure they would understand if I sold it to buy food.'

She tensed, moving to stare at him. 'I am not a tart. I am not a fallen woman. A Jezebel. Or whatever else. I am a…' Her chin rose. 'A singer.' She lowered her face. 'Or I was to be. That evil debacle of a man was to pay me to sing.'

'You *sing*?'

She looked directly at William. 'Yes. Songs. To sing songs. Wren hired me. He'd promised me wages.' She snorted, then caught herself. 'I do have a good voice and the wages were not such a large amount to make me suspicious.' She straightened her fingers, saw blood on the gloves and shuddered. 'I have always been told my voice is a gift.' Her words faded away.

Her hand rested in her lap and her head bowed. 'My songs are in that satchel. With a picture my friend Grace drew of us singing and laughing with Joanna and Rachel.'

'So you are a Songbird.' He reached and tugged at the fingertip of her glove. She didn't need to be staring at blood.

'Not any longer,' she said, pulling away to remove the gloves herself and fold them.

'Nonsense. Don't let one person stand in your way.'

'It's not one person.' Shadowed eyes stared at him. 'It's everyone. Everyone says I should be a governess. Everyone. And this proves it.'

'This proves nothing of the sort.' His words were firm, but Isabel discarded them with a wave of her folded gloves.

'I will never sing again,' she said. 'Madame said it would be the ruin of me and she didn't know I listened so I suppose she was right. I just couldn't believe it—until now. She was *always* right.'

She met the view of the brown eyes. 'Even when we didn't let Madame Dubois know she was right—she was right. I should have learned from my friend Grace how things go awry.'

'And what has happened with this friend, Grace?'

'She explained to me how...' She fluttered her hand at her head before pulling the bodice of her dress for more covering and leaning against the inside of the carriage which smelled a bit like a blacksmith's shop. 'People make mistakes. And I see now that perhaps I should have been happier about my chance to be a governess. Not everyone is so fortunate to have the parents such as I do who are willing to send a daughter away for education.' She winced. 'But I wanted to sing. I truly did. For audiences.'

She remembered the joy flooding her when music sounded. 'I had to know. Wren and I exchanged many letters and I believed him reputable. I had to know if he had a true job for me. I might have suspected that it would be all for naught, but all my life I would have wondered. Perhaps it is worth the risk of death to know.'

'No. It was not.'

His words brooked no argument. She examined him through the fading light. He sat, unselfconscious of her perusal, and it didn't seem that she was being impolite or forward, but just learning what he looked like and trying to learn his thoughts.

But she had to think of her future now.

'I will send a post telling how I was waylaid,' she said. 'I will leave out certain parts and I will hope that Madame Dubois accepts it, and will again reference me to a family. I will be a…' She shut her eyes and forced out the words. 'A governess.'

'The children will be fortunate to have you.'

'I must hope I am allowed to regain my position.'

'A governess could sing to her charges.'

'Of course.'

'Sing for me,' he said.

'No.'

'Please.'

She tried, but only three words came out before her mouth dried. Her voice wavered, cracking, and no longer sounded her own.

'I never want to sing again,' she said. 'I sang because *la vie est trop courte pour boire du mauvais vin*. I wanted a chance to drink the *good* wine.'

'The results can be the same. But do not give up something you love—something so sweet as song.'

'My voice has always brought me notice,' she said. 'Always, and so many times Madame told me that pride goes before a fall and that it doesn't cushion the ground a bit.'

'Songbirds don't have to remain on the ground.'

'My wings have been clipped,' she said.

'I will find you a safe place to have the good wine tonight and tomorrow you may send the post to your friend. You will have many chances to make the children happy in your care.'

'If you would just deliver me to a place where I might find suitable lodging.'

'I know of only one place that would have what you need. My sister's home. She's married and too proper for good health. Tomorrow, my sister can quickly send a messenger to your destination and make up some folderol about how you aided her, causing you to become separated from your carriage. She'll even put together a new garment for you. This will only be a small detour in your travels.'

She let out a breath. 'Thank you.' The words hurt her throat. Wren must have pressed against it more than she'd noticed. She trailed her fingers over her neck, searching for a cut but finding none.

He leaned forward, sliding the wood aside which covered the small trap window. 'Sophia's.' he called out. But before he closed the window, he added, 'Slowly,' before glancing at Isabel and smiling.

That one word wrapped around her, suffusing her with wellbeing.

He relaxed to put an arm at the back of the seat, not touching her skin, but enveloping her all the same. 'So, Miss Songbird, let us introduce ourselves on the way. Just listening to your speaking voice is quite the treat.'

Chapter Three

The carriage creaked to a stop and instantly Isabel saw William's eyes shutter, then he straightened, slipping his arm from behind her.

'If you will wait for a moment,' William said, hand on the door. 'I'd like to send my sister's butler on an errand so you can go into the house without being seen. It's better if it's assumed you arrived with Sophia.'

He lowered his voice. 'And you can trust the coachman to keep his silence, I assure you.' Jumping out, he exited into the dark night. She pushed her hand against the warm leather of the seat, loneliness creeping about her. She wished he hadn't left her—now the memory of the knife resurfaced.

She was alive and, except for a detour, her life was going to continue on just as planned. Now she could embrace being a governess. She'd seen the truth of what a singer's life was really like. Her mother had warned her countless times that people assumed all singers were really paid to do other things. That hadn't mattered then, but now it did.

She shuddered and opened the carriage shade. Enough light filtered from the moon so she could see a mansion. A mansion. William hadn't told her his sister was wealthy. Immediately, she dropped the shade and worked with the pins in her hair, ignoring the sting the movement caused to her arm.

She was arranging pins when the door opened and William looked inside. His lips quirked up. 'Songbird, do not do yourself up too pretty. My sister is used to looking at me.'

Her hands stopped. 'I'm a sight.'

'You—' he reached in, took her hands and pulled her with him, as he backed from the carriage '—are a sight like a swan in the moonlight. And all swans do not have their feathers always perfect. Sometimes the birds flutter about and feathers fly everywhere, but not for one moment do they stop being swans.'

'You're quite flattering.'

'You deserve it,' he said, leaning low so he could speak quietly as they walked up the steps. 'But with three sisters, I've had lots of practice, not that they don't deserve it as well. But my sisters gave me a list once.'

'A list?'

'Yes. A list of compliments. They had sat around one evening and decided what wonderful phrases they should like to hear from me instead of my asking if they had memorised their lessons, or practised pianoforte or were kind to each other. Every time I corrected them in any way, I was to repeat one of their compliments and add one of my own.'

'I should have liked to have had a brother like you.'

Opening the door, he ushered her inside. 'Sophia said she married in spite of having a brother and Rosalind claims she and Harriet are unwed because if I am among the best of men, then she fears for her sanity should she end up with someone only twice as good as I am.'

Gazing at him, she tried to think of suitable words to thank him for what he'd done. But her voice fled. She brushed a hand to her neck, wishing she could find something to say that explained what she felt.

'Oh…' Gently, he took her hand from her throat and his forehead almost touched hers. 'Please don't look so stricken.'

'I owe you—' she breathed out '—so much.' She clutched his lapel to remain upright.

With the lightest touch at the small of her back, he kept her steady, his whisper caressing her. 'I would have done the same for anyone.'

She tightened her clasp on his lapel. 'That only makes you…even better.'

He shook his head, darting a glance upwards, before returning his gaze to hers. 'I'm only two whiskers away from being a drunken, gambling, rakish, penniless, thankless, conceited heir to a viscount. Please don't let anything else get out about me and ruin my carefully earned reputation.'

'You were the only one who came to my rescue and I screamed. I'm sure I did.' She flattened her palm against the wool of his coat. 'I'm so fortunate you were there.'

'I just wish…things had been more like you wanted,' he said and his eyes fell to her arm.

'I couldn't have…' She tugged at the gown's shoulder, aware that only a bare inch held the garment. 'It was almost worth it to know there are men like you in the world.'

He grunted a denial and he watched her hand struggle with the fabric. 'Do not think about that, Isabel.' His words softened into a whisper. 'It is beyond your repair.' He took a smallest lamp from the side table and held it aloft so she could manage the stairs.

When they reached the sitting room, he led her to an armed chair upholstered in burgundy. He lit another lamp and put it on a table at her side.

'I'll get Sophia,' he said, leaving.

She'd expected him to ring for a maid, but he'd acted much like someone of her own means would. Her mother's maid-of-all-work wouldn't have been roused this late in the evening because it would have taken more time than the simple task of fetching someone.

Isabel glanced around the room and found it little different from her parents' home. The lamps were more plentiful and the painting above the fireplace had quite a large frame, but other than that, the chamber could have been in a country squire's house.

William returned, and shook his head. 'She has to put her hair up.'

Immediately Isabel took in a breath.

'Do not concern yourself,' he said, his face reassuring. 'It's Sophie. My sister. The one with—'

'With…?'

A woman walked in, hardly looking old enough not to have her own governess. Her hair frazzled around its pins. The dressing gown had the same capped sleeves of a day dress, but the drape and sheen of a something one could wear at a soirée.

'With the most beautiful smile in the world,' William continued.

William introduced them, talking as smoothly as if they were at a morning call and the day was dawning with the promise of sunbeams and wildflowers.

When Sophia saw Isabel, her mouth opened and she said nothing at first. Then she said, 'Your arm… I must get a cloth to clean your arm.'

Isabel stood. 'It's dried now. And only stings a little. Your brother saved me.'

'Oh, him.' She shrugged the words away. 'I slipped and fell into a stream head first and he tugged me home by my ear because he said I scared him so.' She thrust her hand sideways, giving a punch to William's arm. 'I still haven't forgiven him for making one ear crooked.'

William examined her ears. 'Yes. Hideous. Makes me shudder.'

Sophia waved his words away and stepped towards Isabel. 'So let us get you all mended.'

'Soph—' William interrupted. 'There is one other thing. I would not want to send a rider in the darkness, but you must pen a quick post in the morning for delivery to her employer. Just make up something about her rescuing you and a companion from a horrible attack of wasps or something and how she could not leave you abandoned… You know, the same story you told Aunt

Emilia.' He winked. 'It is a shame to let such a tale fade away when it could be used twice.'

Sophia shook her head. 'I don't think Aunt Emilia believed me.'

William snorted. 'I know she didn't. She told me I must get you married off immediately, so I looked about and tossed a suitable fellow your way.'

Sophia raised her chin, smiled and added drama to her voice. 'And all it took was *one* dance and he was *smitten.*'

'See, Miss Morton…' William tucked his hands behind his back '…she is good at folderol.' He turned to leave, then stopped and looked at his sister. 'You might let Aunt Emilia know of the tale. Just in case.'

'I shall. But she'll not be awake early in the morning. She's attending a dinner at the Brownings' tonight and she'll not be the first one to leave as she has put on her marriage-mart gloves again. She thinks our sisters should not rusticate away in the country.'

'She may be right.'

'Oh, please.' Sophia's voice turned whimsical. 'Once it's known that Ros and Harriet are interested in courting, Aunt Emilia will be sorting out the proposals and you will be complaining because the suitors are not worthy. Aunt Emilia is planning to get an early start on the Season. Even the people who have been in the country for the summer are returning to be at the dinner. Apparently it is quite the event because they all wish to discuss Nash's plans for our town. We can't let Bonaparte outshine us.'

'I'm surprised I found you at home.'

'Only because I do not wish to get into a heated discussion about architecture or Napoleon and prefer to spend the evening with my *smitten* husband.'

'Now you will be hearing about Nash's plans from Aunt Emilia, or her battle plans for capturing beaus for our sisters.' He raised his chin and smiled at Isabel. 'Our aunt does like to go about. Even though she has a home in the country near my father, she prefers her residence here. She considers good society vital.'

'Which means she has to ignore tales of my dear brother,' Sophia inserted.

He inclined his head to his sister and Isabel. 'And now your dear brother must take his leave as I trust two such enterprising women will have this night well in hand.' His glance lingered on Isabel's face, then her injured arm.

'Miss Morton, it might be best if you stayed at my sister's an extra day or so, unless you have a dress with long sleeves with you. That cut on your arm might raise questions.'

'Yes,' Sophia inserted. 'I'll be able to get you a gown with longer sleeves, but wearing too much covering in this heat might cause more notice. You even have a slight bruise…' She tapped a spot near her cheek. 'But after all, the wasps were chasing me at a rapid pace before you flung your bonnet like a sword and frightened them away.'

William's smile turned to Isabel alone. 'Do not let her get too carried away or she will have you saving scores of infants and battalions of soldiers, and it will get difficult to remember the details.' He leaned so close to Isabel that she could feel the flutter of his lashes, but the motion was in her chest. Almost whispering, he said, 'But don't even tell her one tiny little untruth and expect her not to remember every last detail.'

'I heard that,' Sophia said, voice loud. Then she resumed her regular tone. 'It's true.'

William murmured assent and spoke to Isabel. 'I regret we met under such unpleasant circumstances and I hope you forget all about this night soon.'

The doorway framed him, then he left. His footsteps faded into distance and the room became just a room and she could feel the bruise on her face without touching it.

William trod down the stairs, forcing himself not to turn around. He rang for the butler and waited, tapping the pull against the wall.

Finishing the last two buttons of his coat, the butler arrived and asked, 'Yes?'

'I realised my sister has a friend visiting, so I'll not be staying.'

'Yes.' He pulled his coat tight.

'Watch over them.'

'I always do.' The knowledge of the first time William had visited Sophia in the middle of the night with his own key and nearly got his head bashed in by the servant reflected from the man's eyes.

'I know.' William stayed a second longer, acknowledged the memory with a grim-lipped smile and walked out into the night.

The bolt in the door clicked.

William looked at his carriage, the three-quarter moon and the houses with mostly dark windows.

He heard the woman's voice again and turned to the open window well above him. Murmurings and a *'Goodness!'* from Sophia, and then more murmurings and a shocked exclamation. Sophia should know better than to let in the night air, but he stood until one of the carriage horses whinnied and then he turned to go home.

He sat in the carriage, crossed his arms and leaned back into the leathered cushions. A hint of her rose fragrance remained in the vehicle. The knowledge of how close he'd been to leaving Wren's earlier in the night gnawed at him. He needed to push all recollections of the past hours away and think of nothing but the fact the woman was safe, alive and cared for.

The vision of her face when the knife had been at her throat stayed in his mind. He'd been so close to walking out the door and the Songbird's life would have been altered for ever. If not for the waggling feather, he would have.

He ran a hand over his knuckles and swollen fingers, inspecting them. When they healed, he might visit Wren again.

Then he brushed a smear of dried blood away. But before the singer left London, he would make his way to his sister's house and ask Isabel to sing something for him. He smiled. He imagined them standing side by side at his sister's pianoforte and music filtering through the room.

* * *

The thought remained in his head until he walked inside his parlour. The view from the window was not fascinating, but he never seemed to tire of it. He stood at the middle of the three windows looking down and could hardly see outlines in the darkness below. Another row of town houses, just like his. Another row of windows, just like his. He didn't care to see the interiors of them or what lay beyond the panes. He feared he might see a rug, just like his. But he knew he wouldn't see furnishings like his. The room had almost none except for the two tables, the stiff-backed chair and a pretence of a desk with serviceable lamps. The servants' quarters were better fitted than this room, he hoped. The starkness suited him. Kept him from getting too close to the memories of the past where the picture of home could be painted by the fripperies spread about and the little flower shapes sewn into table coverings.

None of that appeared in his domain and his bed was the only softness in the entire house. A large beast of a bed that had once been his grandfather's and had been no easy chore for the workman to reassemble.

But he didn't want to go to bed because he kept reliving the quiet moments with the woman in the carriage, trying to think of the exact tilt of her nose. The colour of her hair was easier to recall and in all the upheaval he wasn't quite sure what had happened to the plume.

He shook his head. He was standing at the window, thinking of a bit of fluff just as a schoolboy would do. His head must have been hit harder than he realised. But the moment he'd stepped into the room at Wren's and seen the knife and her eyes widened in fear had left more than a few scrapes on his hand. The knowledge of how fast a person's life could turn to dust shook him. Now his insides shivered.

His eyes flittered to the decanter on the side table. Half-empty. The servants were not allowed to refill it until it became completely empty. If his father had walked into a room in the family home and not found it full, someone would have heard about it. If not everyone.

His father. William wished the man still looked at the world through hazed eyes.

William resisted the urge to walk forward and put a boot through the bottom glass. That would change the window, but as soon as a servant became aware, the window would be fixed.

One by one he could smash out each pane, yet the world would go on as it always did before. He could not change the way the world rotated and even if he broke the glass, other people would rush to bring the order back.

And his father, after years of a waking sleep, had truly awoken and decided he needed order back and he wanted the world on his path, a path he'd ignored the presence of for years. His father didn't remember the broken panes swept into the dustbin. He didn't remember the shattered glass.

Now, the Viscount just cared that his son be married and provide an heir. He had instructed William much like he might tell him to go to a sideboard and pick a confectionery.

The man planned to force marriage on to his son by any means possible—taking the rents William lived on would accomplish a lot. Removing the funds wouldn't hurt William alone, though, and William knew it. Twelve servants lived in the town house. Thirteen if he counted the little child he pretended not to know about—a boy who had some claim on the cook the housekeeper had hired the year before. He'd only found out about the lad because one of the servants had hidden a badly written note near William's pillow. Apparently life always didn't run smoothly among the staff either.

William took the decanter and filled his glass almost to overflow—just to see how close he could get to the edge without a spill. He placed the decanter on the table and slowly brought the liquid to his lips, not spilling a drop. He drank the liquid in one gulp, enjoying the burn.

The glass still in his hand, he stretched and strode to the windows. The servants needed their employment.

William would somehow get the horses back, then he would attend a soirée and dance with all the unwed ladies. Give his father some hope. Fruitless hope, but it wouldn't do to torment the man.

Everyone would be happy. William would find a way to have the horses returned to the stables. His father would believe a search for a bride had commenced. Sylvester would know his son would inherit the Viscount's title. Everyone satisfied if not happy. End of plan.

William slept well into the next morning and lingered through his morning wash. His dreams had been of birds fluttering about with feathered bonnets.

When dinnertime came, he would be at Sophia's house. He pulled a book from the table where it had sat for a year, planning to read enough of it so he could say he'd finished, then he would return it in time to sit for a meal with his sister, and her guest, and hopefully an evening around the pianoforte. It was only natural that he might want to visit and make sure their plans were progressing well and offer assistance.

With the mostly finished book tucked under his arm and his chin feeling raw from the second shave of the day, he strode to the front door when a carriage pulled to the front of the house.

Sophia didn't have a town coach. It could only be his father.

William put down the book and walked to the staircase before the butler could answer. The front door shook with a violent knock.

William opened the door. His father brushed by him, bodies connecting as a shove, and William stepped back.

His father raised his eyes to his son's face, slammed his beaver hat and gold-tipped cane into William's hand and said, 'Get used to that.' He continued up the stairs. 'I will see that if you are not hanged, then you will be transported. It is apparently your wish.'

Transported? Hanged? His father was daft. Completely. The years of liquid grief had turned his mind into pudding.

The Viscount rushed ahead, more at a run than William had ever seen him. William followed, knowing he didn't want his father's conversation carried to the servants' quarters. His father stopped inside the parlour, whirling around. 'You thankless piece of conceited tripe. You've gambled your name away and mine, too. Generations of our heritage. Destroyed. For ever. By you. I thought you cared more for your sisters than this.'

William put the hat over the globe of a cold lamp and propped the cane against the wall. 'What are you talking about?'

'My sister—' his father jabbed his own chest '—my sister, Emilia, came to me in tears. You are less than a son.' He splayed his hands, fingers arched. He pulled in air through his teeth. 'You called my bluff, only it was not bluff. I merely threatened to circumvent the inheritance laws. But I had no need. You were quite willing to take care of that yourself.'

'I've done nothing wrong.' His voice grated on each word. 'I only wished for the horses.'

The Viscount whipped his head away from William and stared to the windows. 'I cannot even bear the sight of you.' His words raced. 'I didn't think you would perhaps jump to marry someone suitable, but I didn't expect you to destroy our entire heritage.'

'I've done no such thing.'

His father waved his hands in the air. 'You wanted to make sure no woman would consent to wed you. You abducted a woman in daylight, in front of as many witnesses as you could find.'

'Abducted? Are you foxed?' His voice rose. The man had lost his senses.

'Do not try to turn this back at me.' He rushed by

William and to the windows. He stretched his arms at each side of the window, as if holding himself erect. His head dropped.

'Your Aunt Emilia has even begged to say that you were with her to save you. But I have forbidden it. Besides, too many have seen you.'

'The woman was attacked.'

'Attacked? Of course she was attacked. It's said you near dragged a reddish-haired woman screaming from a brothel.'

'No.' William's throat clenched. 'No.'

'Why am I not surprised? I have heard. Always I have heard. I have heard of the night you were foxed and fought the Duke of Wakefield's brother. I have heard of your gambling. But I never thought you to be so low as what transpired last night.'

The Viscount put closed fists over his eyes. 'My son,' he gasped out the words. He pulled his fists away, eyes reddened. 'I caused this. I caused it.' His voice cracked, then gained momentum. 'But I can correct it. You will vacate the premises by the end of a fortnight. I suppose sleep in your new carriage. I do not wish to see you again.' His lips trembled. His voice had the same fury as when he had told William to take the ring from Will's mother's finger on the last night of her life.

The jewellry had slipped easily from her finger and he'd felt as if he had stolen her last breath.

Pushing the memories aside, William turned so he would not see his father's face. The same vice clenched him that had surrounded him so many times before, only this time, he had to use all his might to push it away so he could speak. 'What happened?'

'Tonight,' the older man said, 'I have lost my only son. I could not sup with someone such as you.' He stepped around William, pulling his hat from the shade and grasping the cane.

William turned. 'Father. What is going on?'

The Viscount took his hat, and clenched the cane. 'I must blame myself, William. But it does not change a thing. I shouldn't have mourned your mother so long. I should have opened my eyes before it was too late. But it is now too late.'

He stepped forward, but lowered the walking stick. 'Oh, you showed me. You really did. But I will not ignore such behaviour. No longer. This was beyond the pale. Even for you.'

William squinted at his father. 'The woman is safe at Sophia's house. I took her from Wren's, but she wished for me to.'

'Sophia?' His father started. 'What does she know of this?' His fists clenched. 'I could pay the hangman myself for you attacking an innocent woman.' He stepped back. 'Your sisters. Think of your sisters.' He dipped his head. The room was silent. 'This will reach their ears. They'll be humiliated.'

Attacking an innocent? His father believed William attacked Isabel? The vice gripped again.

'The whole town will hear of it.' His father's voice ended on a high shriek. 'Apparently the talk of your— behaviour became the centre of the dinner. Your aunt was mortified. The whispers have already started and will become shouts. She came to me in tears. She found Sylvester and he agreed that you dragged a woman from Wren's. He said he was so shocked he didn't think to chase you and rescue her until after you had spirited her away in your carriage.'

'I didn't do anything wrong.'

'All the men saw you leave carrying a woman of quality from Wren's. A copper-haired woman with a bruised cheek. The men at cards heard her scream. Saw her in tatters. Blood on her sleeve. You forcing her out the door and into the carriage. Leaving a knife behind. It is thought her body was tossed into the Thames.

'Oh…' William stepped back, reaching a hand to the wall, steadying himself. 'No. No. It is not that. I didn't—'

This… This would destroy his sisters.

'You will never step foot in my house again. You will distance yourself from your sisters for their sake. I hope you care enough for them for that.' His father's eyes twitched.

Events of the night before careened through William's head. He'd done nothing wrong, except perhaps in letting Wren escape a magistrate, but he'd not wanted any notice of the night.

Now his name would be destroyed. The tales of his past weren't enough to grieve his sisters, but with this added, everything would be embellished. The tarnish would never be cleansed.

William took in a breath. 'Father.' He laughed, but could barely manage the sound. 'That is so absurd.' He waved a hand. 'She was to meet me, but was early

and confused at her direction. When she was alighting
the carriage, a dog, obviously trained by a cutpurse,
ran out and startled the horses. The culprit knocked
her about, but Isabel fought back before running into
the back door of Wren's. The criminal chased her and
caught her there.' He hoped no one had truly noticed
her in the shadows before. But he doubted they had. At
first, the bonnet had hidden her face and covered her
hair. She'd remained in shadows, her presence overridden by the woman on the stage. Then, when he'd moved
her outside, her clothing dishevelled—everyone had
noticed them and the light reflected on her hair when
the door opened.

He took a breath, gathering his thoughts. 'The driver
had to keep the horses steady while fighting off the dog
and didn't realise Miss—' If he'd heard her surname,
he'd forgotten it '—my Isabel had exited the carriage
and been attacked.'

His father stared. 'And why would a woman of quality be wishing to meet you there?'

'We had corresponded. We were to go to Gretna
Green. I plan to wed her, but could not start out with
her in such a state. That is why I bought the new carriage. To elope. She is waiting at Sophia's to recover
and then we will marry.'

The heat of the day had collected in the room and
the Viscount rubbed sweat away from his forehead with
the back of his hand.

'She is alive? A reddish-haired woman?'

'Very much alive. She is a good woman. I wish to
marry her. We are betrothed.'

His father examined William's face. 'Without so much of the piffle spread in—did you attack her?'

'No. I could never do that.' He used his eyes to convince his father. 'She didn't realise where she was.'

'You believe her?'

He nodded. 'She is a country squire's daughter. She had no notion.'

'From the country, you say?' He shut his eyes. 'And you have been corresponding with her and she agreed to meet you—'

'Father. We have corresponded many times while she trained to be a governess. We were not certain, with the differences in our station, that people would accept our union. So I thought it best, to avoid dissension, to present Isabel as my wife.'

'You can produce her for view?'

'Of course.'

The Viscount slammed his cane against the door frame. 'I will remember this story well enough. I cannot have my only son accused of defiling a woman. I cannot.'

'I didn't. When she didn't meet me as planned, I found her crouching behind Wren's and without thinking I took her through the place, hoping I might see the cutpurse and have him contained.'

'I could not believe what the others are saying, but I have heard the tales of your courting the women of the *demi-monde*. You are known in every gambling hell and tavern in London. And yet, you say you were with an innocent miss. If she weds you I will know you tell enough of the truth. If she doesn't, I forbid your name spoken to me and I'll not have it said in my presence that I have a son.'

He stopped mid-turn to the door and then returned his gaze to William. 'Should I trust you enough to spend the day at the club laughing at the tale Sylvester is telling because he thinks to get me to switch funds his way and a jest got out of hand?'

'Yes.' The word had the strength of a church bell.

He turned his back to his son. 'I will explain this fluff to your Aunt Emilia and she will begin combating the tales. But you must produce this sweetheart of yours and she must be at your side. And she'd better have red in her hair.'

Every rail on the bannister sounded to have received a thwack from the cane as the Viscount left the house.

William went to the window. His mouth was dry. He put a hand on the wooden shutter running the length of the door. No, the houses across the way were not like his. He swung his leg back, planning to kick out the window, but returned his boot to the carpet. He could not. If he did, they would think him the one cracked and no one would believe him innocent.

He would marry. Isabel must understand. His future depended on her saying yes.

Chapter Four

The clean dress looked more mending thread than cloth, but it did wonders for Isabel's spirit. She held the skirt away from her body and curtsied to her image in the mirror. She dreaded sitting down to dinner with Sophia and her husband because she'd never eaten in such a fine house and she hoped she didn't embarrass herself.

A maid knocked, then entered when Isabel answered. 'Miss, you are requested to the mistress's sitting room.' The woman darted away before Isabel moved.

Truly, she didn't want to step outside the bedchamber. But she must. She must put on a brave face and accept her fate as a governess. Quickly, she practised the brave face in the mirror and then she laughed at herself. To be safe was all that mattered.

She would regain that governess position without losing her reputation. Her parents had sacrificed so that she might attend Madame Dubois's School for Young Ladies and have the best education they could provide.

She could not reward them by failing to be able to care for herself.

When she walked into the sitting room, Sophia wasn't present. A lone figure sat on the sofa. William, legs stretched, his gaze on some distant thought. Her spirit leapt. Isabel rushed forward to thank him again. William rose from the sofa, legs straightening in a controlled slowness.

She lost her thoughts. She'd not seen a man such as him. Ever. He could have trampled any man in one of her novels. This lone man had saved her against a man with a knife. His inside was as magnificent as his outside.

A true rescuer in gentleman's clothing. The cravat, perfect. The waistcoat under his dark coat gold with matching buttons.

'I do not know how I will ever thank you,' she said.

His lips thinned, then turned up. His kept his gaze on her. His eyes had no true happiness in them, but his mouth seemed determined to laugh.

'Marriage?' he asked.

She leaned forward. 'I didn't hear you.'

He clasped his hands behind him. 'Will you be so kind as to wed me? Vows. For ever. All that nonsense.'

She needed two tries before she could speak. For ever? Nonsense? 'You did save my life,' she said. 'Perhaps I could stitch you up a rather nice nightcap. My father quite likes the one I did for him.'

'We have quite a kettle boiling around us,' he said, leaning his shoulders forward and tipping his head close to hers. He smelled better than any perfume she'd ever scented. Perhaps like lilacs, but not flowery. More like something to deflect the scent of shaving and masculinity and things that might tempt a woman.

Yet the words he spoke had no sweet fragrance in them.

For ever? Nonsense? She had dreamt of true love. Of all that 'for ever' and 'nonsense'. And even asked that if there were angels up above, one might send a nice vicar or soldier her way. He didn't need all his teeth, or hair or even the usual number of fingers or toes, and this man seemed to have all that, whereas a man missing a few parts might be more willing to share all his love to find a wife. She wanted someone who gazed upon her as a shining star. Someone who could shower her with love…and perhaps *not* be found in a brothel. Although she could not complain he had been at Wren's the night before, but still that didn't induce her to wed him.

She put a firm, competent look on her face. 'I am quite good at making stockings which keep the feet warm on a cold night,' she said.

He shut his eyes briefly and pulled back, lips upturned, as if they knew no other direction. 'You would not ever know I was about. I doubt I would be home enough you'd notice. You would be a governess of sorts still, but it could be for your own children. One would hope for children to be a part of the endeavour.'

Oh, that was what this was about. The man needed some sons and perhaps he'd only been at Wren's and not noticed the many fine places where a decent woman could be found.

'Children?' She looked past his shoulder to the wall.

'You're not unpleasant to look at,' she said. 'I could recommend several young women who are now at Madame Dubois's School for Young Ladies who would be quite good wives.' She appraised him and fought to keep speaking. William had helped her most efficiently and she should do the same in return. 'What colour hair do you prefer?'

He appraised her, eyes lingering at her head. 'A copper colour. Like sunlight has softened it.'

'Um…' She looked at him. 'I admit, my hair is a good shade. I have heard that all my life. And I can understand you might think to have children with this colour of hair, but it is indeed a bit rare and one cannot count on such a thing.'

'Probably a bit much to expect the sky-blue eyes to go with it.'

Her stomach curled, making it hard to maintain her composure.

'Yes, I'm a bit of an aberration.'

'A lovely aberration.' He paused. He looked at her without flirtation. 'And your voice. I like your speaking voice. It doesn't grate on my ears.'

'Oh, my…' She put her hand to her bodice and ducked her head in the way she did when someone praised her singing. 'You are quite efficient with the compliments. I hope that is one of your own and not from the list.'

He nodded and his lips turned up at one side before speaking. 'You would be surprised how many times a woman's voice has grated on my ears. I have three sisters, remember. So when I called you Songbird, it was not idle. But it would be best for us to wed.'

She put her palm out, touching his coat just above his elbow, giving a brief pat, trying to ease the rejection. *Oh, candlesticks, no one would ever believe she had refused a viscount's son.* 'You do not have to concern yourself with my honour. Your sister has agreed to help me get to Sussex. If that does not work out, I can return to my parents'.' She could not go home in disgrace though. She would have to find a post.

'I am not concerned only about your honour.' His eyes sparkled and his lips, still firm, returned to their rueful smile.

'I know a quite lovely girl of near marriage age,' she said. 'I could see that you have an introduction. Blonde hair. Eyes the same colour as mine.'

'Do they sparkle quite as well as yours do?'

'I'm sure when she looks at you they will quite outshine…' She paused. Cecilia was so sweet and kind and rather younger. An older rake would not do at all. 'She may not quite suit you, though. I think perhaps all my friends remaining at the governess school might be young for you and the ones who graduated with me are quite busy. Perhaps, um…' she stumbled '…a nice widow. A woman with some—knowledge. More your age.'

'I'm twenty-four. Not quite ancient.'

'Oh,' she muttered, 'I thought you older. At least thirty. Closer to thirty-five.' Particularly if he seemed desperate to find a wife.

One brow rose.

'I suspect you have rather included many adventures in those years. I do seem to remember asking if it was your first time at that horrible place and I think you answered that you were long past first times at anything.'

'Except marriage. It would be my first time at marriage.'

'I fear you do not understand the concept.'

'I disagree.' He took a step away. 'I have seen it quite close. Love and all that…conflagration of mindless emotion.' He stopped. 'Isabel. I am quite slogging in the wrong direction. I hate to tell you what has transpired, but I feel I must…'

'The talk is out about my misfortune.' She met his eyes. They confirmed her words. She continued, 'You are asking for my hand in marriage to save my honour.'

He was valiant. No knight could surpass him.

His eyes shut. 'Not entirely.' He stepped forward.

Again, when he stood so close, something about him distracted her thoughts and took them as directly as one might take the bridle of a horse and turn its face in a desired direction.

'I would hope that I would be so noble as to marry to save you, but I am not sure.' He took her fingertips. She could not move.

Now he spoke softly, conveying the importance of his words with his gaze.

'It is said that I ravished you in Wren's. I spirited you out by force. The dishevelment. The torn dress.'

'*You* didn't ravish me. You rescued me.'

'Yes. But to have that untrue story—no matter how it is said—your presence in such a place will cast aspersions on you. I would prefer us both to get out of this as best as possible. I would not wish to spend the rest of my life with the lingering question in the minds of others as to whether I truly attacked you or not.'

She balled her fists within his hands. 'I will tell them. I will tell them all.'

'You may,' he said. 'Other questions will arise that neither of us particularly care to be subjected to. You will be seen as a woman afraid to tell the truth about a wayward viscount's son for fear of repercussions. I do not have a…' He searched for a word. 'A sombre past.'

Her stomach bunched into a gulp and then bounced from one side of itself to the other. 'William, I fear you would not make a good husband.'

'I know I would not. That is one of the reasons I have not considered marriage in the past. I think it a suffocating, strangling gaol. It is not a leg shackle. It is a throat shackle. I have said it is likened to having leeches attached to bleed the body dry and leave it a desiccated shell. Much like the body left behind centuries after death.'

She pulled her hands away. 'You have worked long on this proposal?'

'Twenty-four years.'

'Am I the first to hear it?'

'Yes. This is a first.'

'I dare not ask…'

'I don't think I should talk of my life if we are to be married. Last night I thought never to see you again so I didn't care overmuch. If we might be seeing each other at a marriage ceremony, then I don't care to discuss how I spend my nights.'

'The socks and night caps would probably not make a good gift for you.'

'No.' He gave the saddest smile she'd ever seen. 'All that I ask is that you stand at my side and answer a few words.'

'Those vows and nonsense?' She might end up the desiccated shell, but she was not quite doing as well on her own as she'd hoped. And she had no desire at all to be a governess. None.

'Yes.' He stood. 'I see a bit of concern on your face. But you do not have to worry I will be a brute like Wren. I will not…be unkind.'

She didn't speak.

'Ours would be the most perfect of marriages.'

She lifted her brows.

'Yes. If you have need of me once we are married, you will only have to give a note to my butler and he will see that it is delivered and I will read it immediately. We won't see a great deal of each other. I truly do not like to be home.'

'You did rather help me,' she said. When she looked into his eyes, it was as if they begged her to say no. Forces behind him pushed him her way, much like a pirate would shove a person into the deep. 'Do you not think you are making a terrible mistake?'

He shook his head. 'All my sisters' lives I have been there for them. Perhaps even when they had no one else. I have had one unselfish task, only one, and that has been to see that they are safe and have a home. When that is provided, they content themselves. I cannot bring disgrace upon them. A few tales about my revelry doesn't hurt—that is shrugged away. But that I might harm a woman would not be tolerated. A man who hurts weaker people for his pleasure is condemned. His family—particularly sisters of a marriageable age— would be tarnished.'

He moved to the window, looked out, shook his head and returned to her. His smile was directed inwards, but the question in his eyes was for her alone.

'Can you not think of another solution?' she asked.

'Not at this moment. If I could, I would give it.'

His words rested in her like a wooden ball rolling down a stair, clunking to the bottom.

'If you do not wish to wed,' he said, 'I understand. But, Sophia will be damaged if you do not. So will my other two sisters and my Aunt Emilia. My father will manage to consider Cousin Sylvester his heir. I will be tossed from my home. At least half of the servants will be without employment.'

'You do not play on someone's sympathies…do you?' She brushed her fingertips over the sleeve of his coat. They had only met the night before, but they were not strangers. Nor friends. Nor enemies. But they had shared a moment of decisions together that few ever faced and her life would plunge one direction or the other based on her response.

'And there is the fact that I found you a place to stay last night. Although I understand if you have no wish to marry,' he said. 'I certainly can understand that. Perhaps better than anyone.'

That he could understand her wish not to marry *per-*

haps better than anyone' was not a resounding push in his favour.

'I must give this some thought,' she said. 'But you should give it a great deal more consideration as well. Marriage is about love and holding the other person in the highest esteem. At least it is for me.'

'As a governess you would not be allowed to have a marriage.'

'I can eventually leave a governess post. Or I might fall in love with a tutor, or stable master, or linen draper—on my half-day off. And if that person loves me back, just a little, it is more than you're offering.'

'I'm wealthy.'

She paused. One shouldn't marry for money. But one shouldn't overlook funds either. 'How wealthy?'

'My children will have a governess. A tutor. And if you wed me—' He shrugged. 'Your children will have a governess. A tutor.'

'My son would be a viscount,' she mused.

He frowned. 'Bite your tongue. There is never any rush for that.'

'He would. Just not until he was very old.'

'So we will wed.'

'My daughters would be able to have the finest things.'

He nodded. 'I can also ensure that you have reputable avenues for your talent. I would consider it a way of thanking you for taking on the misfortune of marriage.'

'I don't— Marriage is not such a thing.' She turned away. 'As your wife I wouldn't wish to sing. That's over for me and I can accept that easily.'

'You would be giving your chance at love away, but it would enable more choices for the children you might have. A sacrifice, for sure.'

The clouds inside her head cleared. A mother did such things, or should.

'You may wed me,' she said. She could pretend. Perhaps if she didn't pay attention to the marriage words they would not quite count as much and she could pretend to be a governess with the children away on holiday. That could be pleasant. And she would not mind to have a little family for herself. And if the boys favoured him, oh, she would preen, and it would not be a problem for the daughters to inherit her hair colour or his.

'I don't see that either of us have many other choices. You are all the things a woman would want in a husband,' she said, giving a smile that didn't reach her heart. 'And all the things she would not.'

Isabel sat at the writing desk which had been moved into the room. She didn't feel like opening the ink bottle. She'd never written a letter while wearing a borrowed chemise, but the garment would do her well to sleep in and by the time she woke, her own laundered dress would be dry. She didn't have to worry about choosing matching slippers, as she should be pleased her slippers were mostly free of the muck.

She would be quite the lovely bride in the patched-together dress. Her marriage would take place some time the next day as William was getting the special licence and telling all his friends how delighted he was to be married.

She could marry, or, she could go home in disgrace.

She chose to take the stopper from the ink bottle. The letter would be easiest. She would write her parents of how wonderful everything was as she had met the man of her dreams… She shut her eyes and tapped her closed fist at her forehead. Oh, this news had to be delivered in a letter. They would never believe it if she said it to their faces.

Or they might.

She remembered her father picking daffodils for her mother each spring. Roses in the summer. Walking hand in hand in the crisp autumn air and calling her the best gift of his life—one he could hold each day of the year.

Her parents loved her. She knew it. But when they looked at each other an affection shone in their faces, along with something else. It was much like a clockmaker might want to see how the mechanisms worked to turn the hands of a timepiece. Isabel had imagined how it would feel when her own husband cherished her so.

When she had realised that she was being trained to be a governess and a governess didn't have a husband, she'd felt tossed into a rubbish heap. She could never be loved in the same manner her parents loved each other. She'd put all of her spirit into her song the next time she sang—the very first time she had noticed tears in a listener's eyes. Her dreams had soared. Singers could marry. They could have their own family.

She imagined the devotion she wished for. She began

to write. The man she wrote of in the letter was so deeply devoted that he could not bear to be away from his beloved one moment more. He had cherished her from afar…

She tapped the nib against the inside of the bottle, planning just how it would have been.

Her parents had missed one of the events where the school had let her sing, so that was where she had met William. And he had been instantly smitten. Tears had flooded from his eyes—no, scratch that. He had shed one lone, intense tear as he had thanked her for the overwhelming performance and called her a songbird. She smiled when she penned the word *songbird*. He *had* called her Miss Songbird.

She dipped the pen again. He'd begged, yes, begged that they might correspond. She had refused, most assuredly, but he had managed to get his letters to her, and after great personal dilemma, she read them. Slowly her heart had melted—*but, no*, she'd insisted, she could not neglect her dream to become a governess. Over time, however, his devotion had overtaken her and she had agreed to wed.

William stared at the darkened ceiling in his bedchamber. The ceremony would be in a few hours.

He'd not slept at all. He'd kept remembering the deep love his parents had had for each other and then his mother had died. The world had gone silent that night after her last breath. Then he'd had to remove her cherished ring from her finger. None of them had been the same after that night. His father began to substitute liquid for air.

Love had destroyed his father. Took him from them in the guise of drink. But William didn't blame his father for that weakness.

William had heard the noises the second night after his mother's death and crept to his mother's room. His father had been huddled on the floor, arms around himself, rocking. He'd been crying out his wife's name over and over.

William had pulled the door shut and walked the hallway. Silence had followed, and permeated deep into the walls around him. In the days afterwards, he'd watched the family move about and it had felt as if he watched a play. He could see the actors and hear them. But he wasn't even standing near the stage.

He rolled in the bed, kicking the last of the covers to the floor.

Marriage. Children. Such a risk.

But he didn't love Isabel, so marriage could not destroy their lives. He would not allow her to love him either. He imagined himself standing beside Isabel as the vicar asked—

He had forgotten a vicar. No one might be standing there to marry them.

He'd been so concerned with getting the special licence, the town coach, and telling as many people as he could think of to expect the happy event, he'd forgotten someone to make the words official.

Within moments, his boots were on and his shirt stuffed into his trousers. He tied his cravat as he rushed down the stairs and he had no idea of how to progress but he was certain the butler would know of someone who could perform a marriage.

The butler chuckled as he gave William direction to a vicar's home.

William had had a bit of difficulty finding the house in the darkness, but he banged on the door. He heard a voice grumble out, and then he waited, rubbing his chin, feeling the stubble.

The vicar, a wisp of a man, finally appeared, his hair falling in snowy frazzles around his face and a scrap of a belt around his nightshirt covering. Without speaking, he waved William inside.

'I have a special licence.' William shot out the words. 'I need to be married quickly.

'Is the babe arriving now?' the vicar asked, tugging the belt tight.

'No,' William said, taking a step back. 'There's no child.'

'Well, then, what's the rush?' He squinted.

'I'm marrying today and I didn't remember I needed someone to speak the words.'

'Are you going to battle?' the man questioned. 'Leaving soon?'

'No.' William shook his head. 'I just need to be married.'

'Ah.' Again the man tugged on the tie at his waist and then stepped back, peering through squinted lids. 'You might come back after breakfast and I'll decide then.'

The speck of a man was saying no? 'It's your job.'

'A young man pounding on my door in the middle of

the night when there is not a babe arriving before morning makes me concerned that he might not be considering the options.'

William tightened his stance. 'I cannot go into the details. Just tell me who might be able to say a few quick words to take care of this for me.'

'I suppose *you should* prepare us a pot of tea and tell me about it.'

'Tea?' William gasped out. 'I do not know how to make tea.'

The man grunted. 'And you expect to be able to handle a marriage?'

'The servants will handle the tea.'

'Would you like my advice?' the vicar asked.

'No. But if I stand here much longer I suppose I will be hearing it.'

'Yes. And I know how to make tea, so I do have more knowledge than you on some things and I am not rushing about in the wee hours. So perhaps you should come in.' He walked away as he talked. 'You owe me that for waking me. And if your reason for pounding on my door has merit, then I can take care of the marriage for you.'

William ducked his head, stepping into the scent of tallow candles and well-settled dust. A floorboard creaked under his foot.

'Come into the kitchen with me and I'll light a candle,' the vicar said. 'Don't bother bolting the door. I always open it anyway, no matter what kind of person is pounding.' He chuckled in William's direction.

After the kettle started, he whisked a glass and wine

bottle from a shelf. After placing the glass in front of William, he poured without asking and then concerned himself with his own drink.

'So,' the older man asked after he finished preparations and settled to sip his tea, 'what is all the rush about?'

'A young woman and I need to be married. We do not wish for any tales about us to be spread.'

'A compromising position?'

'You could say that.'

'Perhaps you're overreacting. Tales can fade.'

William snorted. 'Not this one.' He leaned forward. 'I know what I am to do. We are to be married and we won't cause interruption in each other's lives.'

'I have never heard of a marriage which does not cause some interruption in life.'

'I have the funds to see that it happens,' William said. He stopped. 'I am very adept at dealing with such things. I can live separately if needed.'

'Marriage. The specialness in part is that it cannot be walked away from. That is what makes it different than, say, not marriage. Love is fickle, though.'

'We are not in love.'

The vicar sputtered into his tea and set down his cup.

William continued. 'We are in agreement. She and I have discussed it. I told her what nonsense love is.'

'Ah.' The vicar nodded. 'You shouldn't have told the truth on that. Not even to me. But if she agreed with that, then I suppose she will have no one to blame but herself.' He chuckled, and mumbled, 'Do not expect that reprieve, however.'

'Isabel is not like that.'

'You've known her long?'

'Long enough.'

'A lifetime can be not long enough to know what a woman is like before you marry her—from what I've seen.'

'The woman *I am* going to marry is…' He paused. 'She's almost alone in the world, or that's how she feels. I don't want her to be alone. I may not be able to give her everything, but I can give her a home, safety and a haven. She'll have servants. Children, perhaps.'

In a flash of memory, he could see his parents laughing at the table and then his father throwing crockery about after her death, acting in the same manner as Rosalind when she'd been cross. Only he could not send his father to his room and tell him that the governess would not be reading him a bedtime story.

His father had never even raised his voice before his wife died. Never acted anything but sensible and selfless. Then he'd become senseless—and selfish.

William's eyes flickered to the small man who stared into him. 'I need to marry her—for my own purpose, but it is not an entirely bad thing for her. Without me, she will likely remain unmarried and not have children of her own.'

'Why do you think she won't find someone else? Is she unappealing?'

'I wouldn't say she is unappealing. In fact, she is too appealing—to be safe—alone in the world. It isn't beauty, though I am not saying she isn't.' William smiled, staring at the empty glass. 'She has this copper-coloured hair.' He held out his hand, thumb touching forefinger, making the movement as if holding a strand. 'The light shone on it and she had her bonnet off, and the other men saw it and they saw her eyes, and ten years from now, she could walk into a room and they will remember her.'

'There are other ways to protect a woman besides marriage.'

William let out a deep breath. 'Not this one.' He put the glass on the table and leaned back, stretching his legs. 'Not this one. She's been at a school in the country or she would have had suitors lining up. Even at the school, someone found her who wished to take advantage.'

The minister stood. 'You think to love her later.'

'No.' William breathed out the word. 'I don't. That could never happen.'

'If she is so appealing—' He moved, standing by a shelf with a basin on it, keeping his back to William. 'Another man should easily fall in love with her.'

'That's true. But I've seen what love does—I'm not in favour of it.'

'My wife might agree with you,' he said. 'But you might fall in love if the two of you are married.'

'No. I do not have it in me.' William considered the words.

'How does she feel about you,' the vicar asked, 'this daft woman who has agreed to wed you?'

'She doesn't know me.'

The man turned around, wiping his hands on a cloth from beside the basin. 'I would say she doesn't.' He

Chapter Five

Isabel examined her patched dress and stained shoes. She'd once wondered what she'd choose to be married in. It wasn't this.

Her invisible groom's father, Viscount Langford, sat in Sophia's overstuffed chair as if it were his throne. He patted a chair arm and stared, emotionless.

'It'll just be a few minutes more,' Sophia said, perching at the end of the sofa and resting one hand on the brocade between them. The other hand held a fan that flitted more than any butterfly wings. 'And William will be here. He's not really late yet.'

Isabel raised her head in acknowledgement.

'If he doesn't appear, I will find him and drag him here myself.' Langford stood, walked behind the sofa and patted his daughter's shoulder.

'This almost reminds me of the day—' Sophia stopped fanning, glanced at her hand, then spoke to Isabel. 'One day, in the past, my sisters and I waited for Father and William to return. It was in August, too, and a much warmer day than this.'

'Do not speak of your mother today,' the Viscount commanded. 'If she were here, William would have married long before now.'

Isabel stood, turned to the Viscount, gave a small bow of her head, and put a smile on her face. 'William—' she fluttered her hand over her heart and paused '—was waiting for me. His whole lifetime. So it will not concern me to wait a few moments for him.'

Thoughts flickered in his eyes. 'Welcome to the family. I do beg your pardon if anything I have said this morning offended you and I beg forgiveness for the errors I have made in bringing up my son, which I feel are about to be visited on your head.'

She gave the assured blink she used for the audience before she sang. 'Then when my husband does not do quite as I expect, I will keep my words kind to him and my ire will be directed in your direction.'

He turned halfway from her. His voice was soft. 'Do as you must.' Then he turned back to her. 'Isabel, I will be prepared for your visits.'

Laughter sounded as a door on the lower floor opened. A scattershot of noises sounded.

Sophia and the Viscount looked around as if a gunshot had landed nearby and no one knew which direction it came from.

Sophia's words were a whisper and she looked to the ceiling. 'Thank you.'

The Viscount turned to the wall and sighed, then said, 'What did I do?'

Isabel could not think which face to use and she settled on the one she used at the governess school after she sang and everyone praised her.

William appeared at the doorway, with two men behind him, one with a book under his arm. William hadn't shaved. Isabel couldn't concentrate on the greetings around her, but examined William. He only looked her way a half-second or less. Blazing determination flashed in his eyes. The same stare he'd had when he'd pounced on Wren.

Then the cleric made some jest about reading the right portion of the prayer book. William glared and the other man's eyes darted downwards, but his smile beamed. She wondered if the Book of Common Prayer had a section for words said at funerals because that would be the only jest she could think of to use.

The wedding would not fool anyone present that it was a love match. She in her patched clothes and him appearing as if he'd just rolled from a bed.

She glanced to the door. A quick dart and she could be down the stairs. She opened her mouth, thinking to conjure up another aunt. She could rush away to retrieve her aunt to attend the wedding, but then she shook the thoughts away. William had saved her and he wished to protect his sisters.

The cleric spoke to William, patting him on the back. William swayed and she could have sworn the older man gripped the back of his coat to hold him steady.

Now she knew why men often had a friend at the side when they spoke their vows.

'Let us begin.' The cleric moved, directing the other man to stand by William.

'Miss,' the cleric said, taking the Book of Common Prayer from under his arm and looking to the vacant spot beside William.

She bit her lip and looked at the empty place at William's side. She would be standing there a long time.

She moved into place, but not quite. Another person could have stood between them. Stepping sideways, he put his hand around her waist. For a moment his fingers rested at her side. Then a tug and she had no choice but to follow his clasp. She squeaked and her feet caught up with her body.

They were close. Very close. And he was strong. Her hip tingled where it brushed against his side. The tingles spread around her body. This could work.

The minister opened his mouth to speak, then closed it. Then opened it again, looking at William and not at the book. Then he shook his head.

'We shall proceed.' William spoke. It wasn't a question. He dropped his hand away from Isabel, and cleared his voice.

Internally, Isabel stumbled, but nothing changed in front of her face so she didn't think she'd really moved. She leaned closer to him, her bare arm against the sleeve of his coat, and she took in an easing breath.

The Book of Common Prayer opened and the world outside the windows stopped. Isabel became a wife and she couldn't hear the words but his arm rested against hers, comforting.

In the last dress and pair of shoes she would have

ever chosen, she wed William, and even though he looked as if he'd fallen from a horse and smelled of an alehouse, he'd charged a man with a knife to save her and he'd married a stranger to protect his sisters. She stole a glance at him. Behind the ragged façade, she was certain some part of him wished for the marriage. He'd pulled her to his side and she'd felt it.

William listened to each word, committing them to memory. Blast. He had not expected them to sound in his head as if blared from a trumpet. Nor had he expected them to sound so real and sincere.

Words. They were just words. But they weren't like any he'd ever heard before. He was listening to a decree of the rest of his life. Vows of spiritual portent, spoken from a prayer book, with family around, to bond. Marriage had not been invented by a sane man. The vicar was right after all. The process was necessary for the sake of the children and the record-keeping of whom they belonged to. One didn't want to pass a title too far from the lineage.

She stood beside him, chin high, eyes forward, pale and…kissable lips.

He'd never kissed her, though it wouldn't be a problem. He'd held her in the carriage. If not for her misfortune, he would have kept the coachman driving circles in the town all night. He never seen a woman so *just right* as her. Tall enough for him. Short enough for him. Curved and straight enough. Just right.

All things considered, Isabel was a fortunate choice. His thoughts raced among the other ladies of his acquaintance. What if he had rescued one of them? She would be standing beside him now.

He imagined someone else at his side and felt a shudder. He had certainly missed cannon fire on that regard. At least fortune had chosen Miss—Isabel. He had forgotten her name again, but it would not be a concern now. She was Isabel Balfour now—which didn't quite seem to fit her. Yet speaking the vows with someone other than her would have been—unfathomable. In relief, he huffed a sigh—just at the moment the vicar pronounced them man and wife together.

His sister hissed.

The vicar tutted and William shut his eyes. That was something that could not be explained away.

Then the vicar prayed over them. And prayed. And prayed. The ceremony ended and the air dripped with the heat of the day.

William glanced at Isabel. No songbird's feathers had ever drooped more. A stab into his midsection. Guilt. Remorse. Anger at the ironic situation. All flashed into him.

She looked at him and when her eyes met his, the wilt disappeared. In his whole life no woman's eyes had ever pinched in such a way when she gazed at his face.

Pleasantries sounded and everyone disappeared from the room, except William, his wife and his father.

The Viscount's eyes rested on Isabel. 'I wish you both all the best. And I am pleased to have you as a daughter.' He took her left hand and pulled it to his gaze, looking at her wedding band. His eyes darted to William's long enough to spear him and back to her simple gold band, then to her face. 'Isabel, if I can ever be of any assistance to you in any way, please do not hesitate to contact me. I will accept your criticism freely and direct it in the proper direction.'

He looked at his son. 'Let me know when the heir is on the way.'

William blinked once in acknowledgement that he'd heard and his father left the room.

'Well, we are married,' his Songbird chirped, but her profile had quite a strong jaw. William offered his arm. She took it without looking in his direction and then a sigh exploded from her lips. If candles had been lit nearby, that blast would have easily extinguished them.

This would require something expensive or rare. It always worked for his sisters.

'Perhaps we could take a ride in my carriage and I might select a gift for you,' he said.

'Oh… Thank you so very much, but I do not need a thing. Your sister has sent for my trunk—she is so thoughtful. She also instructed a burly footman to Wren's as I mentioned that my satchel is there.' She paused. 'She is quite thoughtful.' Her face ever so innocent, she sighed.

'I didn't mean it the way it sounded,' he said. 'I was merely thinking how fortunate I was to have you by my side instead of someone else.'

'I am sure that is how everyone took it. Husband.' She stepped to the stairs and he followed. 'For ever… nonsense…' She sighed again, much in the same way a cat's hiss might turn into a growl.

Chapter Six

He'd taken Isabel around London after the marriage even though she'd refused to shop. He'd made sure she could later and let her know where he had accounts.

At his town house, he'd shown his bride to her room. She'd immediately spotted the trunk and while the door hadn't slammed in his face, or even shut, it had been nudged his direction, but his boot had stopped it. He'd left her when she'd hugged a dress to her face and the sniffles had started. It wasn't even a pretty dress. He'd had a good look at it when he'd said her name and she'd flung the clothing past him.

So, he'd moved to his room, took off his boots, stripped to his shirt and trousers and lay on the bed, giving her some time to orient herself before he returned.

Isabel was more in agreement with his plan for marriage than anyone else he could have chosen. She'd not even wanted to shop with him. And the little nudge of the door hadn't been an accident. She would be the perfect wife once she stopped sniffling and throwing things at him. He didn't blame her.

He would make it up to her. He would.

He promised he would get her a beautiful piece of jewellery soon. If there was one thing he had learned, the bigger the mistake; the bigger the gift. And sometimes it was best to wait before delivery so that it didn't get thrown back.

He shook his head. He was a rake. What kind of rake was reluctant to visit his own wife's bed on their wedding night? It was just that she'd felt so fragile in the carriage. And then the tears. She'd hugged some garment and cried. He didn't wish to cause her more pain and so soon after the attack. She had to be bruised as she'd fallen to the floor. His own ribs still hurt.

The turns of the past few days passed through his mind and he realised he hadn't slept the night before, and his eyelids weighted him down until a sound woke him.

Tap. Tap. Tap. He looked to the door. No servant would be…on this night.

Tap!

He opened the door, and a rigid, wan face glared. 'It is my wedding night and I would prefer to get some sleep and I cannot because I feel like you are going to slip into my room any second.' She paused. Her hair had been taken from the knot and cascaded about her shoulders. 'Where have you been?'

Just enough light illuminated her to give her the gentleness of a lost waif.

'I fell asleep.'

'Well, that is a good plan.' She whirled away.

He took a step, following her. He reached to clasp her arm. 'Please.' Gently, he led her back to the chamber.

'My ribs,' he said and patted over them. 'I should have told you.' In truth, he'd had many worse bruises, but a woman shouldn't be alone on her wedding night. Neither should a man for that matter. 'And I didn't ask about the cut on your shoulder.'

'It's well enough.'

He led her beside the light and her hair showed glints of the copper. 'Isabel.' He touched the strands, letting them slide through his fingers, and he remembered a tale of a woman whose hair was so alive that she could let it down at her window and a prince could climb it to be at her side. He felt like the man trying to find the princess.

Burying his face against the silkiness, he slowly pulled her close, breathing in the soap-clean scent mixed with a reminder of spring flowers. *Just right.* She was not just right. She was perfection.

'I told the truth about the sigh,' he said. 'I thought of my misfortune, should someone else have been at my side at that moment.'

'Surely you—'

'I could not imagine how lucky I was to have you there instead of anyone else.'

Isabel put her palms out and a fortress of male was at her fingertips. Instead of fear to have a male so close, his strength flowed into her.

'Are you hurt badly?' she whispered.

He rested his face against her hair. 'It does not hurt at all, but…you're certainly making it feel much better.' His thin shirt was no barrier to the chest beneath. Warmth raced from her fingertips into her heart and she splayed her hands to feel more. She had not realised. He had not looked so formidable only inches away, nor so gentle.

Kisses sprinkled her whole body with sparks of warmth.

He stepped aside, pulled off his shirt and leaned into the light. Purpled skin, half the size of a boot.

She reached out, swirling her hand along just above the skin, not touching. 'I am so sorry.'

'I'm not.'

He clasped his hand over her wrist and moved her hand to the centre of his torso, just above his waistband. He pulled her hand close. Her fingers spread naturally, fitting against the taut skin. He trailed her fingers upwards, moving them over the ribs, the orbs, the lines and swirls of his chest.

Silken. Taut. Flexible and firm.

She'd never heard a song written about such an experience, never understood why people acted in manners not suitable to their station. In one brush of her hand against William's chest she understood things no one could have explained if they'd spoken for a million years.

Like a creature burrowing against another for shelter, William put his face closer to hers. 'Isabel… Is…I don't think we've kissed before. I wanted to—I wanted to lean towards you and kiss you during the wedding. I ached to do it.'

He loosed his clasp and took his hand away, but her fingers stayed above his heart. He touched his lips to her nose, petal-light, brown velvety eyes watching blue.

'Our first,' he whispered. 'But do not try to keep count, because if you can do so the night will be counted a miserable failure in my eyes.'

The world disappeared when he pulled her close and melded her into his arms. Her mind could not think past the feel of being held and she became light as thistle-down, and wafted along on the warmth, held aloft by the rushing breaths. The soft brush of lips against lips joined them in a world of nothing but their heartbeats.

She didn't know when the sash on her gown loosened and the garments fell away. But somehow, without her knowledge, William removed her clothing and his, and lifted her to the bed.

Their bodies twined close, skin heating skin, and for once, warmth on an August night soothed.

He paused, pushing himself up so that she looked into his eyes. The darkened room didn't allow her to see the exactness of his features, but she could visualise him easily. His lips were parted and he studied her face, then moved to the side enough that he could reach to her cheek. She didn't feel the touch, but his hand heated much like sunbeams travelling over the skin.

His fingertips dropped to her skin, moving to her jawline and down her neck to her shoulder. He trailed down her arm and took her hand, putting it against his cheek, moving to place a kiss against her palm. The bristles of his face mixed with the softness of his lips. She traced his jaw, taking in the transition to a world she'd not known existed. Tendrils of his hair brushed against her knuckles.

'Isabel,' he whispered, so softly she knew it was not a question, but a caress with words.

He moved forward to kiss her, but something inside her had changed so that the tilt forward seemed to take a thousand moments, but she savoured each one.

His lips, warm and moist, took her thoughts away so that she could only feel.

His hands brushed over her breasts, bringing the feel of a caress to her entire body. He outlined her hips, her stomach, and pulled her against him, his hardness between them.

Again the warmth of the night became a balm as the slickness of his heated body bonding to hers swathed them in a cocoon of togetherness.

When he entered her, the murmurings whispered into her ear made her feel more protected and loved than she'd ever imagined at any moment of her life.

In some knowledge she didn't know how she'd gained, William did all he could to protect and cherish her with his body.

William stood at the side of the bed, looking down. His head kept lowering as he fell asleep on his feet and then he'd raise it and jolt himself awake. She lay so still and looked more fragile than any glass figurine with her resting lips, the lashes resting over closed eyes and the skin pale in the moonlight.

He leaned over her and brushed a kiss at her hair, hoping she would wake. She didn't move. Then he brushed a knuckle against her cheek, and her eyelids flickered and she rolled over.

Stepping away he turned, controlling his breathing. She was well. She would remain well.

He should have met Isabel in her chamber. Even after she'd knocked on his door, he could have easily walked her back to her room and then left as she fell asleep.

He was not cad enough that he could ask her to leave his bed, and he didn't think she had plans to go. If she had, she would have left earlier.

He could not become attached. He could not experience anything deeper than he might feel for any other person. To care enough that you didn't want to hurt someone was how it should be. But he could not care enough that the person could damage him. If he had learned one thing in his life, that was it.

He didn't don his trousers or shirt, but slowly began gathering his clothing. Devil take it. His face itched. He touched it again. This would be the second day without shaving and he simply could not stand another moment of it.

But he couldn't ring for his valet and ask the man to simply ignore the woman in his bed—the wife in his bed.

This was what the vicar had meant about marriage, but William had been too absorbed to see. A wife did differ from a mistress. He'd not expected that since no love was involved.

The simple act of declaration of marriage in front of a few witnesses and it wasn't just nonsensical words. But he had suspected that all along.

His thoughts had tried to warn him when he'd not been able to think the night before. He'd babbled on to the vicar as if he'd swallowed a crate of ale, but he'd not had any spirits until the one before the wedding, hoping it would steady him. The portent of knowledge, and the sleeplessness, had taken him out at the knees and gutted what was left of his thoughts.

This oddness, at seeing Isabel asleep in his bed, helpless in her slumber, was a reminder of all the conflagration he'd experienced during the past days. Surely, soon this would dissipate. Distance would help.

With his clothing bundled in one hand and his boots in the other, he made it out the door and pulled it closed behind him. In the hallway, he dressed, resting his back against the wall as he tugged on his boots.

Marriage had reduced him to—secreting himself out of a married woman's bed in the night as if she might have a husband appear at any moment.

He would have to find another place to stay, at least temporarily until he had accepted the routine of someone living in his house. But he could not turn to his friends. He would be the laughingstock. *So, Will, wife toss you out on the wedding night? What didn't you know how to do?*

He would go to his sister's house. He wouldn't have to explain there. It wasn't as if he hadn't stayed there many times before when he'd been playing cards with her husband, or talking with her, and the night had flitted away. The servants always let him in as if he owned the property.

Someone knocked at the door and Isabel's eyes opened wide and she pulled the covers to her neck, feeling the strange slide of bed fabric against bare skin. She was in the middle of a monstrously large bed, she was naked and she was alone.

'Yes?' she asked, that being the only word she could think of. William. He didn't wish to startle her.

'Pardon.' A male voice, rising high at the end, as if his foot had been trampled. Not William. 'Later, sir.'

Oh, that was most likely William's valet to wake him.

She looked around the room. He was not about, nor were his boots, nor any sign of the clothing, except hers.

Well.

She jumped out of bed, dressed as best as she could and darted to her room. How did one approach the servants and ask where one's husband had wandered off to? She could not pen this in a note to the butler.

Back in her chamber, she sat on the mussed covers where she had tossed about the night before waiting to see if Mr Husband remembered he had got married. She reflected on what a small bed the room contained. Oh, it fitted her shape perfectly, but didn't quite measure up to his chamber.

Little embers grew inside her, fanned by every deep breath she inhaled.

She stood, arms crossed, and examined the bed. The room was not nearly as nice as she'd thought it the night before. Oh, it was beautiful and pleasant, all the things a woman could wish for if she had not awoken alone in a much larger tester bed.

No lovely posts raising high in the room to declare the owner worthy of the best.

She tamped her hand over the covers. Lumps under. She was certain.

This was what he had meant about marriage. The tenderness of the night before was like the empty—smaller bed. It had…a rather nice cover, but underneath it was just workable. Nothing alive in it.

Oh, what a fool she was for neglecting to believe the truth told to her.

She whirled around, saw her face in the mirror and picked up her brush and pointed at the reflection. 'He told you. He didn't wish to be married. Vows and nonsense. Vows and nonsense.' She combed her hair and reminded herself that it was not his fault. None of it. He had rescued her.

They had met in a brothel, lest she forget. He was not a saint. He was probably back at Wren's hoping to… win something.

She put her brush on the table.

It wasn't as if she cared for him overmuch. Her feelings for him only stemmed from the fact that he had saved her life. He could have turned and left her to Wren. None of the other men there had even noticed her—so she was indeed fortunate he had seen something other than his ale and the lightskirt trying to entice him.

This day would have started very differently if not

for William. Very. She didn't want to contemplate how. She would be in worse shape if she'd returned to her parents. Disgraced. And *only* disgraced might be an overly hopeful thought.

She looked around the room. He'd married her. Kept her from being a governess. She needed not be so harsh on him. Not that there was a thing wrong with being a governess. She just didn't wish to be one. Or at the moment, a wife.

She refused to sigh and hissed instead.

Her stomach plagued her. The same way it had hurt the morning after her parents had left her at Madame Dubois's School for Young Ladies. They had waved goodbye and said it would not be long before they would be back for her. And she'd really thought they would leave and realise how they could not continue on without their one and only child and return. Even the next morning she had expected them back at any moment and was reprimanded by Madame Dubois for running to the windows.

She had just known they would miss her so badly that they would return. Every day she had expected her mother to rush in, tears streaming down her face, arms outstretched, and pull Isabel close and say she could not bear another moment without her precious daughter.

Finally her parents had returned on the appointed day and the hug had been tight, the smile sincere, and then they had all got into the carriage and Isabel had talked and talked and talked and her mother had not once mentioned the absolute misery of having Isabel away from home. Not once.

Isabel had been the most wonderful daughter ever on holiday from the school, showing her parents all the things she had learned. She had assisted her mother without being asked and had even helped the maid-of-all-work, who had said Isabel was the best child she'd ever seen and that she had missed her terribly and it was so good to have her home again. The maid-of-all-work had hugged her three times when she'd first seen Isabel. Three.

And then when the holiday was over, her parents had taken her back to Madame Dubois's School for Young Ladies Who Were Tossed from Their Homes and left her again. Isabel had not spoken on the trip and she didn't think her parents had even noticed. Again they had waved goodbye and smiled at her.

Then Grace had rushed to Isabel and had hugged her and said she had missed her. Joanna and Rachel had mentioned how much they had missed all their dearest friends.

Still, Isabel had not felt as alone the first day of the school as she did on her first day of marriage. No noise of other students chattering and playing reached her ears. No instructions shouted about. Perhaps she would have liked being a governess more than she realised. Over time she would have sneaked into those children's hearts and they would have missed her *terribly* on her half-day off.

Chapter Seven

'William.' His sister's voice.

The door opened a peep. He raised his head from the pillow.

'William.'

'Stubble it, Soph. I'm trying to sleep.'

She was halfway into the room. 'You look hideous.'

'Thank you. Go away.' He kept his eyes shut. Feigning sleep never worked, but one could hope.

'The maid told me you were here,' Sophia called out rather more cheerily and loudly than necessary.

He tamped the pillow with his hand, still not looking at her. 'She was right.'

'I was married a whole week before I showed up on your doorstep and you sent me right back home again.'

He felt the depression of the mattress as she sat.

'So what did you do?' she asked.

He didn't answer.

Then she laughed. 'Oh, I remember. At the wedding. Oh, that was endearing.' She mocked a man's gruffness. 'I now pronounce you married.' Then her voice rose and she emitted a very feminine, six-syllable sigh.

He half-opened one eye. 'I meant nothing. I was pleased to be wed and thankful I had found Isabel. I sighed because it had taken me so long.'

'Didn't take her long to toss you out.'

'She didn't.'

The mattress shifted as she rose. 'I'm sure she didn't.'

'Send some hot water this way.'

'I think I shall visit Isabel.'

He opened his eyes and snapped out the words. 'I forbid it.'

'Mmm…' she said at the doorway. 'Remember what you said to me? That sometimes it was fine for me to pretend to be wrong even when I was right because sometimes men were just too thick-headed to see what a treasure was before them.'

'I would have said that the sky was made of gooseberries if it would have convinced you to go home.'

'The sky is made of gooseberries, but you may stay as long as you wish. I will send some water for you, though, because you have a forest growing on your face—' The last of her words were lost in the closing of the door.

This would not do. He merely suffered from the shock of the wedding and the fact that the country miss had not known the proper rules of marriage. A wife didn't visit her husband's bed. And he had simply not been thinking when she appeared or he could have handled it so diplomatically and swept her up into his arms and whisked her down the hallway into her room.

He realised he had to go home. He'd had some rest now and he could see things much more clearly. Once he got the ragged mess of a beard taken care of he would go home. He would explain the way of the *ton* to her. Bedchambers were sacred by morning light. He could no more stay in her bed and risk the ladies' maid walking in than she could stay in his bed and be awakened by the—

Oh.

Walking inside the doorway to his house, the familiar scent of lemon let William know his housekeeper had been working.

His steps lightened as he moved to his private chambers to drop off his coat and then he would find Isabel.

Inside the room, he stilled. He could see nothing different. Nothing. Yet, he felt he'd stepped into someone else's room and not his own. Perhaps it was some lingering perfume or just the knowledge that she'd been there that disconcerted him.

But he supposed it was normal. Even his sisters rarely visited his town house and he'd invited no other woman inside, ever. The servants were mostly hidden in their duties. Sylvester sometimes visited, but was never invited. One allowed for Sylvester.

The room was no different. He was no different. And the woman in his home had no ties on him other than the fact that they had married. An arrangement that would suit them both for their futures. The vows were just words. But very loud ones, he admitted. Ones still ringing deep within.

William had escaped the need for courtship. He was as pleased with his wife as if he had chosen her from a fashion-plate magazine. The house was certainly big enough for the two of them, though he wasn't certain how he would have felt if he'd walked into the bedchamber and she'd been inside.

Well, he smiled, shutting his eyes briefly. He wouldn't have minded in one regard. His shoulders relaxed.

He examined the room. The bed. The walls. Everything was the same. Except the folded paper on the nightstand. He moved to it, picking up a note.

He stared at the words decorated with swirls and loops. She'd asked for his presence in her bedchamber.

Well, if one were to lose one's privacy, then it could have a pleasant side.

A night of little sleep with all the events around him—well, two nights of little sleep had disconcerted him. He must not let his imagination take him down some path that only he saw.

If she asked him of his whereabouts in the night, he would tell her. He would reassure her that he would bring no disgrace on her.

He strode the hallway to her bedchamber just as a maid exited the door and his eyes flickered to the servant. She scurried away, but his hand went out, stopping the door before it closed.

Isabel hummed beyond the door, unaware of his presence. The sound flashed into him like a gunshot wrapped in velvet. He could not move. Her voice, even without words, controlled his heartbeats and whispered endearments.

His fingers tightened on the wood and he listened, his body swathed in the sense of song and Isabel.

Oh, he had not planned for this.

The humming stopped suddenly and he blinked, deserted.

He stepped inside. Isabel stood in front of the window. Light haloed her copper hair and emphasised the contours of her clothing.

One blink of the lashes over azure and his words fell to their knees. 'Good morning.' He could think of nothing else.

Her smile knotted around him and he had to shake himself internally to step back into his realm.

'I have a plan.' She moved as if a wind had lifted her an inch taller. 'A plan you will like so much.'

Yes. He stopped the word from falling from his lips. He needed to hear her voice. He waited.

'I will change my name.' She clasped her hands to her chest. 'You can tell everyone I am away visiting my family and then, after time has passed—' She shivered with excitement. Her eyes shone. 'You can tell everyone I am dead.' She tilted her head to the side. 'You cannot marry again, but…' she shrugged one shoulder '…you do not want a wife.' Then her face brightened. 'I will tell only my family and my dearest friends I am still alive.'

Dead. Dead? The word flamed inside him, dried his mouth, slapped him back into the world he'd left behind. He didn't know if he'd spoken or not. And her face, it didn't shudder in fear at the words passing through her fragile lips, nor did she gasp at the finality of what she said.

'Yes. I will change my name, alter my hair, use face powder, perhaps spectacles and I will find a reputable place away—far away.'

She might have said more. He could not comprehend. His legs tightened. He turned himself into a wall of stone. 'No.'

'Why is that not a grand plan?' Eyes clear and innocent fluttered at him.

He took everything he felt from his words and his body, and made himself an empty slate. 'I need an heir.'

She put a hand on her hip and pointed out the window. 'Tell your cousin to get married. It shouldn't all fall on your shoulders.'

'It doesn't work that way and you know it.'

'I was not born to be a governess. But I don't think I was born to be a wife either.' She indicated the inkstand. 'I was just writing to my friend Joanna and I didn't know what to tell her, so I told her almost nothing but that I was married and would write more later. That is when I realised how confused I was with the events raining about like a tempest. We don't know each other and yet we are married.'

'I know you well enough. You are a good wife— these past few hours. I see no reason for that to change.'

She cleared her throat, which if he was not mistaken was a feminine growl. The sound pulled him back into the light.

'It's not working out too well,' she said.

'I thought you might want to stay in London, if for no other reason than to sing again.'

She shuddered. 'I do have a good voice, but singing doesn't appeal any more. I cannot bear the thought of it.'

She stepped back into the light, rubbing under her chin. 'Some moments I can still feel the knife. Mr Wren had watched me from the audience and I had not suspected it anything but enjoyment of the song. And he had such other plans. I walked about with pride, singing, and I was no different than a hare playing in a field being watched by a hawk.'

William's mind raced ahead. His mouth dried. The thought of other men viewing Isabel tumbled around inside him. He would certainly make sure she had a strong servant with her when she ventured about and he'd tell the coachman personally to keep close to Isabel when she was outside the house. He didn't want any harm to come her way. Instantly, he added plans to tell the butler to hire a sturdy servant who could always be spared when Isabel went out.

She waved a hand. 'I will disguise myself if I leave London. You will not have to fear anything. And if by some chance I am recognised you can merely say some sort of truth. Perhaps that I disappeared and you lied to protect me. That you feared me mad.' She smiled. 'A dead, mad wife would surely cause you no censure, but sympathy. If I need to act like Lady Macbeth, I can. I am quite good with theatrics.' She shivered and let her hands wrangle over each other.

'You are quite good with the imagination.' He'd seen

the same smugness she wore on each of his sisters'
faces—when they were not listening to a word of reason and had no intention of unlocking their ears.

'You're needed here,' he continued, his words almost
a retreat because dealing with his sisters had taught him
that was the best way of attack. 'While you were born
to sing, I was born to be a viscount, to produce children and take care of the properties that I inherit. And
I rather hoped you would help with some of the parts of
that which I cannot possibly manage alone.'

Her hands stilled, but remained clasped. She looked
at the floor. 'I am sorry that my leaving will prevent
the heirs, but I do not know how I could leave children
behind, so…perhaps I should go soon.'

'It doesn't work that way, either.'

She twirled and plopped down on the bed. 'I have
your interests at heart, of course. I know you do not
want to be married.' Her shoulders wobbled, but it
wasn't in weakness, more of a stance he'd seen on a
bull as it locked hooves into the ground, ready to charge
ahead.

Life with Sophia, Rosalind and Harriet had prepared
him for this. 'You are very correct.' His sisters would
have pulled a face, but Isabel had not heard him make
that same remark a score of times.

He gave her a chance to absorb how correct she was,
then added, 'We do not have to think of ourselves as
married. We are merely two friendly people under the
same roof.' With his sisters, he would have retreated
before they realised they'd been contradicted, but they

were used to his instruction. Instead, he planted his feet firm. 'Friendly.'

Dismay flitted across her face, but then she looked up.

Her shoulders relaxed. 'But I could go for a while to the Americas. Do not rule out the value of having a wife who doesn't live in the same country.'

This would not be the time to agree. 'I want you with me.'

'But you left. In the night,' she said.

'I went to Sophia's.'

'You left.'

'Yes. I felt the need to.'

'I understand.' Her lips tightened after speaking. She looked at the healing mark on her arm. 'I suppose it is all right.'

'We hardly know each other.'

'Which can only be corrected one way.'

He moved to her and knelt on one knee. He clasped her fingers and waited until her eyes met his. 'I do not have it in me…to form a close attachment.'

'Not if you are leaving before morning.'

He squeezed her fingers, hoping to soften the determined chin with his earnest words. 'I can't change the side of the world the sun rises on. I can't change much in this life. I had thought to love before, but I discovered it cannot be done.'

'Give me a chance. Just to know that you like me would be pleasant.'

'I do like you, Isabel. Of course, I do.' *Of course. Of course.*

'Then why does it matter that I stay?' she asked.

'I need an heir.' The next words almost hurt his mouth and he chose them carefully, realising them for the first time himself. 'And I would not mind some respectability in my life. While I don't intend to become a doddering old saint, I would like, should I have children, for them to have a pleasant childhood. I would like them to have a mother, and a woman trained such as yourself would be the best, absolute best, mother a child could have.'

She lowered her chin and gazed up. 'I was not the top student at the governess school.'

'I'm sure you'll make a good mother.'

She looked at the side table. 'If they were my own little ones, I think it might be wise if a true governess were hired—I did not pay as much attention to the lessons as perhaps I should. I planned to forget every study as soon as I walked from the door.' She clucked her tongue. 'Sometimes my plans are successful.'

'You'll be able to love the children and that's what's important.'

'Of course.' Her smile beamed. 'I did like it when a new student arrived and I loved them all. Miss Fanworth sometimes chose me to take them around the first few days, but she never chose me to help them with lessons.'

'I can help with the studies,' he said, leaning just close enough that he could get a whiff of roses. 'And you can bring sunshine into their lives.'

'I could.'

He rubbed the knuckles of her hand against his

cheek. 'And why don't you get a larger bed—one big enough for two to be comfortable?'

A quick dart of her head took her full expression from his view.

'And would you be spending the night in it?'

'It would not do for a lady's maid to walk in to help you wake and find me half-naked.'

'My parents were quite comfortable to sleep in the same room. It is not entirely unreasonable. A servant can wait until summoned.'

'But the town house is large enough for comfort. In the country, roosters crow to wake the house. Here, servants open the curtains.'

She took in a breath and her eyes didn't return to him. 'It is indeed unfortunate that no roosters are about.' Pulling her fingers from his, she tapped her chin. 'But, in that case, I want to keep my present sleeping place. In the night, I need to be able to feel both sides of the bed.'

'I understand.'

She took in a breath and moved her body aside and hopped to her feet. 'So do I. I will not trouble you. You will not even know I am here. I will send notes to the butler when I need something from you and he will relay it. You need not see me except for the briefest moments and a few events needed for respectability. I know that I owe you and I will repay you in heirs.'

At the door, she grasped the frame, but turned to him. 'Please do not get too attached to me as I do think the idea of moving and changing my name has much merit.'

In two steps he was at the door.

'Is—' He put his hand over the one she rested on the door frame, holding her steady. 'You must give me your word you will not act on that thought.'

'I would ne—'

'Isabel.' Innocent, innocent, innocent eyes stared at him. 'Your word.' He could not risk her rushing off to some destination only she thought wise.

A frown. A pause. 'I will not leave.' She met his eyes. 'I will make this my home. I will make this a home.'

Chapter Eight

Isabel listened to the clattering of the carriage wheels over stones and the sound vibrated into her ears and stayed. The maid sat beside her. The servant was a good two score older and would be the proper chaperon. Isabel didn't want to be alone. Choosing whom to call on was easy because the only person she knew was William's sister and the driver knew the direction there.

She had to get something in her head other than the repeat of marriage vows and a sigh. And the memory of William's eyes begging her forgiveness while his words ran through her like a pike.

The maid darted a look at Isabel.

'It is just…nothing…' She kept her next sigh internal. It was nothing. Her marriage. Nothing. She felt no different. Just odd. Everything around her except her clothing was different. Even her name.

The clatter of thoughts in her head didn't cease when the carriage stopped. She didn't want to leave the vehicle, but she put her hand on the door, and descended.

She had to speak to someone and William's sister was most likely to understand. Besides, Sophia already knew the details and Isabel would not have to guard her words.

Once inside Sophia's home, she was taken to the sitting room with light-coloured walls and matching brocade on the sofa. This was a far cry from Madame's school where all the furnishings could withstand constant use. In the centre of the room, a small table for a tea service had an oval rug under it and two chairs were aligned for easy conversation, with the sofa just on the other side in case two more people wished to join in.

This was the same room she'd visited before, and yet, she didn't recall any of it.

She waited, careful not to disturb anything. A clock pealed in the distance and a dog barked several times, then stopped.

Finally Sophia entered the room, steps slow. She took a breath. 'He is not here.'

They only knew one person in common. Thoughts buffeted Isabel. Sophia thought William had already left the marriage. 'I know.'

Sophia's lips turned up. Her face eased. 'He *was* here. Almost all night.' She added the last words quickly. 'He has a chamber of his own here. He often comes to the house early in the morning and sends his coach home. Then we have breakfast and he falls asleep, and slips out in the evening.'

Sophia indicated Isabel sit, but Sophia remained standing.

'Does he talk much?' Isabel asked, making herself comfortable.

'No. But we don't have a lot to say. It is almost like a pair of slippers who've been stored side by side. He goes his places and I go mine, but we spend time together while nothing else is happening.'

'Oh.' Isabel imagined herself as another pair of slippers. Now she understood the marriage William wanted. But she preferred to be the same shoe and match. The one that was part of a pair.

She dismissed her thoughts. The marriage was still fresh. It would take at least a few days for him to understand how wonderful it was to have a wife. A cold thought hit her. Just as it had taken her parents a few days to understand how much they missed her and return.

Sophia interrupted Isabel's memories. 'William says you have a voice like a songbird.'

'I am pleased with it.' Isabel smiled.

'Would you sing something for me? I would like to hear it.'

Isabel opened her mouth, then stopped. Never before had she felt the slightest hesitation for singing. If someone asked a question, she had to prevent herself from giving the answer in song.

Shaking her head, she touched her throat. 'I can't. Today I woke up with a soreness and it would hurt to sing.'

'Later, then?' Sophia asked.

'Of course.' Isabel smiled, but her thoughts didn't match her face. Her desire to sing had fled in the same way a clock that had ticked a whole lifetime suddenly stopped and would not work again. She could not bear the thought of being watched while singing. Just could not. And it had been her favourite part of the performance before.

'I look forward to meeting your sisters and your husband,' Isabel said, turning the conversation in a different direction.

Sitting in the chair adjacent to Isabel, Sophia shrugged. 'You'll know sooner or later—my husband and William do not get on overly well. They are friendly.'

'It is not uncommon for a man to not think someone good enough for his sister.'

'It's not that.' She waved away the words. 'My husband is a few years older and he treats me as if I were born on a cloud and my feet shouldn't touch the ground. He feels William does not take life seriously enough.' She grimaced. 'William does take life seriously. Too seriously, I think.'

That was not quite how Isabel saw him. She raised her brows in question.

'He is quite determined to wring all the excitement out of it he can,' Sophia said. 'He may be out at all hours but it is a seriousness in itself—to grasp the spice of life. I became aware of it about a year after our mother died. He does not talk of what he does much. Sometimes he checks with the man-of-affairs to see how the finances are going and watches over what our sisters are doing. He has been counting on Aunt Emilia to find them matches. Usually, he is ready to sleep when he is here as he has been awake the night.'

'I do not know where he is right now, but he's not at his town house sleeping the day away.' She smiled to take any censure out of her words. 'But you know how we met so it is not as if it is a love match. I don't think he quite wants that.'

Calling it a friendship was even an overestimation. She would have liked nothing better to have been discovering his life from him, but instead she sat with his sister.

'I once had hope…' Sophia ran her fingers along the wooden arm of the chair, letting her words fall away into the room. 'I am only a year younger than he and closest to him. I was twelve when our mother died and our father grieved so much that William had nothing to do but take things in hand. My brother was quite the stickler with us. As he watched over us and made certain our lamps were out at a decent hour, he then bribed the coachman to take him about. He was tall even then and his ready smile helped get him wherever he wished to go. He told me the older men had no trouble testing the young pup's mettle and challenging him to keep up with them.' She grimaced behind her smile. 'He did, I'm sure.'

Isabel remembered his form flashing across in front of her as he tackled Mr Wren. 'Did he ever have cause to fight with someone?'

'I would imagine he did after our mother died. He would say he fell from a horse, and yet, he'd taken Father's carriage. The stories he tells me are all suitable for a grandmother's ears. My husband has privately mentioned a few escapades of my brother and they weren't saintly. William laughs it away when I ask and will not give a direct answer.' She paused. 'He never angers with me, except when I would jest at him about one of my friends hoping for his notice or ask him when he might marry. That is the only time he would anger. He would stay away longer as well.'

Isabel straightened her shoulders. William married because of his love for his sisters. He protected them. He wouldn't have wed her if not for the disgrace that would have been visited upon him and his family otherwise. She mustn't forget that.

'I do not want to be too inquisitive.' She used the same downward chin movement and the tilt of her head that could capture an audience's awareness. 'But has he ever been in love before?' Her demeanour was relaxed, but her heart braced for the reply. If he had been in love once, then he could fall in love again.

The thought jarred her. She wanted him to love her. Very much. And it was not as if she loved him. She'd been serious when she mentioned wanting to leave. Leaving could be much happier than loving someone who gave the highest regard to a friendly marriage. A Mr Grebbins.

Sophia laughed, leaning forward. 'You do not have to be jealous. I can assure you. Not long ago I asked him the same question. If you could have seen his face, you would have known he told the truth. He told me to bite my tongue. I have never known of any woman he has mentioned by name, although my husband has heard that William attended Drury Lane with someone on his arm.'

'I am so relieved.' Her shoulders dropped, but her smile might not have fooled friends who had seen her perform. William had not been in love. He'd started his adulthood earlier than many, yet had not even mentioned a woman by name to his sister.

'Does the—?' Sophia started, but then shrugged away her words.

'What?' Isabel asked. 'Please tell me what you were going to say.'

'I was going to ask about the ring. If he has mentioned it, or if you have it and have chosen not to wear it. I have not seen it since the night our mother died. William surely has it still.'

Isabel forced her hands to remain still and her eyes not to glance at the plain band on her finger. 'I haven't seen it.'

On the table beside her, Sophia touched the base of the lamp, turning it, staring into the glass. 'Our mother always wore the ring. The night she died, I was at the door because I'd heard a flurry of movement and knew something had happened. Father insisted William take the jewellery. Told him he must marry some day and it would be his wife's. William shouted he could not take something she loved so much. Father insisted.'

Isabel glanced at the gold band on her finger. It was like her own mother's wedding ring and her mother's band was a reflection of love. Now, the gloss on Isabel's seemed a jester's laugh, as practised as the words of songs.

She remembered the expression on her parents' faces

when they saw the other person enter the room—enchantment.

Kind Mr Grebbins and his wife had visited her parents often and both had the kindest words. Mrs Grebbins reminded Isabel of a fluffy hen clucking, preening happily in the sun, but almost unaware her husband was in the room. Mr Grebbins smiled often, in the way of a grandfather not seeing much more than a blurred shape.

Isabel had overheard her mother and father discussing how lonely the couple was. Mr Grebbins's first wife had died in childbirth and his heart had died with her. He'd married again, but he'd never danced with the same dash as he had with his first wife, nor had he laughed so heartily. He made the best of it and didn't bemoan his lot in life as Mrs Grebbins was a good sort, he was a good sort and that is what good sorts did. They had spent thirty years of their lives together. Good-sort years.

Mr and Mrs Grebbins had always ambled back to their home—silent—their shadows remaining alone, never touching.

Love is priceless and cannot blossom for every couple, her mother had said, and then her parents had shared a lingering glance.

At William's town house, when Isabel had left, William had wished her well with all the courtesy of Mr Grebbins suggesting to his wife they might leave before darkness descended.

Chapter Nine

Matrimony didn't agree with him. In fact, the whole house seemed out of sorts since his marriage. A fortnight should have been enough time for them to adjust. If it had been a manor, he would have called it Bumbling Hall. Cook didn't seem able to adjust to the circumstance of his asking for breakfast.

'My apologies.' The servant bowed her head as she exited his breakfast room, after replacing the drink. 'I brought you the mistress's chocolate and she does not wish for hers to be spiced as you do.'

He nodded, taking a sip from the glass left behind. The chocolate still wasn't correct. He tasted it again, drinking half of it to see if he could discern exactly what error had been made. He paused, realising why it tasted bland. His cook had not made morning chocolate for him in years. The only time he drank it was at Sophia's and he'd got used to the way her cook prepared it. If he ended the night at his own home, he sipped a brandy as he prepared for bed.

He left, returning to his sitting room. The newspaper lay on the table, but he had no wish to read it. He preferred his news from the club, either by men who had participated or men who'd seen it. Almost always the stories varied, but he sorted out the truth from them.

He picked up the print anyway. Reading through it, he then slapped it back down. Old news. He should have taken to the clubs. He would not make such a mistake tonight. All his friends would be abed now so he had no reason to trot out.

Sylvester had congratulated William on finding a bride who didn't curtail the nights out and said he planned to do the same.

He looked closer at the arm of the chair and pulled a bit of feather from it, then flicked the fluff aside.

William wasn't even certain if Isabel knew he was home or not.

Isabel was not like his sisters, always managing to burst upon him with some question, or leave this or that frippery for the servants to put away.

Moving to the door, he opened it and returned to his chair.

She'd not spoken with him since she had suggested she could leave and change her name. Perhaps that had been too imaginative, but still, she'd offered.

William had left each night at dusk since their wedding night, until the last one. He'd been arriving home some time after midnight because she'd listened and he didn't return before she fell asleep.

She could not imagine that Husband would be expecting her to provide an heir without his help. She'd also kept the smaller bed and although it had started as a rebellion of sorts, she'd considered it carefully and kept the plan. She looked at the paper in her hand, blowing to dry the inkspot she'd mistakenly made. Well, her penmanship never would win any notice.

She would not be able to send this letter to Grace. She hoped that Grace might meet William some day and draw a picture of him. Grace could sketch up anyone's face so quickly.

After Isabel realised she was to be married, she'd written to Grace, Rachel, and Joanna. Isabel had spent the entire day writing to everyone she knew—making sure they all knew of her good fortune so they would not suspect she'd made a judgement in error. She'd only admitted to Grace that the marriage was not exactly a love match, but more of a union of two sensible people in exact understanding of each other. Isabel's teeth had ached after writing the letters, but she was certain it conveyed a certain sophistication and a smattering of newly gained maturity.

Isabel knew she was indeed more fortunate than Grace, with the uncertainty of finding a child, and how horrible it was that Grace had not been able to keep the little one in the first place.

'Isabel.' William's voice interrupted her thoughts. She started. She hadn't heard him enter her sitting room. Her throat tightened and she nearly knocked the paper from the table. She caught it in mid-air and looked his way. His white cravat looped in a single knot. His face was freshly shaven, which jolted her. The other men she'd met had never looked anything but whisker-peeled after a shave.

She couldn't stare, he'd think her a twit. If she spoke, well, then she'd have to find words somewhere within her and she couldn't think of any.

'You look lost.' He took a step inside. 'What *are* you thinking of?'

Grace. Grace could rescue her once again. She couldn't tell him of Grace's misfortune, but she could talk of her schoolmate. 'My friend Grace, and how she used to make up tales about how the owner, Madame Dubois, obtained the governess school. My favourite was that she was a highwayman in her youth and robbed a merchant of all his gold. But one of the girls said her father insisted that the land was once owned by a peer. Madame spoke so elegantly, and I knew she was from France, that I could believe her somehow close to the aristocracy.'

Isabel picked up the paper she wrote on. 'Madame didn't like my favourite songs and told me I was only to sing ones approved by Miss Fanworth. Miss Fanworth approved few I liked.'

Isabel thought back to the excitement of watching the girls laugh and gasp when she sang the most gruesome songs, or sniffle when she chose a mournful tune.

But she had no more wishes to perform. The night at Mr Wren's had cured that.

'Are you settling in to your satisfaction?' he asked, lowering down into the easy chair across from her. The undersized chair gave him the appearance of even longer limbs.

'I am.'

'I don't know if I'm doing so well,' he said, laughing quietly. 'I've been home more these past few days than I'm used to.'

Her brows rose. 'You're serious?' He'd hardly been home at all.

'Usually I'm at Sophia's house. The club. Lord Robert has gambling events which last all night to several days, and he prefers them away from his home, so he finds a place where we can stay comfortably during breaks in the play.'

'Do you not like the town house?'

'It has my bed, a roof, room for the servants. That's all that matters.'

'It's a little sparse.'

He looked around the room. 'I suppose. I don't like tripping over furniture or lots of little cloths decorating here and there in a room.'

'Would you mind if I added just a few things?'

'Whatever you want to do is fine with me. Just not too many things that look like undergarments tossed about.'

'Table scarves?'

'That's why I have the inside shutters on the windows. I didn't want the look of chemises or a grandfather's coat hanging out to dry.'

'You've succeeded. It looks like you've either just moved in or are about to move out.'

He laughed, stretching one leg. 'I suppose you could be right on both counts. Sometimes that's how it feels.'

She studied him to see if he told the truth.

'Don't be concerned,' he said. 'I'll be visiting my father soon and I'll make sure the town house is in my name completely so that it can be yours for the rest of your life. You'll always have a home of your own now.'

'But, I…' She'd wanted him to say a home of their own. It wasn't as if she wanted him to say he loved her, but they were living together, married, and she wanted him to feel as if he belonged with her. 'I want you to like the house.'

His eyes wandered around the room. 'I like the windows in the front and I don't see you changing them.' He brushed back the hair at his temple. 'If you dislike the house, I can set my man-of-affairs on the search for another.'

'Oh, no.' She raised both palms. 'I just want you to feel like it matters to you. Like a home should feel.' She paused. 'I would hope.'

He put his elbow on the arm of the chair and raised his hand to prop his chin on it. He settled into the relaxed pose and watched her. 'It already feels more like a home than at any other day since I've moved in. No one moved above stairs before you arrived. Now, servants rush by with a plate of food leaving an aroma of a cooked meal behind. Or I hear you moving, or see you in the hallway and your cheeks light up just the barest, and your eyes smile, and I feel I've been bestowed a piece of treasure no one else even knows exists.'

She saw glints of a similar treasure behind his eyes.

'Thank you.' Warmth infused her cheeks, but she wasn't embarrassed.

'A songbird. Who doesn't have to be caged. Who flits

around and brings cheer. In this instance, my father was right. Marriage is an honourable state.'

He stood, planning to bend down to kiss her, but if he did, she might think it a sign of more affection than he could give.

He walked by, hoping she would retire early, and moved to his bedchamber.

William opened his nightstand drawer. Isabel had taken him at his word about penning notes. He lifted the last note passed along by the butler, opened it and read again. Isabel mentioned at both the beginning and end that it wasn't necessary for him to attend Lady Howell's soirée. He returned the note to the others, then flipped through them. The one before had mentioned the dress she'd purchased while out with his sister and she'd suggested the garment as suitable for an evening event. She'd also mentioned her wish to show them as deeply in love to the *ton* so no one would ever, ever hint of any impropriety of the past. For his future sons and daughters. Sisters. And himself.

Nothing truly personal was in the notes, yet he'd kept each one. The words of each breezed into the mind as if dashed from a smiling pen. Yet when he read the pages one after the other, the breeziness seemed procured.

Sadness touched him. Probably leftover-marriage tightness. He'd privately asked one of his older friends about the feelings a man might have after the deed was done and the answer had been little more than a shoulder shrug, and a discourse on the sanctity of friendships away from home, good libations, and how a lizard had been on the wall in 1797, or was it ninety-eight? That had helped tremendously and convinced him to spend another quiet night at home.

Waistcoat unbuttoned, he opened the bedchamber door, stepping into the hallway as Isabel rushed from her own room, a blast of feathers on her head. Even her reticule was feathered. He hoped there were no winds.

He paused as she caught sight of him. 'I thought to tell you I don't wish to attend Lady Howell's dance.'

Her lips rose at the sides. 'I don't either.' But something beyond the sky-blue eyes dimmed.

He didn't want to attend that soirée, but blue was his favourite colour, particularly when it had the sparkle of gemstones. He even liked the darkening blue of the sky before a storm. But he didn't like the dreary blue of sadness. 'But perhaps we should go.'

Her eyes brightened, then faded. She clasped her reticule in both hands. 'I do not know. It will...I don't want people to think I have married you for your...'

'Good looks?' he asked, raising his brows.

She opened her mouth briefly. Her cheeks reddened. She walked forward and slapped his arm lightly with the bag, causing a wisp of feather to break free and float between them.

'Oh, be serious,' she said, leaving, 'no one will think that.'

Chapter Ten

William didn't know if Isabel was aware he'd entered the parlour. He'd stopped at the doorway, watching. She was dressed for the soirée early, waiting for him.

She gazed out the middle window of the three, framed by the opening. If butterflies could become women, then Isabel had once had wings. It wasn't that she flitted around, although she could. Her reddish hair had the splash of colour that caught the eye and perhaps the same texture of a wing. The pale ball gown had hardly any hue in it except for the two flowing ties that attached at the back of her sleeves and flowed behind her. The fluttery azure fabric trailed down the back of her gown.

How did one manage a butterfly?

'Shall we leave?' he asked. Her reticule and fan lay in the chair beside him. To see someone else's property so at home in the chamber surprised him.

She didn't move. 'I suppose it is time.' She drew in a breath. 'I should not be worried. In the past, I stood in front of people easily. It's just now, it seems more daunting. The only person there I will know is your sister and she has said that her husband will certainly ask me to dance. I've met him.' She looked at her accessories. 'I do wish I didn't feel so much that I will be noticed out of kindness or curiosity.'

He leaned against the frame. He couldn't suggest they stay home that night. She needed to be comfortable in society and, with her nature, she would be as soon as she had a chance.

William snorted. 'You will dance many times,' he said. Cousin Sylvester would be sure to ask her as well. 'If my cousin approaches you, he will push the conversation in the direction of Wren's. He is an inquisitive little snipe, but we are related and he does have my horses.'

She turned, the fluttery ribbons of her sleeves emphasising movement. 'I won't mind.' Then her eyes widened before closing tightly. 'But sadly...' An internal wind buffeted her. Then she gazed again at him. 'But how can I talk of such an event at a soirée? I was indeed too frightened to move. If not for your presence, I would have expired from fright.' She touched the tip of her glove to her eye and wiped an imagined tear.

He watched and she gazed back. Within moments, her eyes saddened so much he wanted to reach to her, but then her lips turned up. 'I have heard but never tested it, that men do not always know how to speak with a tearful woman and might change the subject quickly.'

'You're quite good. How does one know if the tears are real?'

'They're real,' she said, lifting her brows. 'Always.' Isabel stared at him with wide-eyed innocence, causing him an inward chuckle. Sometimes her naivety appeared skin-deep to him. He wondered, if under the fluff and nonsense, hidden even from herself, an old spirit fought to reconcile with the world.

He held out his arm. 'Shall we leave?'

Her silent laughter brightened the room. She twirled and then closed the distance between them, the scent of roses swirling in the air.

He lifted the reticule and fan, holding them in her direction. She took them.

'Do you need anything else before we go?' he asked.

'Might you fetch me a compliment?'

Lightly he rested his hand at her back, the contact warming him and bringing a flush to her cheeks. He closed out all other moments by leaning in, whispering so his breath touched her ear, 'Compliments could not even begin to do justice to what I see.'

Her fan tip moved up, sliding down the smooth skin of his cheek, and stopping just over his heart. 'I think you managed it quite well.' She examined him. 'And I suppose your words of flattery are always real?'

'Never doubt them.'

She gave a tiny joust with her fan before putting it to her side. 'I won't.'

She turned, preceding him, and his fingers stretched so that the ties from her gown slid through them like gossamer.

* * *

Isabel gauged everyone in the room had known each other since before she was born. She was certain even the younger women had inherited some knowledge of each other well before birth. One woman raised a glass to her lips and three glittering bracelets slid on her glove. Four musicians played and only about twenty people bustled about in the room.

William led her to a woman and introduced her.

'So at last we meet your love,' the lady responded.

William's smile beamed. But his expression froze for just that instant the word *love* lingered in the air.

Their eyes caught. 'Yes, we have not been *wed* long,' she said, looking adoringly at him. Now *wed* caused his warm brown eyes to have flecks that looked like spear tips. She didn't wish to end the evening impaled so she struck the offensive words from her vocabulary.

Apparently, he didn't like profane speech.

'Ah.' A voice at her elbow jarred her. No one had been standing there a second ago. 'I believe no introductions are necessary for me,' the voice said.

'They are.' William's smile never faltered, as he introduced his cousin to her.

From a direct view, Sylvester's delicate features and long-limbed stance would have made artists ask him to pose, but when his head turned and she saw his profile Isabel noticed that, when in shadows, he could have passed for a well-attired weasel, in a handsome sort of way.

'May I have the first of what I expect to be many,

many dances throughout the years?' Sylvester bowed as he spoke.

William answered as Sylvester finished the question, 'As long as you mind your manners.' The commanding inflection in his voice couldn't be mistaken.

'Correct,' Sylvester answered, holding his arm for her to grasp. 'I could never do anything else with my enchanting new cousin.'

Sylvester whisked her away for a dance and she dodged his conversation easily. One didn't attend a governess school without having lessons in how to handle impertinent questions.

When the dance ended, he led her to the refreshments, and she suspected it was because the other guests had abandoned the area to begin a reel.

'I am impressed,' he said. 'Both with my cousin's choice and your ability to dance, not just with your feet, but with words as well, manoeuvring the talk back to me each time I spoke of Will.'

'The two of you are quite close and I'm sure you know all there is to know of him and only wish to learn my thoughts on the matter. I assure you, I feel the deepest loyalty to William Balfour.'

He grinned in response. 'My loyalty to him comes and goes, and I know it is not possible yet for you to have found out all the cracks and crevices in our world.'

'I would like to never find them out. So you may keep your silence.'

'Ah, Cousin. You speak the impossible.' He handed her a lemon drink, which surprised her as she expected him to give her the punch. 'I was merely a pawn in the elders' plan to shake William into the game of producing an heir. William may have let it slip to Mother that he never, ever intended to go through the uncertainty of watching children mature and having the responsibility. He may have felt that Harriet's birth contributed to his mother's illness. Everyone else thought so.'

'Your mother would scheme so?'

'It is not scheming—it is her family concern. She feels she didn't assist William enough when his mother died and she is making it correct now.'

The pianoforte sounded and the violinists began. Sylvester stepped closer so he could hear her.

Isabel took in a breath. 'He was hardly more than a child when his mother died. He couldn't have been expected to handle it all on his own. And yet I understand he certainly did much of it.'

'I would say he did all of it. Including the care of his father. The Viscount was near bedfast after the death just because he could not go on. My own mother had her hands full with her family and could not help. William had three sisters. Grieving.'

'He grieved, too.'

'I doubt his sisters let him.' Assured words.

She indicated a glass of the drink for him, but he shook his head.

'William often confided to me he expected never to marry,' he said, 'and part of that was because he wished never to have the worries of children. When I heard you were trained as a governess, the marriage made sense. A woman experienced in care for little ones. William has said to me many times that he managed his sisters and he does not wish to become a parent again. After Harriet got lost in the woods, I heard his recriminations to himself. When Sophia noted how dashing the foxed soldier was and thought he might need a wife to write to, William rushed straight to Mother to get her help. He now has enlisted her assistance on getting the other two wed also. Said she had had good luck with Sophia's marriage.'

She could not follow his conversation well because her mind had fixed on the first part of it. 'I don't think that my training as a governess mattered.'

'I would not bet the stables on that. Not that I do not think any man would find you appealing for a wife.' His cheeks reddened. 'But William was sincere in his intention not to wed. But I can see—' His face brightened more and he reached for the glass nearest and gulped down some of the lemon drink. Made a face and looked at the glass and swallowed as if trying to get the last vestiges from his taste. 'A governess. A person to care for the children. You know what I mean.'

'Yes. But, he is close to his sisters.'

'In a distant way. He is nearer Sophia now that she has married and has a husband to care for her. If you'll note, even the horses, Marvel and Ivory, were at his father's home. William prefers a wide swathe around him.'

'Thank you for keeping your cousin's confidences.'

'I have,' he said, leaving and tossing a wink her way. 'With family.'

He moved to the outer doors where William now stood and both began talking.

She didn't doubt a word Sylvester said. William had put some distance between himself and everyone else. It could have started when his mother died, or when he realised she was sick. Or earlier. It didn't matter.

Isabel took the lemon drink, finished it and noted the punch with reluctance. She was not sure how it had been mixed. She had heard the drinks ladies mixed for themselves often had more strength than what might be found in the men's glasses.

Isabel reached for a drink. The punch had its use. She was stranded in a sea of jewellery and wanted something to float about on.

On her first day at what she'd then called Madame Dubois's School for Abandoned Young Ladies, her parents had done exactly the same. They had introduced her, smiled all around and then she'd been on her own.

Her mother had made her leave her doll at home, telling her that she was all grown up. She didn't know what had happened to that plaything, but it would be nice to have her now, except, she supposed, the punch was the more mature version.

The liquid slid into her stomach, marking progress with heat. No, she'd never had any drink mixed quite so liberally. Putting the rim of the glass to her lips, she took an even tinier sip than before. Oh, she could quite shake the jewellery if she wished to.

More dancing. The music was quite good. The dancers were quite accomplished. The world was quite perfect around her. Just like the first day of school. Society, even a children's one, didn't allow cowering in the corner. Sipping very, very slowly, she examined the room, ignoring the glittery baubles.

This event was to set the stage for the rest of her life. She smiled and replaced the glass, reminding herself that no one could see beyond a confident smile into quivering insides.

Something bumped her from behind and she turned, a turban brushing her face. White hair straggled from the head-covering and one eye had a milky frost and the other a clear chill.

'Pardon.' The woman spoke. 'I have no time for proper introductions. One of my many faults. Not that I have many.' She looked to her right. 'You're not dancing. You should, you know. Does wonders for the complexion. I swear by it.' She chuckled. 'I'm at least eighty and I don't look a day over seventy-eight.'

'I would agree.'

'And your name is?'

'Isabel Balfour. I am married to the Viscount's son. He is—'

'Wait.' The woman raised a hand, stopping the words. Her gloves swallowed her thin arms. 'You may call me Lady Howell. If you forget, just think of a dog and its bark and then its howl at the moon.' Her nose wrinkled. 'That's how I remember it.'

She looked at Isabel's stomach. 'And are you increasing?'

'No. No.' Isabel narrowed her eyes, whispering.

'Well, you better get your mind to it,' the older woman said, voice strident. 'That's your duty now. Heirs.' She put a gnarled finger out. 'I had six in the first six years of marriage. Not many can carry that feat off. The trick is that the first one was very early—very early.' She leaned in and grinned. 'The second—I wasted no time.' She counted on her fingers. 'Three and four, twins. Five, well, what can I say, I had too much wine in celebration of finding a wet nurse for the twins. By six I put my foot down and said, I'd done my duty. I told Lord Howell to keep his distance. He howled.' She patted Isabel's arm. 'My favourite thing to tell people is how Howell howled. He never recovered fully.'

'I do think it would be nice to have children.'

The woman's lips tightened and her lower jaw jutted forward as she appraised Isabel. 'I recommend you stop at three. By the fourth child, they tend to put a strain on your temper.' She turned away.

Isabel heard her mumble as she left. 'The little chit cannot carry on a conversation.'

Then Lady Howell walked up to another sea of jewellery. The music ended and words jumped out from within the room. 'William Balfour's wife doesn't know her place in society.' All the faces turned Isabel's way.

The musicians even stared at her. How could they know who the woman spoke of? But apparently they did. They'd probably played at many soirées for the same people. This world was no bigger than a teacup and she was being examined as a speck in the bottom of the cup.

William stepped to her elbow and took her hand to pull it to his lips, then tuck it at his arm. 'Yes, she does know her place, Lady Howell. It is at my side.' He shot a look at the musicians and the next song began softly, easing the silence. 'Now we must be leaving, Lady Howell. Duties await us.'

He stood by his bed, hand on the post. He hadn't known the right words to say in the carriage and he suspected there weren't any. At least not that he could think of.

Leaving her alone at the soirée had been a mistake, but he'd been trying to get those horses—which could have waited.

He wanted to make it up to her. Neither of them deserved what had happened. At least she didn't. Society was not always easy for women who didn't live in it from birth.

Isabel shouldn't be belittled, except perhaps for keeping that ridiculously small bed.

Ridiculously small.

Somehow it had become a battlement. A territorial stake of some sort that he didn't understand. Why, the whole house was hers to command. Everything but his personal effects. And the valet. And the butler. But he wasn't certain she quite understood about the butler.

He pulled the tail of his shirt from his trousers. His boots were already put away. Reaching for his dressing gown, he placed it over the back of a chair and moved to the hallway.

'Isabel…' he opened the door and stuck his head in, inhaling the scent of roses and soaps '…it's too early to sleep.'

'No it's not. Not for me. Go away.' She rolled, putting her back to him. 'I have a headache that starts at my feet and goes straight to my forehead. The slippers were too tight.'

He left the door open. Moving to a chair, he picked it up and placed it closer to the bed. He sat, clasped his fingers lightly and stretched his legs, one foot moving to her counterpane. His heel rested at a covered mound which hid her leg.

'I know you're here for your duty,' she said.

'If I must, I must.'

He moved his feet to the floor, scooted his chair closer and pulled the cover from her foot and took it in his hands. Warm and delicate. She slid her foot aside, but he caught it. Covering her foot with his grasp, he kneaded the bottom with both thumbs. Her foot tilted towards him.

He pressed against each muscle, easing away tension, rubbing over the skin, soothing it.

'That is better than a warm bath,' she said.

He reached out, caressing the other toes with the same care. 'Is your headache any better?'

'I had thought not to wear those slippers again, but I do like the colour and if you could do this afterwards, I might keep them. Would save you the cost of another pair.'

'But is your headache any better?'

'I am not sure.'

He continued, sweeping his hands to ankles, kneading and rubbing. 'I suppose it will take me a while to get there, but I shall.' He continued sweeping his hands just above her heels. 'But not in that bed.'

'So,' she said. 'You will not do your duty while I am in this bed.'

He nudged her foot. 'Duty. That word is hideous.' He stood. 'Move over.'

'I thought you said…'

'Duty has nothing to do with it. Share the mattress.'

'There is not room in this bed for two people. It only holds me.'

'I noticed. Give me some room.' One knee on the bed, he wedged himself in beside her, tossing the covers away and rolling her to face him. 'See, it holds two people, except for my feet.' He moved one leg up and draped it over her thigh and adjusted close. The same delicate scent he'd noticed when he'd walked into the room engulfed him. 'I'm sorry you didn't enjoy the soirée. I didn't either.'

'I thought Lady Howell's invitation sincere.'

'It was—for her. If it makes you feel better, she has called me a tosspot and I believe she called my father a lovestruck chit.'

'It doesn't. Now I feel sad for you and your father. Well, for your father.' She snuggled. 'Are you a tosspot?'

'Who knows?' He shrugged.

Chapter Eleven

Arms tightened around her, embracing her so completely she could feel nothing but maleness and heart-beats. A wall of strength caressing her with the lightest touch. She'd never felt so safe.

Her hand clasped his side, over the cloth of his shirt, and her fingertips brushed back and forth, the friction the cloth created under her hand bringing his skin alive to her touch. 'Do you think you are a tosspot?'

'You are intent on that question.'

'And you do not wish to answer.'

His chest moved with a slow intake of breath, giving her room to get closer and yet, when he breathed out, she remained burrowed against him. 'I drink more than many, but not as much as I did. Several years ago, I noticed my friends were sotted every night and I was there as often as not.'

The room was silent before he continued, his words pulling her inside his thoughts. 'I wondered if I could go a fortnight without drink. On the sixth day, I was at the club and the scent of spirits lingered in the air so much I could think of nothing else. I was surrounded by desire for it. I ached for it.'

He stopped speaking. She pressed at his side. 'Well?'

'Sylvester put a drink in front of me and I sat with it for hours. But I refused. I went to Sophia's and slept a few hours until morning and then drank chocolate while I waited for her to wake. I drank possibly three glasses in three hours of waiting for my sister who'd decided to sleep in. Luckily, her cook makes very good chocolate.'

'I didn't like it so well as what the cook makes here. Your sister's burns the mouth.'

'Ah, yes. It's very good.'

'Did you finish the fortnight?'

'Of course. I didn't doubt it. I refused to let my want for it overcome what I truly desired and my biggest want was to be in control of the liquid. I didn't have to drink. Since then I have not felt as if it matters so much whether I have drink or not. On occasion, I even have a child's drink called milk. I have also discovered that one of my servants can take a jug to a home just outside of town and find water that tastes wondrous and refreshes my thirst better than anything. It is the best thing I've ever tasted.' He laughed. 'I can be as particular about the water I drink as some men are about their brandy. Makes all the difference. Even the tea is better.'

His hand ran the length of her back stopping as it slid to her hip. His face moved closer and his kiss barely brushed her lips. Tremors raced in her body. 'The best thing I've tasted, except for one other thing.'

His kiss didn't have the hint of brandy, or anything

but the freshness of him. 'That is much better than any drink.'

She hugged him tight, the length of his body pressing hers. The bed could have been half the size and they both would have fit. She could feel nothing in the world but him and it was the best feeling she'd ever had.

He pulled back, leaving one whisper of his lips against hers before breaking contact, and leaving her dazed with the loss.

'Isabel. I may not have been entirely honest with you.' He sat up, moving from the bed and reaching back to scoop her up into his arms. 'I will do my duty.'

She gasped, but her arms slipped around his neck. He moved, widening his stance, maintaining his balance.

'I am not at all concerned about the duty to the title,' he said. 'I am concerned about my duty to you. I simply cannot leave you in such a small bed. I cannot.'

'I am happy with it.' She put her arm around his neck. 'I mean that.'

'Well, you must give my bed one more chance.' Their faces close, he took her out the door. 'But do not destroy my manly pride.'

When they reached his bedchamber, she noticed the light flowing through the doorway. 'You left the door open. You planned this.'

He took her inside and the scent of shaving soap lingered in the air. 'I said I was a tosspot, not a fool.' He stopped in mid-stride. 'I must tell you that tonight—' His face rested near her ear. 'I would have built scaffolding to your window to hold you in my arms.'

A burst of warmth hit her when his nose nuzzled

at her ear, his voice barely aloud. 'And it would have been worth it.'

He turned so she could see his bed. 'We need more than that little pillow of a mattress you sleep on.'

With a sweep of his arms, he tossed her on to the bed and then he followed, landing around her, his weight cushioned by his arms.

'How is your headache?' He ran his fingers over her cheek, leaving warm rivulets larger than the path of his touch.

'It is completely gone.' She put one hand up, feeling the tendrils where his hair brushed his collar.

'Now,' he said, enfolding her in his arms, 'let me tell you how sorry I am that you had a bad experience tonight.' He squeezed lightly. 'But it's over.'

He'd just hugged her.

'That did make me feel better.' She reached out, clasped the front of his shirt and tugged.

He chuckled and squeezed her again and again and again, each time almost taking her breath away. 'Even better now?' The laughter in his voice, along with the hug, accepted her.

'Don't squash me in two pieces.' She lay in the crook of his arm.

'I wouldn't want to squash you in one piece.' He put a hand at her stomach. Waves of something delicious reverberated within her. 'Although in that tiny bed you have… See how much nicer this is.'

'I don't see that I have that much more room in it.' She wriggled against him. 'I can't even reach out my arm.'

He rolled her so that they lay facing each other, side

by side. 'Oh, by all means, reach out your arms all you wish, as long as it is in this direction.'

She pretended to push at his chest. He didn't move. She pushed. He still didn't move. He studied her, squinting. 'That's not what I meant.'

Reversing the direction, she tugged at his side. He tumbled against her. 'Ah, yes,' he said, breathing the words into her ear. She moved her head so their lips could meet and he pressed against her. Hunger grew inside her. She could not get close enough.

He tugged his shirt aside, moving apart long enough to pull it over his head.

Without her moving, his mouth found hers and he grasped the ties of her chemise, his fingers smoothing them, reaching to the very last of the ribbons, straightening, bringing the skin beneath the fastening to life before he slipped the knot loose.

He touched the chemise, his hands smoothing over the skin underneath while the garment moved up with each caress.

His legs brushed hers. A rough texture against the softness of her skin. Pleasure tingled from each movement.

He lifted the garment over her head and, as he pulled it up, his skin replaced where the fabric had touched. He could not possibly be surrounding her as closely as the clothing, but he did. She couldn't feel any other sensation of the bed, or time or presence except him.

'Songbird,' he whispered in her ear, the words hitting her in the way of music, a music shared by their bodies.

He cupped the underside of her breast and his face

moved over it, the sensation of the roughened chin and smooth lips interspersing one with the other.

His hand at her thigh caused her to writhe towards him, but he held her back, using touch to bring her to a crescendo of sensations, overpowering her with gentleness.

Then he moved his body close, sliding above her, his eyes holding her, until he shifted, enveloping her with their joining.

His shoulders held his chest above her and she pulled, but William's strength kept his weight from crushing down and her body moved up to meet his.

Their breathing increased, until the pause, and her heart stilled.

Neither moved, savouring one last second of togetherness, before he rolled to clasp her close at his side.

William stared overhead, Isabel nestled in the crook of his arms and her fingers swirled over his chest. She felt more comfortable against him than his own heartbeats felt in his body.

'Are you asleep?' she asked.

'Yes. I have been for this past hour.'

She laughed. 'Then I had best leave before you wake because I don't think I will be able to survive much more.'

He hugged her close, giving him a completeness he'd never felt before.

'You feel so strong,' she said. 'As if you are twice my strength.' Her palm flattened and stilled.

'You jest,' he whispered and rolled, keeping her

in his arms to stop above her. 'I am three times your strength at least. Four on a good day.'

She pushed at his chest, but he swooped down to cover her face with kisses before he rolled to his back again.

This was not working as he'd hoped. In truth, he didn't feel stronger, but weaker. He could not force himself to roll from the bed.

'Is this not better than being a governess?' he asked.

'I don't know it is that much different,' she said. 'My charge is just much more difficult to command. Did you not learn when you were a child that you must obey the governess?'

'No. I am quite certain only my sisters had a governess. I had a tutor. My father would step into the room as I studied my lessons and make certain to check with the instructor to ask what I was being taught. He was always enquiring if I had learned my numbers that day. Sometimes my mother would insist the tutor work with my sisters. Father would bluster that they didn't need to learn, because they were to marry. She would tell him that their husbands might need help understanding the sums.'

'I think I would have liked your mother.'

A grunt of agreement. Both his mother and father had seen that his days were filled with learning and responsibility. At least until his mother became ill. When she failed, the world changed. When the Viscount lost his wife, he lost all care for the world.

'We'd just finished a portrait sitting when my mother became ill. The paint wasn't dry. Immediately after her death, my father commissioned a larger portrait just of her. It still hangs in the library.'

The portrait was impossible to miss. His father had sat in the room days on end staring at the likeness, twisting her handkerchief in his hand. William had hardly ever entered the room. Seeing his mother's face had been like having a blade in his stomach. It reminded him that she was no longer with them. Seeing his father sitting there, dazed, lost to them, willingly, had been worse than his mother's death.

'I don't like to talk of it,' he said. 'The past is gone. It was not that hard for me to put it behind me. I loved Mother dearly, but it just was not the terrible tragedy for me that it was for my sisters. Oh, they carried on so.' He bumped his head against hers. 'You would not believe the tears. Rosalind was six and giving in to grief too much and would not leave her room, just as Father would not leave the portrait. We had to do something. Sophia and I picked Rosalind up. I had her under the arms and Sophia her feet and we carried her down the stairway. It is a wonder we didn't kill ourselves. Sophia had tears rolling down her cheeks. Then we locked Rosalind out of the house and told her she could not return until she stopped crying.'

'Did it work?'

'She totally destroyed the window, but she was not crying when she found us and told us we could not lock her out of the house. She said she would burn the house down before she let us do that. I believed her. Rosalind is strong-willed. The fuss upset Harriet. I had to drag her from under the bed, then she was afraid the house would catch afire while she was asleep and the nursery maid would not wake and we would all die. So she would not sleep unless Sophia and I were with her and then Rosalind had to be there as well because…I cannot remember why. Oh, yes. Harriet was afraid that if we let Rosalind sleep anywhere else she would start the house afire. She convinced Rosalind to stay with her and things got better.'

For three months his sisters had all slept in one bed and he had put two chairs together and tried to sleep. He'd hardly been able to get any rest. Then he'd started leaving the house after his sisters slept. He'd felt guilt for leaving that first night, but his father had remained staring at the portrait and William had not been able to stand another moment of the grief. The men at the tavern had welcomed him and they'd all known his mother had died. They'd drunk to life and laughter and pretty lasses.

Isabel's arms tightened at his waist. 'You were so young to deal with that.'

He snorted. 'I was not. I was a man at thirteen. When I was fourteen I discovered that my mother's cousin had diverted nearly four hundred pounds of my father's funds. Then, when I was away at university, at first Sophia would help me keep an eye on Father's affairs.'

Things had changed while he was at university. Rosalind and Harriet became more interested in the funds, particularly after he let them keep a portion of all increases to themselves. That had been a profitable decision. Rosalind had signed their father's name on to a letter hiring a quite good land steward.

'Rosalind became quite good at forgery and understanding accounts. Harriet reads all she can find about crops and livestock, and shares the information with the tenants. Harriet knows the number of eggs any breed of chicken should lay in the first year and how much the amount of eggs will decline in the second. She has also informed me that if a chicken starts laying eggs with thin shells, a solution is to crush eggshells and put them about for the chickens to peck. Father barely knows how the eggs get on the table.'

William turned to Isabel. He brushed a kiss on her nose, gave her a squeeze to pull her close and then rolled from the bed.

The most fortunate thing of the night had happened when he talked of the past. 'I cannot sleep this early.' He dropped another kiss on her forehead, softening his words. 'Goodnight, Songbird.'

Those last words were safe. They sounded pleasant, but meant nothing. He would go to the club and possibly visit Sophia later. One didn't want to start a habit which might be hard to break.

Isabel sat in front of the window, letting the evening light shine on the paper so she wouldn't have to have a lamp.

William had arrived home around midday. She'd heard his footsteps and then the door of his room closed, and nothing else.

Having him home pleased her, but she wished it didn't. It would be best if she celebrated his leaving.

Sylvester's words returned to her. William had taken

care of his sisters when he should have had someone caring for him. The memories of grief and responsibility had blended, causing him not to wish for children.

A maid opened and closed a door, bringing Isabel her tea.

'French apricot biscuits,' the maid said. Isabel nodded.

The maid opened the door to exit, holding the empty tray, then stepped sideways to give William room to enter.

Looking at the paper, she ignored his presence and gave a puff, pretending to dry ink.

'You should put on a performance for my sisters. I would like to see it as well.'

'I wasn't married when I wished to sing. I was younger.' Something had changed after the night at Wren's. The way the men had watched the singer. Before, she'd not minded the eyes on her. Loved the attention. After watching the singer warble and the men leering, now she could only think of the faded shading and the filth in the corner and the scurrying of insects. Just the thought tightened her stomach in the most unpleasant way.

Her eyes locked on his boots.

He knelt, holding her desk with one hand to keep himself easily balanced, but his face was now lower and she couldn't escape his examination.

'Sing a quick song. Just for me. Nothing particular. A lullaby.'

She shook her head and brushed across the papers with her fingertips.

'I can hear you hum when I am in the hallway.'

'I don't hum.'

He stared at her.

'I tried to sing for your sister Sophia and I could not. Never before had that happened. Not ever close to that. But the words were frozen inside me.'

The night she'd been attacked, she'd feared Wren might destroy her voice with the knife. He hadn't, but the blade had reached into her spirit and taken away her wish to sing.

'Isabel. You can't lock that voice away. It is a part of you. You must let others hear it as well.'

'No. Just the thought of singing in front of people now…' She touched her stomach, trying to brush away the coldness.

Chapter Twelve

He was a fool.

He let himself out the door and walked to the mews, escaping his house. Before, he'd wanted to go to the taverns and clubs, but now he felt forced away. Because he knew what would happen if he stayed in. He'd not be able to turn away from her as easily as he'd turned from the drink.

He wasn't deserting Isabel, but he could not bear the thoughts buffeting himself another second. He had one foot in the memories of the past and another dangling in Isabel's direction to be pulled even deeper into the strangling world of emotions.

He had a chamber that had a suitable bed and he could have used it. He just didn't want to be mired in thoughts and when Isabel was near he acted on impulse, and then his mind followed. The actions he liked; the thoughts he could do without.

He ran his fingers through his hair and ignored the darkness around him, reminding himself of the saying that it was darkest before the day dawned. But it was also dark in the light when grief took the day and choked it lifeless. If not for the nights of drinking and revelry, he could not have survived the past.

Three grieving sisters trying to find their footing and a father who could not move didn't spread joy and sunshine all about.

Some things were best forgotten. Thinking of the past only put one back into it. Life wasn't to be lived in memories, but in experiences. Forward at full rush, letting the wind of revelry breeze the thoughts away suited him best.

He owed Isabel nothing, other than material things and, of course, not to bring her public disgrace. He had saved her and in return had had little choice except marriage.

All in all, he felt rather fortunate when he truly considered the options of a wife other than Isabel. In fact, the one good thing of this was that Isabel would have been his choice had he wished to marry, but he hadn't.

He planned out the next few days of his life. He would work to get the horses back and he would spend an enjoyable time doing so. A few nights with his friends at the clubs should clear his mind.

'Are you going to stare at the cards all night?' Sylvester asked.

With a small shake of his head, William pulled a card from his hand and put it on the table. He'd lost again. He didn't care.

Lord Robert, younger brother of the Duke of Wake-field, made a rude jest. Sylvester laughed. The Duke didn't. William hadn't thought the comment insulting Sylvester humorous either.

The ale tasted off. He kept hearing Isabel's voice, and the tune she hummed. He stood. 'I'm finished.'

Sylvester looked his way, smiling. 'Leaving early?'

'I just want to go. My luck with cards is dismal to-night. Next time should be better.' He'd spent the last few nights running around the clubs with Sylvester and staying up all night.

When he returned home to sleep in the day, Isabel had been moving about in the house. He was certain she'd known he was trying to rest and had strolled about slamming doors. One could not accidentally create that much noise in the hallway outside his bedchamber door.

'I imagine you do,' Sylvester said. 'Ready to beg her forgiveness. You've not fooled me. I know she's got her chemise knotted around your private parts. You're going to be wearing a bonnet if you give in.' He leaned towards William.

'I told you we didn't have a disagreement,' he said. 'We are getting along quite well. She has no complaints of anything I say or do.'

'Unlike the rest of us,' Sylvester said. 'But go along home. You'd best enjoy the fruits of marriage if you have to wear the fripperies. If a woman such as she asked me to wear a bonnet, I would ask which colour was her favourite.' He paused. 'Which colour do you choose, Will?'

William clamped a hand on his cousin's shoulder. 'You should be so fortunate as to wed someone like Isabel.'

'I married a dainty little doll,' Lord Robert said, 'and the next thing I knew she had feet bigger than mine and had filled the house with crying babies, plus all her cousins and her mother, grandmother and grandfather.' He mused, almost whispering, 'I married one woman and ended up with a village under my roof.'

The Duke of Wakefield didn't raise his eyes. 'You just didn't find the right woman.'

'Because she does not exist,' Lord Robert grumbled, thrusting a finger under his eyepatch and rubbing at the eye he'd lost long ago. 'Even my mistress is more trouble than she's worth. I had to tell her I am with my wife tonight just so I can get some respite from her.'

The Duke of Wakefield stood, his chair clattering back, tossing his cards face-up on the table. 'I can see why you men prefer each other's company instead of a wife's.' His voice choked on the last word. 'A woman might expect something out of a conversation.' His eyes misted and he turned on his heel and stomped from the room.

'Blast,' Lord Robert said. 'He's acted like he's wearing a coat of brambles since his wife passed away.'

William stared after the Duke. Wakefield's loss had been months before. Months. In the early part of the year.

Lord Robert adjusted the patch, stared at the disarray on the table and then sorted the funds from the cards.

'That was a winning hand he forfeited. You can tell that my brother has never met my mistress. She doesn't expect anything out of a conversation.'

'Neither do my horses,' Sylvester said, glancing at William. 'I'm planning to dash off to see them. Autumn is a good time to visit the country. Marvel and Ivory should be ridden and not just by stable hands. If you want to see how they're faring, and take in the countryside, you might trot down to the estate with me, Will.'

'I'll think about it,' William strode to the hallway, leaving—going home. He had no desire to go to the country, but he kept remembering the pain in Wakefield's voice. The Duchess had been rather insipid, in William's opinion. Love had altered the Duke's mind.

The night air had cooled, giving a liveliness to the darkness. His mood lightened as the sharper air hit his face. He had no wish to be anywhere else. In a few moments he would be home and he would not have to see Isabel, but surely it would cause no harm to speak with her.

He frowned. He was rushing home like some besotted fool. A few more times of such and he would be strangled by those corset ties.

When he stepped into his house, his butler met him with a note, then whisked away.

Isabel had written to tell him that she was spending the night at Sophia's and would return later on the morrow than she expected. Of course, Sophia had invited him, too. He crumpled the paper and let it fall to the floor. Just as well.

He bent and swept the paper into his hand, smoothed and folded it. He'd have enough for a bonfire by Christmastime.

Walking up the stairs, he stopped at his room only long enough to add the notes to the rest, then he moved down the hallway. At her chamber, he opened her door and peered inside, just to make sure she hadn't returned. He knew full well the butler would have told him if Isabel was at home, but perhaps she'd returned and the servant hadn't seen her.

He inhaled, enjoying the soft scent. Roses again. Taking off his coat, he tossed it over a chair and added his waistcoat. Sitting on the dismal bed, he flattened his hand and pushed into the mattress. It should have been replaced years ago, but he'd had no reason to do so in the past.

Removing his boots, he let them fall to the side. Stretching, he lay down. His feet dangled at the end of the bed.

He had to find a way to cleanse her from his thoughts. He remembered staring at the glass of amber liquid. The feeling of power when he no longer wanted the taste in his mouth and could stand and walk away.

In her room, the presence of Isabel engulfed him. He breathed in deeply, noting only the barest hint of roses in the air. He imagined the taste of her, the lightness of his knuckles brushing against her skin and the way her eyes reflected the blue of the sky.

He imagined her twirling, taking in the world like a flower taking in the morning rain and savouring the drops on petals and the flourishing moments of being alive and at the height of a bloom.

He ached for her.

He rolled from the bed, grabbed his clothing and strode from the room, shutting the door with a slam which was much too muted for his own comfort.

He could hear Isabel at the stairway. She had not jested when she'd written that she would be home later than expected.

The paper tightened in his grasp. Footsteps tapped. Tap. Tap. Pause. Tap. Tap. Tap. He could imagine her stopping. One could almost read her thoughts by her movement. She would come in and beg his pardon for being about while he was at home. He was certain of it. Isabel was a generous-spirited person.

He lowered the paper and peered over it.

She stopped long enough to glance in, wave a parcel in his direction and then strolled by the door. A maid followed her, bowing under the weight of her load. He folded the paper, rolled it and popped it against his knee.

He would get someone to summon her. Or send her a note. They must talk. Not a single one of the parcels could have been a larger bed. Perhaps he should just move the little puff of furniture out of the room himself.

The soft voice jolted his reverie. 'Are you ill?' she asked. He'd not heard her step into the room. He looked up. She closed half the distance between them and peered at him with wide eyes.

He forgot. He forgot what he was so angry at her for. 'I am fine,' he answered. 'I didn't sleep well.'

'It is rather early for you to be awake.'

Her eyes blinked with the innocence of a babe and weakened something inside him so that he felt as if he were the one taking his first steps. Wobbling.

He unfurled the paper and looked at it again. 'I hope you had a good visit with Sophia.' The words reminded him. She had not alerted him beforehand of her plans. What if…what if she'd instructed the coachman to take her to her parents' home, or what if she'd decided to go to somewhere and sing something and someone had been about with evil plans? 'You must be careful when you are out.'

'Oh…' she raised her brows '…I took a maid. The burly one. And your coachman…'

'It is a dangerous world. As you well know.'

'Yes. Your sister has told me about the many times you have gathered bruises in the night hours.' She brightened. 'I admit. You dived at Wren as if you had done it before and I cannot complain.' She glanced at him. 'Have you had call to use your fists before?'

'Not in Wren's. Now let us change the subject.'

'Certainly. I don't wish to talk about Wren.' She raised her brows. 'Have you had many fights?'

'No. How is Sophia?'

'She is fine. How many fights?'

'I didn't keep records. And did you enjoy your visit?'

'Very much. She told of a time she thought your nose had been broken and you said you stumbled into a chair.'

'It was inconveniently in the hands of a man who also bumped his nose against it before the night was over.

And has that oaf of a husband of Sophia's whittled any more wooden hearts for her?'

'He whittles hearts for her?' Eyes gauged William's face.

'Yes. He's daft.' Inside William smiled. Subject changed. 'I'm surprised she didn't show them to you. Pulled them out every time I saw her for months afterwards.' Couldn't change that subject easily either. *You should marry,* Sophia had mentioned. Once. Each minute.

'We talked of everything from corsets to Christmas.' She beamed. 'I never thought to have a sister. And now I have three. Sophia plans a gathering with your other two sisters so I can meet them soon. I am looking forward to it.'

'Some post arrived for you.' He pointed to the letter on the table.

She opened it and read, and kept her eyes on the page. It could not take that long to peruse.

'What is it?' he asked, moving to her.

'From my mother. I did want her to think this a love match, at least for a time.' She handed it to him. 'She is not much for writing letters.'

He read, resisting the urge to shred the pages. 'She does not truly see you. I should write her and tell her the error in her words. But I am sure she does not realise what she said.'

Isabel's hand touched her plain wedding band. 'I didn't want her to know the truth any more than you wanted them to think you attacked me.'

He folded the missive, eyes on it. 'Did you need to

keep this?' Before she answered, he ripped it across, across again and then once more. 'If you save something that brings you unhappiness, it is like saving a stone for an enemy to throw at you again and again.'

Her azure eyes stared at him.

'It does not bring me unhappiness. It is just my mother's way of speaking. She does not always hear what she says.' Isabel watched him as if he'd lost his mind.

He held the torn paper to her. 'Burn it.'

'William.' She examined him. 'She didn't say anything dreadful.'

Returning to his chair, he picked up the newsprint. 'I just didn't like the way—Isabel, I am out of sorts today. I lost at cards the other night.'

'A large sum?' she asked.

He shook his head. 'No. I simply do not like to lose.'

'No one does, William. That is what makes winning so grand.'

'I do not need the grandness.' He had been reading the same publication for days now and the words had kept fading into the blue of Isabel's eyes. Perhaps once he went away he'd be able to think of something besides the azure.

'Thank you for the kindness you've shown.' She closed her fist over the papers. 'I'll toss this into the fireplace.'

She walked over, leaned his way and put a kiss on his forehead. Of all the places to kiss… He was not five years old. Then she turned to leave and something inside him plummeted.

The realisation of his dismay at her turning away

caused another bolt of something in his chest. His feet were on the ground, but his life didn't feel connected to him any more.

'I need to go to my father's home.' He did. He didn't feel he belonged in his house any more. He'd not spent a lot of time in it before, which had not mattered at the time. But now it did. In truth, William could hardly bear to spend so much time gambling now and counted the hours until he could return to the town house, only it didn't feel the same as it did.

And he longed for the scent of roses.

He just needed to get past this one hurdle of newness. Before the marriage, he had not wanted to be at home. But now he felt displaced from it by Isabel.

To go to the country could be reviving. The town house kept them too much in proximity. An outing could divert him. He needed a change from the blue eyes and wistfulness in them. It was not fair for her to have him underfoot so much. A woman learning a new home in a new town didn't need to be stumbling over a man as well.

He wasn't happy at the taverns, listening to the boasts and jests of the other men as they talked of their conquests, while he thought of Isabel.

'A change could do well for both of us.' He didn't look at her when he spoke. He could not bear to see innocent hope reflected from her gaze, or dismay, or relief at his departure. 'My cousin Sylvester is leaving to go to the country and invited me. If I go, I'll be able to purchase the horses back. You'll find your footing in the house without tripping over me. Sophia will be near if you need anything. And I'll have a messenger at hand for you to deliver notes as often as you wish.'

Notes, Isabel thought. Her arm would expire with the number of notes she could pen to him if that was what he wished to see instead of her.

'How long will you be gone?'

'I have not thought about it. With Sylvester, you never know what will happen. And Harriet has written that my father has been in the attic moving things here and there. It seems as if he has decided to look at every scrap of the past my mother touched. Rosalind worries that he has suggested some endeavours to my man-of-affairs that she doubts will be productive. Father has been so removed from the world he does not realise what we've done in the past decade.'

'He doesn't listen to your sisters?'

'As of last time we spoke, he didn't listen much to anyone. But it is good for him to be taking more notice of things. It's just that it is not needed now and he should find other ways to amuse himself than in prodding around in the affairs of the estate. We have managed well for years without his interference and we don't need him to muddle things now.'

'Perhaps he wants the feeling of being needed.'

William didn't move. 'It is a little late for that.' He took the newsprint from the floor and glanced at it again. 'But I will give him a listen. All the care of him shouldn't fall on Rosalind and Harriet.'

'Are you sure it is care of him that he needs? Perhaps he needs you to care *for* him.'

He turned and mused, 'I should take Harriet this paper as it has mention of events that could be planned for the Season. Perhaps she'll decide to stay with Sophia and attend the soirées. She refused last year.'

'William. Are you listening at all?'

Brown eyes landed on her, but flicked away. 'He is our father. Of course we care for him. Did we not manage his affairs—although I know it benefited us as well? We kept the roof over his head, the windows clear for the sun he could not see to shine in on him and took care of all around him. Soph, Ros and Harriet cajoled him to move about. I threatened.' He opened the paper, turning the pages, searching.

'So now he understands what you wished for and can do it.' Isabel stepped closer, almost against the newsprint.

William kept searching the words. '*Now* he wants to meddle in our work, but he must simply be shown that it is not needed. I will do as I did with my sisters who could be cajoled with a promise of fripperies. He will be soothed by the thought that two of his children have wed—two more could and soon he could have grand-children—something he claimed a necessity.' He folded the paper to the section he wanted. 'Yes, this should do for Harriet.'

'William, do you not think it unpleasant when your father wished you to wed?'

'I am merely dangling the possibility. I will not fuss if she doesn't wish to marry. Rosalind can stay unwed, too, for all I care. But they have stayed in the country to watch Father and I don't wish him to ruin their lives because they believe he needs them. I have fought against his neglect in the past and I will not let it happen because they have compassion for a man who had none for them.'

He tossed the paper into the chair. 'You were not there when he turned his back on his daughters. I really do not see any problem with him understanding our wishes. After all, now there is the possibility of an heir to mention and bring him to the realisation that we are no longer infants and can care for ourselves without help.'

He stepped to the window, glanced out and then said, 'I can understand his feeling that I was old enough to be left on my own when Mother died, but I cannot believe he ignored my sisters. Mother would have wept.'

'Yes, some females do not like to be ignored.' She didn't linger, but moved to the door. 'You do not have to tell me goodbye,' she said. 'It will be little different anyway.'

Chapter Thirteen

She had received two notes from William. One mentioned the need for him to help his father longer as the man was trying to comprehend records William now realised the Viscount had never ever noticed. Not even when his wife was alive. William wished Isabel all the best and appreciated the notes.

She didn't quite think the last bit of the statement was written with the utmost sincerity.

The note she had received a fortnight before expressed that he would return soon, perhaps within days, and mentioned his happiness that she had met Rosalind and Harriet, and he wished Isabel all the best and so forth. It was surely a coincidence he'd written the second time after his sisters had returned to the country. They'd been quite curious that she'd not travelled with him, nor received a post from him, and they were certain he'd been getting hers. She'd mentioned a need to stay home to take care of her…aunt…who lived nearby. When the women remarked on their wish to meet the aunt, sadly, the aunt could not as she was quite reclusive. She always feared strangers would steal her gold.

When she'd said those words, Isabel feared she'd gone too far, so she'd added the mention of her aunt having no gold.

Isabel sighed. Soon, she expected she'd be writing letters to the imaginary aunt, thanking her for all the times she'd been helpful.

She'd like to write to her mother, but once her mother had asked Isabel to save the letters until she had five to combine as the cost to receive posts was dear.

If not for music she didn't think she would have ever managed happily at the school. Grace had heard her singing to a rag doll Isabel had traded her best hair ribbons for and asked to hear it again. She'd managed to feel at home at Madame Dubois's school after she began to sing with the others. And now she had made the town house her home.

If she were not to be loved wholly, then so be it. She could be married and yet happy. Some day. She hoped.

A spinster. She thought of Madame Dubois. A spinster. Not one to smile easily, if at all.

Isabel wrote a letter to William, telling him she was getting on quite well and wishing him all the best. She looked at the words and tossed the letter into the fire. She would not write him again.

Then she examined her room, picked up a fresh sheet of paper and her pen. Now she was wed and— she tapped the pen at her cheek—she assumed she had quite a lot of funds at her disposal. Definitely more than she had ever had before. When William's man-of-affairs arrived the fortnight before asking if there had been a mistake on the purchase, and she'd reassured him, he'd not returned.

No one had said a word about the new gowns and she quite liked the camel colour of the new pelisse she had. Trim had been added with wool dyed a lighter colour and frazzled to give a furry appearance around the hem, and adorned the shoulders like epaulettes. The sleeves purposefully gathered just above the elbow and flowed to the base of her thumb. The coat covered her from chin to heel in warmth.

She'd wanted to wear it earlier, but the weather hadn't cooled enough yet, even though Christmas wasn't far away.

She would be spending the holiday with Sophia as Isabel's mother had told her the trip would not be practical. Isabel's father's gout was flaring.

She had no idea if William might even appear on Christmas Day. And if she and the servants were to spend most of the days alone, then as mistress of the house she would begin the season as she wished it. She wished to have holly all about. Taper candles. Evergreen to the ceiling. She'd already given the housekeeper instructions to add some greenery about, telling her to replace it if it became dried before Christmas. Just no mistletoe as it caused her…aunt to cry. Because Uncle Horace, who had died, always pulled his wife into his arms and rained kisses about the tip of her nose—Isabel stopped to add that she had her aunt's exact nose and features—but Uncle Horace loved Aunt so much that he could not see mistletoe without clasping Aunt to his breast.

The housekeeper and Isabel had both given a sniffle when Isabel could not go on. She'd pulled herself together, until she noted something in the housekeeper's eyes.

Isabel realised she'd gone too far, spoken too much, of a couple who didn't exist. And the housekeeper was not thinking of Aunt and Uncle. She was thinking of a couple much nearer.

'That will be all.' Isabel held her chin high and left the room.

William gently pulled the ribbons of his horse and waited as Ivory took her time to stop. He looked up into the windows of his home. According to his butler's post it was painted in the same calming cream colour as he'd left it. She'd even had inside shutters repainted that closed over the parlour windows.

William had left behind the butler's messages, along with the man-of-affairs' letters, but he'd kept Isabel's in the portmanteau and he wondered if any ink remained in the house.

From the outside it looked exactly as he'd left it.

He'd had to return. With each post, he'd felt he lost a bit of grasp on his world. The paint. The two chairs sent to be re-upholstered.

The days with his father had been a trial. The man had forbidden the funds necessary to update the tenants' properties, thinking it far too much of an expense. They'd had to go back over the ledgers, take him to various properties, show him past repairs and it had been a trial for them all.

His father boasted to everyone they met of William's marriage. Twice he'd asked his son if a little one might be on the way and expressing worry that his son was away from his new bride.

But in the moments he was alone, with no more fanfare than a bird's wing, Isabel's face would flutter into his mind and he'd tried to push it away. But he'd kept noticing every time he saw something blue and he'd compare it to the colour of her eyes. Conversations outdoors were hard, because he'd kept glancing overhead.

The time spent with his father and then at Sylvester's country house had dragged and dragged, but Sylvester's mother had taken ill just as William was about to return to London. William could not leave while knowing Aunt Emilia might pass at any moment. Aunt Emilia had finally begun to speak and could take food, and a few days later all could tell she was on the mend.

And his father had even mentioned the coming holiday season, encouraging Harriet and Rosalind to begin the decorations early—a vast change from the past when he'd not been aware of a single sprig of holly.

William walked into the house, noting the scent of paint. He sent someone to care for Ivory, then paused. The house felt like home. Someone's home. Isabel's.

He stepped into the sitting room, but became immobile except for his eyes. The windows were still in place or he wouldn't have recognised the room. He perused each item. Sprigs of greenery dotted the room. He noted the new painting above the mantel—a landscape of a country glen. *That* along with the pianoforte had been noted by the man-of-affairs in a rather rushed post, mentioning their prices. The cost of the two items totalled almost as much as he'd paid for the town house and he'd grumbled over the expense of the house.

He didn't recognise his world any more. Just as when his mother had passed away.

He moved to the doorway of Isabel's sitting room. Paper rested on each flat surface. Isabel, lost in concentration, sat at a desk, her pen in her hand. The only thing that looked like home to him. Stepping close, he had to say her name. He wanted to hear the words. 'Isabel.'

She jumped and sheets fluttered about his head. He caught one. 'You interrupted my letter writing.' She tossed her pen on to the blotter and blinked several times at him, her lips remaining in a firm line. 'You did not knock.'

'No. I thought you might wish to know the horses have been given to me.'

'What horses?' She stood.

'Ivory and Marvel.'

She picked up the paper strewn at her feet, then reached to pull the one from his hand and added it to the others in her grasp. She straightened them. 'I was very concerned about the horses. Wondered about them daily.' She turned her head to the side. 'Every day I wondered how dear Ivory and Marvel were faring.' She gazed at the papers. 'Of course, I didn't expect you to write and tell me how they were.' She held up two fingers in a pinch just wide enough he could see one bit of icy blue. 'Just that much time would have been all it would have taken.'

'I wrote. And I wrote to my sister once and I sent a message to the butler once. I have been kept informed.'

She sighed—and he could hear melody in it and it lasted long enough for a sentence in a song.

Papers flew up over her head again. 'I have shopping to do.' She made a brushing-away movement with her hand. He didn't leave.

She left the room momentarily and returned to the doorway, wearing a brown pelisse and carrying a bonnet with a small plume. The plume fluttered as she talked. 'And Sophia is expecting me afterwards.'

She turned, pulling the door closed, but reversed direction and poked her head back around it, one hand holding the wood firm. 'She has been so concerned about Marvel and Ivory. We have talked of little else.'

He clasped the door, immobilising it. He could not take his own gaze away. 'I think this is our first disagreement.'

'Oh, no.' She lowered her chin and fixed him with a gaze. 'It is just the first you are aware of.'

'My Aunt Emilia became ill.'

'I know. Sophia informed me. Thank you for letting her know when her Aunt Emilia was on the mend. She passed the news of the illness and the recovery along to me as you requested. Also the concern you had for me. Thank you.'

He flicked away the words with a blink. 'It was a serious time, Isabel. Rosalind and Harriet needed me to speak some sense into my father so he did not send us all into poverty. My sisters had tried and despaired, and Father wrested the control back, as he well could. It seems my marriage has made him take note of a world of things he's ignored for years. Now he wishes to make up for lost time. He has years to catch up on. And he would not listen to Rosalind. I had to convince him the girls know what they are doing and he can learn from them.'

She studied his face. 'Did it hurt your writing hand?'

'I didn't think you'd find it odd that I didn't correspond.' His eyes roamed around the room, taking time so she could note the appraisal. 'You have managed to find ways to keep yourself busy.'

He pulled the door wide so she could go before him and she returned to the room.

'You noticed.' Her smile brought the outdoors sunshine closer. 'I hope you like the changes.'

'Of course.' He examined the room. He could not tell her he wished the changes gone. He sat on the sofa and put his arm along the back. 'Do you have any more renovations planned?'

'Not at the moment.' She raised her brows and walked into the room, also spending more time examining the furnishings than warranted. 'But I have a cat. He's not a handsome cat, but he's very lovable once he becomes acquainted and if he's not startled.'

'I am sure it is a quite suitable cat.' The new arrival William's butler had mentioned during the entire contents of one post and said that he had personally overseen the hair-removal process from the rugs, daily, but he had not perfected a method to remove scratches on furniture or boots.

'Rambler.' Her voice rose with authority. 'He was meowing most pitifully at the gate and someone had thrown something at him. I had to save him.'

He reached out, picking a hair from the sofa and letting it drift to the rug. 'The cat is black?'

'Yes. Just do not get too close. He does take a bit of getting used to. The butler claims deep concern that his owner misses him and has sent out servants daily to find his owner. We don't expect success.

'I should tell you…' She forced a smile. 'I might have overspent on the painting. But in time I am sure it will increase in value. Mr Lawrence is quite good.'

'Thomas Lawrence?'

She paused, eyes down. 'I do not believe that was his given name. He said that I can return it and receive the funds back.' She examined the painting, the wistfulness of her own face matching that portrayed in the oils.

'Do you like it?' He wanted to see her eyes sparkle again.

'Not as much as I thought.'

'I am pleased you've made the house comfortable for you.' Easy words to say. 'But please do not select any houses or large properties without discussing it with my man-of-affairs. He has quite a good business sense about him. He purchased the Roubiliac sculpture—which I don't see about.'

'It is gone. The cat toppled it and it landed somehow against the grate and collected a quite unsightly chip.'

He inhaled and exhaled completely before speaking. 'Well, I only bought it as an investment.'

Her brows rose. 'Just how much money do you have?'

'Enough to make you content.'

She put her hands behind her back and moved to him with a swaying motion that reminded him of a wary creature sneaking up on a meal. 'How much funds do you think it takes to make one happy?'

'Happy. I am not sure if that is possible to purchase. But content, I think, can be.'

'Are you content?'

He leaned forward, fingers steepled together, chin down and eyes direct into hers. 'Isabel. We are doing quite well with this marriage. I would like to think we are both content with each other, or will be as the years pass. I will be certain not to cause tales which might distress you.'

Her chin rose. 'Your sister has told me of your parents' deep love. My parents have a—' her eyes became lost '—a considerable amount of love for each other.'

'It is quite unnecessary in our marriage.' He had to make certain they were in agreement on this. He'd already been considering moving out for Isabel's own good. If she were to fall in love with him, and anything were to happen to him, he could not bear the thought of her world turning black.

She tensed. 'My parents find it pleasing.' She had understood that she didn't matter quite so much in her parents' lives as they did to each other, but she'd hoped for that same devotion so many times. She'd thought that once William returned and saw the house with the changes she'd made to make it feel a home, that perhaps he'd realise he'd missed her just a little and he'd like the town house better. She didn't expect as many hugs as the maid had given her upon first returning from the school, but a lingering glance would have been nice.

'Isabel. It's not for everyone and it isn't healthy.'

'Healthy?' She almost squeaked.

'To get so mired in another's life. It's not something I would wish for you.'

'I am willing to take the risk.'

'You shouldn't. You've not seen what it can do.' He stood and his eyes glanced at the doorway. 'I suppose I should let my friends know I am back in town.'

'You've not yet let them know you've returned?'

He shook his head. 'I took each day as it happened, so I couldn't let anyone know of the dates.'

'Then perhaps you could wait just a bit to return to them. I've been wishing so much to see my friend in the country, Joanna. She is with her husband, Luke, visiting his father and has asked if we might like to join them at the Earl's family home. I've always wanted to see Pensum Manor.'

'I've visited it in Hertfordshire once with my parents. It's a fine estate. I'll have my valet return the portmanteau to the carriage and prepare for another trip.'

'You really do not like being in this house much, do you?' She'd thought the extra furniture she'd added might make it more comfortable for both of them, but she'd not been able to fool herself into thinking it the home she wanted and apparently it did no more for him.

'Not more or less than any other. They are all the same to me.'

'No place is really your home. Not even here.'

'If it doesn't leak, one roof is much the same as another roof. If it has a mattress that I can sleep on easily, one bed is the same as another. It doesn't matter much where they are.'

'I like making this my home. I thought you might like it more, too. You had hardly a stick of furniture.'

'It's just because I am practical.'

'Would you not miss me if I were gone?'

'Isabel.' His face clouded. 'We have discussed it. You will not move and change your name. We've agreed on that.'

'I can go to Pensum Manor on my own,' she said. 'I could pretend we are having a quarrel and then…' She forced a smile. 'I will get the butler to send me a post in a few days. I will pen it now. And then I will read it privately and confess that I must return as you are… threatening to throw yourself on a pyre if I do not return. Or something even more eventful.'

'You cannot involve the staff in your—'

'Yes, I can. I have only not considered it before because I didn't think of it. I'm not yet accustomed to having so many helpful people about at my disposal.'

'The pyre is rather dramatic.'

She frowned. 'Well, saying you are going to throw yourself into a candle will not impress anyone.'

'I'll go with you,' he said. 'It's colder out and I could not risk you travelling alone in the winter. Something could happen to the carriage, or the horses, and you would be stranded.'

Isabel clasped her fingers together with an effort to keep herself from twirling about. He was going with her. 'Can you pretend to be quite fond of me whilst we are there?'

He blinked, but his face softened. 'I am fond of you.' Then the stiffness returned to his jaw. 'Very much so.'

The carriage rumbled along on the way to Pensum Manor, springs creaking, jostling the seat, causing Isabel's head to bob a bit and occasionally bumping her against William. The interior of the vehicle blended the scent of William's shaving soap with the remnant earthiness of a brief rain shower. Occasional bursts of wind blew a few faded leaves from the trees and made her feel the path had been created just for that moment.

Even the birds flitted about, seeming more active than she remembered. She turned to ask him if he knew the names of them, then paused. He watched her, eyes twinkling.

'What is so humorous?' She studied him.

'You were humming with the movement of the carriage.'

'I was not.' Her hand fluttered to rest on the side of the window.

He chuckled, reached up and took a strand of her hair that had escaped, wrapping it into a curl before releasing it. 'You were indeed. The moment you started watching the birds you began to hum. I wanted to join you.'

Shrugging, she said, 'I won't do it again.'

He pulled her fingers to his lips, kissed them and released them. Eyes still gentle, lips still smiling, he tilted his head to her. 'You may sing for me any time. The melodies you hum are delightful. I enjoy listening. Please continue.'

She touched her left hand to her throat. 'No. The moment has passed.'

His movements in half-time, he reached out with his left hand, taking her hand from her neck. She'd not re-alised his right arm rested over her shoulders, until his fingers brushed at her shoulder, cradling her. His eyes, soft and softening her, completed the blanket of warmth. 'You can't leave something so much a part of you be-hind for ever. It would be like leaving behind…' His arm tensed against her shoulders and his voice rough-ened. 'A child.'

Even his arm didn't warm her now. She focused on the window, thoughts of the past and the school, and how she'd dreamed many times that her parents had left her at an orphanage and never visited her again.

'Did you dream?' she asked.

He didn't answer, but when she turned to him, his face questioned.

'Of your mother,' she added. 'After she died.'

'No.' A simple word, tossed out, with no emotion in it. And none in his face.

She'd extinguished the warmth, just as if she'd snuffed a candle. She snuggled back and his arm re-mained at her shoulders and the carriage rumbled along, a boulder of a man beside her. She didn't want to be alone.

She rested her hand on his thigh.

His fingers clasped over hers. 'I didn't dream of her then,' he said. 'Sophia would tell me each time she did and would cry. She dreamed of her every night for months and months. Only recently—have I started dreaming of the past. Of the moments during the first year.'

'I learned a trick that makes the bad dreams stop,' she said. 'It works. I swear by it.'

'What?' He drawled the word.

She pulled her free hand up, making a light fist. 'Right before you go to sleep, you clench your teeth on your knuckle and you think of what you don't wish to dream of. It works.'

His chest vibrated and she looked into eyes that welcomed her back. 'Ah…I don't think I understand. I will crawl into your bed and let you show me just how it should be done.'

Her jaw moved nearer him. 'It only works if you do it. Alone. I distinctly remember. Alone.'

'Alone? I will just keep the dreams then.'

He held her still and dusted a kiss in her hair. 'I've heard that kissing a freckle on a woman works just as well.'

'I suppose it could…' She snuggled against him, and returned her gaze to the window, wishing the trip could last for ever, but it seemed to be over in seconds.

The grounds of the estate came into view and she could hardly believe it. Even being a governess at a mansion so grand would be an accomplishment.

When the carriage rolled to the front of Pensum

Manor, the first thing she saw was her friend Joanna walking hand and hand with Luke in the gardens of his father's home.

The vehicle had hardly stopped before Isabel jumped out, rushing to her friend.

The moments were delightful as William stepped behind her and introductions were completed.

She felt a part of a fable, in which only goodness thrived and no hint of shadows surrounded them— except the brisk air seeped through her coat, chilling her. They walked into the front doors and she tried not to shiver as she left the cold behind.

The first days passed swiftly, but by the third, Isabel sensed an unease in William. He kept watching the other couple as if he disapproved of their affection.

'Stop frowning,' she said, after pulling him away from the other couple as they walked in the garden.

'What are you talking about?' he asked.

At the other edge of the gardens, Luke turned to pick up a…brown leaf. They appeared fascinated by something as simple as a leaf in which its tree had long past lost interest. She couldn't tell what they discussed.

She shaded her eyes against the sunlight and examined the couple. Yes, they were entranced in each other and saw only sunshine in the brown, wintery day.

'It is not so bad, surely, being in love?' she asked, taking her hand from her forehead. He watched her.

'Luke and Joanna seem happy with it. My sister seems satisfied with it.' Just the slightest shrug.

'Sophia's husband is quite thrilled with her.'

He frowned, dismissing the importance of the statement. 'Yes. He throws himself at her feet and is like a puppy begging for her affection.'

'Please don't inform him or Sophia of your opinion.'

'I once told my sister, and she insisted I leave her house and not return.'

'How did you get her to let you go back?'

'I showed up the next morning as always. She saw me at breakfast and was silent for a while and then started telling me how wrong I was.'

'You were wrong. Sophia and I often discuss your errors. Some days it is our favourite thing to speak of.'

His brows gave a quick flick. 'Thank you for informing me.'

She splayed fingertips at her lips and gasped. 'I have besmirched you. I didn't mean such a breach of manners.' She breathed deeply. 'An error.' Then her demeanour became her own. She gave a bow. 'You may challenge me to a duel. We can have a chuck-farthing contest.'

He chuckled. 'I have no spare coins. And lest you forget, Songbird, I have been in many drinking establishments in my day and, on occasion, we test our skills.'

'Lest you forget, I have been to a governess school. In addition to our lessons from our teachers, we also took pride in challenging each other. We played draughts for serious stakes and chuck farthing was the game I preferred.'

'But I only have a few coins with me.'

'You don't need any. I will lend you some. But don't

expect any leniency because you haven't been to a governess school.'

Dashing to the house, she went to her room and found the small pouch the butler had collected for her. Returning outside, she held the bag in the air and shook it. 'I will halve this with you but do not get too attached to the coins, Balfour.'

She untied the string, pulled it open and said, 'Hold out your hand.'

He did and halfpennies tumbled into his grasp.

She stared into his palm, counted and took one back. 'Now we are equal. Do not try to take unfair advantage before the game begins. I assure you, I'm skilled.'

Their eyes met.

'I do not even know how many the bag holds,' he said.

'You will have to trust me.' She smiled. 'Although I would advise against it from this point on.'

'Where did you get coins?' he asked.

'Your butler collected them for me. He is anxious to do my every bidding.' She smiled. 'As we speak, he is having a day of respite with a very nice bottle of your wine.'

'You cannot—he is my servant. I didn't give him permission.'

'I did. I asked him if his loyalty could be purchased and he assured me that was impossible as I had it already because my status as mistress of the house commanded his allegiance second to yours. For such a display of service, I could not help but gift him with a token.'

'You must discuss bribes with me first.' He closed a fist over the coin.

She leaned forward so her side pressed against his hand and her nose tilted so high it nearly reached his. 'Shall we decide that with the coin, Balfour?'

'Songbird, you are out of your league.' He glanced around, grinning. 'We must be private about this. I would not want anyone to think my wife willing to wager away the household funds.'

He took her arm and they darted into the wooded area. At the first clearing they stopped.

'You may be a gentleman and dig the hole.'

'My pleasure.' He took a stick and in moments the freshly disturbed dirt scented the air and he had a small indentation prepared. He stepped back, drew a line in the soil, then tossed the stick to the ground. 'You go first.'

'You will not be able to play by the rules and win against me and I am not certain you can cheat and win.' Isabel held the coin high for his view. 'You see, one of the girls I played against, Grace, was quite good. So please—toss. I want to see what competition you offer.'

'I have wagered against all sorts of men in the tavern.'

'But none as good as Grace, I'd wager.' She smiled. 'Toe to the line and prepare yourself to see how haughty words taste.'

He did and tossed. His coin landed near the indention.

She pitched. The coins rested side by side.

He took her arm, gently led her back a few steps,

took his boot heel and made another line. Their eyes met. 'It's time to be serious.'

She gathered her coins to break the tie. With her teeth tightened, she toed the line and took aim. Tossing, the coin landed half a width from the hole. She curtsied to it. 'Go ahead, Balfour.' She lifted the edge of her skirt so she could walk delicately by him, then she brushed his shoulder. 'Show me what you can do.'

His eyes widened. 'I shall.'

Toeing the mark, he aimed.

Just as he threw, she called out, 'Concentrate.'

The toss fell short of hers.

She moved beside him and smiled. 'You will have to do better than that.' She collected the coins they'd tossed, made a show of dusting the dirt from them and strutted his way.

She held a coin up, rubbed her fingers over it and aimed.

Just as she moved to throw, he moved so close his breath brushed her ear. 'Concentrate. Take your time and concentrate.'

She took a step away, swallowed to lessen the shivers he'd caused inside her and just tossed. She blinked quickly when the coin landed on the mark. Letting out a pleased murmur, she swaggered. 'I think it's your turn. Aim carefully.'

'Looks like I'll have to,' he said. He pitched and won. He grinned. 'I would like to raise the stakes.'

'Oh?'

He nodded. 'Hairpins.'

She considered it. 'How serious are you?'

'Plenty.'

'A pin equals a knock.'

'What?' he asked.

'A knock on my door before entering my room.'

He shook his head.

'You don't have to play if you fear losing.' She flounced closer. 'I'm not worried about losing.'

'Then I shall raise my stakes,' he said. 'Butler's responsibilities. I want them discussed with me before any changes are made.'

'Hairpins. Staffing. You are asking a lot.'

'We will take it one at a time. Unless you're scared.'

'No,' she said. 'Not at all. Let us begin. For door knocks versus hairpins.' Swirling around, she bit the inside of her lip, aimed and threw. It landed and she gritted her teeth and pinched her eyes shut.

His next throw landed on target.

'Good try,' he said, stepping to pull a pin from her hair and placing it in his pocket. 'Let's try again.'

Brushing at her hair, she said, 'Lucky toss.'

'Do you really believe that?' His voice was soft. 'Then, double the stakes.'

'You're on.'

He won two more pins before she had a run of luck and won three knocks on her door. She was going for a fourth, when he suggested her discussing the butler's duties with him before making changes versus all the hairpins.

She agreed.

She touched his arm, stopping not just the movement in his toss, but in his whole body. Leaning forward, she blew on the coin in his hand. 'For luck.' Then she stepped behind him.

He turned to her, concentration on his face. 'This works better.' Snaking an arm around her waist, he pulled her close for a quick kiss, then he resumed the game. But he missed further than either had done before.

Her toss did no better and went far wide the other direction. Victory was impossible to determine.

'I need more luck,' he said, putting a hand at her waist.

'I think not.' She backed away several steps. 'I plan to win.'

'So do I.' He followed and again soft lips closed over hers. The kiss took her thoughts and, when it ended, his eyes took control as his hands released her.

Then he turned, and pitched, and the coin touched the mark.

'Ah,' he said. 'My mistake the first time was in kissing to give you luck. This last time was for my good fortune.'

His lips met just against hers. Shudders raced in her body as he pulled her close. Her fingers loosened and the purse fell to the ground.

She had no idea how long they'd stood, when he pulled back. It took her a moment before she realised why he'd stopped. Voices. Joanna and Luke calling to them.

'We're here,' William called out. He took her hand and they walked together on the path towards the house. Joanna and Luke strolled up to them.

Joanna's eyes sparkled as she glanced to Isabel's hair. 'Er…we were getting worried when you didn't show up for breakfast, but I see you didn't get lost.'

'We merely lost track of the time while we wandered these lovely grounds and discussed our household,' William said, putting a hand at his wife's back.

'Discussing the household,' Luke said, turning to take Joanna's arm as they moved to lead the way back to the house. 'There's a lot to be said for it.'

William pulled a leaf from Isabel's hair and held it for her to see before letting it flutter to the ground. 'I agree.'

'I know it's a bit cold,' Joanna said, 'but tonight I planned a starlight picnic. I thought we might leave early to enjoy the sunset.'

Horses were readied and Isabel rode with the others to find a bonfire and blankets spread with a feast already laid out. A kettle warmed near the fire, the smell of cider mingling with the burning logs.

As Isabel sat with Joanna, the men trekked about to gather more wood before the night completely darkened.

'Have you heard more of Grace?' Joanna asked, holding a mug in both hands.

'No,' Isabel answered, taking a stick to poke at the edge of the fire.

'I remember when Grace started being ill every morning,' Joanna said. 'You were laughing when you said the same thing had happened to a relative and the family had been gifted with a new baby within the year.'

'Grace turned white, put her hand over her mouth and ran from the room. I didn't even realise what I'd said until I saw her face.' Embers flared as the stick dislodged a log.

'I'll never forget that moment.'

'Without Miss Fanworth, I hate to think what would have happened. She was there the night Grace needed her so much,' Isabel added. 'I held Miss Fanworth in the highest regard before, but after that, I thought her near sainthood.'

'She always seemed to know how to do everything. She made a poultice for your sting when you decided to make a pet of a bee,' Joanna said.

'I thought it a pretty insect. It didn't seem to want to sting me when I picked the flower and I thought it might be happy in my room. Miss Fanworth understood.' Isabel straightened, and then laughed. 'She always understood. But I used to get so angry at Madame Dubois, because she didn't like the songs I made up.'

'Perhaps the two of you would have got along better if you'd not called her Madame Dubious.'

'I didn't realise she was behind me.' Isabel tossed the stick on to the flames.

'Isabel, she was *always* behind you because you were *always* dancing into disaster.'

'Not my Isabel,' William said, dragging up a limb and snapping it into smaller pieces as he talked.

'Have you ever had to keep her from getting herself into a misadventure?' Joanna asked William.

'She's been so reserved since our marriage that I cannot imagine such an event.' Words delivered smoothly. He cracked the biggest part of the limb in two pieces as Luke walked up and placed his bundle of wood on to William's.

William settled beside Isabel. She tried to still the moment in her mind. The stars and firelight, and William beside her.

'Well, when you have children, the daughters might be spirited,' Joanna said.

At that sentence, William's movements stilled momentarily before he answered, though his words were spoken in the same tone as before. 'That will be wonderful.'

Joanna's eyes darted to William's face.

'William can handle high spirits,' Isabel said, knowing Joanna saw too much. 'He has three sisters and they are all splendid.'

'You're right.' The tension of William's posture lessened. In the firelight, his smile looked sincere. 'I can only hope our daughters take after Isabel.'

Isabel didn't move, except for a quick flight of her eyes to William. 'And I hope they have his strength,' she said.

Joanna nodded. 'I feel the same way about Luke.'

Luke gave her a smile and started discussing the times his family had gathered on the property to search for a perfect yule log.

When they finished the meal, Joanna and her husband stared at the stars while the fire crackled behind them. William watched Isabel, sitting alone, staring not overhead, but at the burning logs. The fire's glow lit her face, but gave her a melancholy air.

When he realised she looked cold, he moved his blanket, surprised to notice they'd sat long enough for dew to fall on to the covering. Then he wrapped the covering around her. She started, as if she'd forgotten he was there.

'Could we walk?' she asked.

He reached for Isabel, pulling her to her feet, and away from the flickering glow. Dried leaves crunched under their feet and they left the blanket behind.

Isabel spoke low. 'Did you mean that—about daughters taking after me?'

'Of course.' His voice rumbled and he pulled her into the haven of his arm. 'Oh, Isabel...' An underlying humour lit his words. He pulled her even closer, warming himself more than any fire ever could. 'You should never doubt such a thing. I would even hope our sons have your spirit.'

'That spirit has caused me some trouble. It has caused you some trouble.'

'Oh, it has caused me no trouble, except for my concern for you.' His arms remained around her, cradling. His fingertips brushed a curl back from her forehead.

Only Isabel's presence seemed to ease the barrier he felt between himself and the others, though he didn't think anyone else knew of it. In some ways, he envied the others' innocence. But he didn't have it and never would. He'd lost it long ago. Like a hanging you could never un-see, he'd seen the way loss into another person took hold. The two could become one, which meant the control of one's body was given up to the other and to the whims of fate. Fate had a wicked sense of mischief.

'Do you care for me?'

'How could I not?'

'That wasn't a resounding yes,' she muttered.

'I'm giving a resounding *yes*,' he said.

'Wonderful...' The word trailed away.

'I don't have the innocence of my youth any more.' That had died with his mother and if it could be taken a second time, then it had been drowned by his father's drink.

Isabel's presence lightened the memories, though. She took his mind from them and jarred something inside him that he'd not known remained. Some ember of the past that lingered inside him. The last spark of family left that he could feel.

Even if he had not been forced to wed her, he realised he would have wanted to. He could not stand the thought of her wedding someone else. She deserved the highest respect and the most tender care. He would help her regain her dream.

He pulled her knuckles to his lips for a kiss, savouring the delicate feel of her skin. 'Songbird. The pretence is not doing either of us any good. And I am not sure we are convincing your friend of anything as she keeps studying us. Let's leave tomorrow at first light.' He released her hand.

'I—I don't want to hurt my friends' feelings,' she said.

'I'll explain to Luke. He's newly married, more so than us. I can convince him easily that we wish to spend some time preparing for the holidays.'

'I have enjoyed the pretence.'

'I'm glad you did. But we need to return to London if we don't wish to risk becoming stuck on muddy roads. If the clouds are any indication, we could have rain. I'd like to be in London if the temperature drops.'

'I do want to return that painting before the artist forgets he promised that,' she said.

'The one by the Lawrence no one has ever heard of?'

'Yes. I decided I quite hate it. The wooded glen is nice, but I would like something more fitting to the room. More fitting to the home.'

'What about a picture relating to music?'

She shook her head.

'But you are a songbird,' he said.

'Not any more.'

'You should reconsider that, Isabel. That is the gift I hope for you to give yourself. The return of your desire to become a songstress.' He wanted her to erase the attack from her memory and continue with her desire to sing.

He could see her vision of them as a couple reflected in her eyes. He must stop this togetherness with Isabel before it progressed any further. She could not understand it was for her own good as well. If something should happen to him, he would certainly not want her burying herself in bombazine, covering the large mirror in her old bedchamber and staring at the wall.

William took Isabel's hand, held it high above her head and twirled her, pulling her into a spin until she couldn't keep up and she fell into his arms. He rocked back and forth lightly, his face pressing against her cool cheek, sharing the heat of his body.

'I cannot let you freeze,' he whispered into her ear. 'You are turning into an icicle.'

'I'm not any longer,' she said.

'I suppose you're right. Perhaps I was the one who needed warming.' He spoke the truth. He wished he could feel the warmth of her to his core and the same innocence he saw in her face. But he didn't even remember what it felt like.

'You pulled us away from the fire to get warm?'

'Yes.' His voice was low. 'One can't argue with a successful plan.'

His hands moved to hold her waist. 'Now look at the stars.'

She did and he twirled her again and again, making them spin in her eyes, and stopped by pulling her close, keeping her solid against him while letting the world regain momentum.

'Now,' he said, after raining kisses on her face, 'let us bid your friends goodbye as they do seem to wish to be alone.'

'Are you trying to escape the togetherness of the night?'

He shook his head. 'No. I've seen many other nights like this, but instead of a camp fire, there was lamplight and a book and my mother would read aloud when I was very young. Then my father took over the reading.'

'You must miss her terribly.'

He shook his head. 'She was sick so much at the end.'

He forced a laugh. 'Isabel. I can see by the tilt of your head that you're feeling sad for the boy with no mother, but truly by then I was grown. My sisters were the trial for me. They needed my help.'

'I don't want to feel like another person you need to help.'

He held her in his arms and tried to force his heart to beat for her and pound with love. He waited. Because if he could not love Isabel, then he knew he could never love another person.

Chapter Fourteen

Isabel considered the trip a success. She and William hadn't spoken much during the return home, but the silence had been companionable. William had laughed when he recounted the chuck-farthing game. His smile had sparked something that made her feel treasured. He'd even kept a few of her hairpins as a memento of their game.

She closed her eyes tight, taking time to think of William's tenderness. Then she stared at the blank page of her letter to Grace.

Isabel twirled a wisp of hair which had escaped from her bun, wrapping it into a curl. Surely it would be acceptable to tell Grace about the wonderful moments shared with William at Pensum Manor. If it sounded as if William had fallen in love, well, that was just how the words unfolded.

She wouldn't tell Grace that Miss Fanworth had written, expressing concern over Madame's health. The doctor had been called to bleed Madame, so surely she would recover soon.

The pen scratched as she wrote the salutation, but she stopped while deciding what to say about the marriage.

Isabel nibbled a biscuit when William walked into the room. Her heart jolted, but she distracted him from her gaze by extending her arm to the painting of the wooded glen. 'I hate this picture more each time I see it.' She left her biscuit and stood in front of the art, hands on her hips. 'In fact, I think I should return it today.'

She tiptoed and reached for the painting. In seconds, William was at her back, his shaving soap engulfing her as his arms spread against her and he helped lower the painting. She could sense the individual threads of his coat sleeves against her arms. She could not feel the colour black, but in a way she did—not the sombre dark of mourning but the enveloping warmth of his coat, in the same peaceful manner a pleasant nap might surround one as a dream begins—the moment when the world around fades into fairy tale.

He slipped the painting from her grasp.

'I do not want this ending up like the Roubiliac,' he said.

'If I choose several that I like, would you mind making the final decision? I do not want to keep exchanging them.'

He put the painting against the wall and turned to her.

She could see it in his eyes. The refusal.

'Never mind,' she said, closing the space between them. She patted his elbow, then let her hand drop away.

'I don't know what I was thinking. And, truly…' she grimaced '…it shouldn't be hard for me to select something new. I can have a grand time of it and take the maid along for her opinion.'

'The maid?'

'Bessie. She helped me select this one. It's a pleasant painting, but…' she ran her hand slowly along the gilded wood at the top of the frame, then stopped movement '…not for me.'

'Perhaps Sophia. She has an eye for such things.'

He touched the wood, his forefinger at the edge of hers. From a distance one would not have been able to see the space between them.

'I really wish you would go,' she said.

'Then let us get another picture for you. It will only take a few moments to select a painting. I will attend to it with you and you will have to leave Bessie to her own devices.' He shook his head. 'We should be friends. It will make the rest of it easier.'

Friends to make the rest of it *easier?* She looked up into a face she couldn't read.

'I wish for you to sing again, Isabel. I've listened to you hum. At Pensum Manor, I spoke with your friend Joanna while you weren't in the room and she said your voice is magnificent.'

'I cannot stomach the thought of performing. I cannot. Not again. It…the memories of the knife at my throat. What if someone, anyone, heard me sing and truly thought I was singing for them when I wasn't? What thoughts might someone have? Mr Wren said men

imagined my eyes wanting them. My lips on their body.'
She shuddered.

'Isabel. You must toss that from your mind as the
words of a brothel owner. His life deals in such things.
Men who are like that will not be in the audience—they
will be at Wren's. And if one man thinks such, it is on
him, not you. If he is going to think vulgar thoughts, he
would think them if you were reading a prayer book.'

'I can't sing again around others. I cannot.'

'You'll learn how to again. You must push yourself
into it.'

Stepping to the side, she picked up a piece of evergreen that had fallen from the mantel when they'd
moved the painting. She held it close to her nose before putting it into place. She kept her shoulder turned
in his direction and locked her gaze with his. 'I could
say the same for you. And our marriage.'

'You can't squeeze water out of a rock.' No smile
flashed at her.

'If you are as heartless as you think to be, then
spending a few moments with a new friend at the holiday season shouldn't be too much of a hardship. So let's
select a painting and spend the day at shops.'

'Songbird, that sounds almost as pleasant as listening to a beautiful voice. Since I'm going with you, will
you sing for me?'

She shook her head.

'Very well. I'll go to the shops and content myself
with your speaking voice, and perhaps you'll even hum
a bit. I'd like to spend the day with you.'

She gave herself a moment, then moved so that the

toes of her slippers almost touched the toes of his boots. She put both her palms at his cheeks, the feel of his skin thundering in her body. She tiptoed and, with eyes open, she kissed, moving just so that the barest amount of lips brushed briefly, then she moved away. Neither blinked. 'What are your plans for Christmas?'

'I have not finalised them.'

She covered her confusion by sitting on the sofa and looking to the window. 'Sophia has invited me to Christmas dinner.' She had assumed they would attend together, although Sophia had warned her that William hadn't attended in the past. He'd refused and said he ate with friends, but she suspected he stayed alone.

'Do you wish to travel to your parents?' he asked.

She shook her head. 'No. I would not wish to be on the road in winter and taking the servants from their family. I'm quite happy to be dining with your sister Sophia on that day. We've already been discussing the puddings we might like.'

She splayed her fingers and patted her knees with several quick taps. 'I have made friends with your sisters and have Rambler. I am beginning as I should go on. For Christmas I have instructed the cook that the servants should have a splendid dinner and will be free from their duties except for the absolutely most dire ones on Christmas Day.'

'Do not expect me to be here.'

She ignored the words. 'The time we spent at Joanna's was one of the best times of my life,' she said.

He sat across from her and reached for a biscuit.

'It was enjoyable for me as well.' He moved forward

and tapped the back of her hand. 'You are indeed a delightful woman.'

Bursts of warmth exploded with his touch, but his eyes didn't give her the contentment she had wished for.

She touched the handle of the tea cup, but didn't lift it. Keeping her eyes on the china, she asked. 'Did you not think we shared something—precious in the country?'

'I did.'

The richness of his voice reassured her, until she looked into his face.

'I've not felt quite so since my youth. I felt more alive than in a long time.' His lips pressed into a smile. The kind one formed when not thinking happy thoughts. 'I thought of little else when I returned. Your friends are very absorbed in one another. Much like my mother and father were.'

He pulled back and interlaced his fingers. His gaze drifted to the window. 'I felt compelled into that moment. Different. I had to leave to think about what was happening. I'd thought I might be changing. That I'd see things differently. But I've examined my thoughts over and over and over and I'm not the same as others are. I care for people, but the thoughts of them fade as soon as they are out of my sight.'

He stood, returning to stare at the painting. His back was to her and his voice softened. 'It would be foolish of us to fall into any traps that might cause us regret later.' He stood. 'Our marriage is perfect, Isabel. I am thankful for it. It is not some heart prattle which absorbs and taints the outlook. It is a marriage as successful people have had for centuries. A joining of a man and woman who each continue to follow the path they were meant to follow. It is as near perfect as it could be.'

'I want more.'

His head bowed. 'I am so sorry. Three years ago, one of my best friends was thrown from his horse and died within hours. At the funeral, Sylvester was in tears. Everyone talked of it for days at the club and I did the best I could to commiserate and offer condolences, but I didn't feel the loss. It has been three years and I've had not one moment of sadness.'

'You care for the horses, though.'

'Yes. They're good stock. I've had them for years and they should be treated well—but still, if they were to die, I don't know that I would mourn. I don't believe I would.'

He lifted his head and turned back to her. She'd never seen such compassion—or pity, she wasn't sure which—in the eyes that watched her.

He reached into his pocket, stepped to the table by her reticule and put something on the table. A tiny click sounded when it touched the wood. 'Your hairpins. I know you won them in truth. It was kind of you to make the game longer by letting it play out as it did. But I don't know what I was thinking to keep them, except as enjoyment of our game, the pleasure of your company and a chance to make the wagering last longer.'

He left and his boots tapped down the stairway and she heard him calling last-minute instructions to his butler to have someone prepare the painting for return and ready the carriage.

She moved to the table, picked up the pins, tossed them into the burning coals and left the room.

William stood in the tiniest shop he'd ever been in. It barely contained the three of them, but the paintings were floor to ceiling.

'Another by the very talented Mr Lawww-rence.' The man's footsteps clacked along and he drawled the word out as he showed them the painting. One empty place must have been from the art Isabel purchased.

'It is exceptional.' Isabel examined the painting of a sad child with a sad mother. Isabel's gloved hands clasped. Her coat quite covered her. In the back, the collar came above the bonnet edge and he didn't know quite how they both managed to keep in place. Her bonnet was unlike any he'd ever seen. Darker brown, and circular, but edged all around by a wide row of wispy feathers which never stayed still even when she did.

And yet, the garment didn't overpower her. He surmised that whatever footwear she had on added to her height and the extra fluff of feathers made her appear even taller. She appeared as tall as he stood in his bare feet.

'Very.' William stared at the signature. T. Lawrence. But this was not by Thomas Lawrence although it was similar in style.

'I would prefer to think about it.'

'Ah.' The man's shoulders slumped.

Isabel's actions mirrored the man's. Then she chatted with the proprietor for a few moments. William watched as the man melted under the infusion of blue eyes, siren's voice and something else that he could not quite name.

The man shook his head. William's attention flashed from Isabel to the conversation. The proprietor had just suggested he had a painting in the back which he might show her.

When he brought it out, the aroma of paint lingered around it. A little girl sat alone on a bench in the central part of the picture, her face shadowed by the bonnet. The trees and greenery in the background faded away and emphasised the girl, hands clasped, thinking thoughts a viewer could only guess at.

'It's not finished.' The proprietor smiled, looking at the art. 'I'm Theodore Lawrence Bryant.'

'Perhaps you might sign this one with that name,' William suggested.

The man shrugged. 'I should. But the other sells better even as I tell the people I painted them. I suppose they put it on the wall and hope no one asks too many questions.'

William stepped closer to the art. He looked at Isabel. 'Could you change the hair colour on the little girl to something closer to this?' He held his hand by Isabel's face.

'Most certainly.' The man stood taller.

'And perhaps, in the tree behind her, birds—listening. And a tiny, *tiny* feathery fluff in the bonnet.'

'I'm sure I could add those,' he said.

'Please send it to my home when finished and, if Isabel likes it, we will keep it.'

'Most certainly.' The proprietor looked at William.

'But your friends will be more impressed with a T. Lawrence painting than a Theodore Bryant.'

'I'm not purchasing it for them.' William looked at Isabel and, in one second, he glimpsed something that caused a feeling of his heart rolling down an embankment. He couldn't decipher if the look in her eyes made him need to clasp her tight to be saved or if the gaze was thrusting him into a chasm deeper than his father had been in.

Quickly, he led her from the room and guided her to the carriage, ignoring the howl of the wind and the darkening clouds which dampened the air. But before he got to the steps, something caught the corner of his eye.

He turned to see Lord Robert and his brother, the Duke of Wakefield, trudging towards them. With each step, the Duke's coat beat the air like a raven's wings.

Isabel felt William's pause and turned to see what had captured his attention. Two men walked in their direction and the older one looked up. Recognition chased the sadness from his lips, but not his eyes.

'Balfour.' The older man's thick silvery hair gave him an air of knowledge and his shoulders gave him a fortress of sturdiness.

Isabel sensed William's indecision. Lines of strain appeared at his temples.

In brief sentences, William introduced the Duke of Wakefield and Lord Robert, the Duke's younger brother.

'So pleased to meet you,' Wakefield said, warmth infusing his words to Isabel. 'I played cards with Balfour recently. He is a happier man now that he's married.'

Isabel examined the Duke's eyes for falsehood.

William stilled.

'It does me good to see a young man so in love.' The Duke's smile faded like a snowflake on a warm coat. 'I remember so well...'

William's stance tightened, one foot pointed away, ready to trudge off. 'We must be going. I would not want anyone to catch a chill.'

'Nor would I,' the Duke said.

The only thing appearing cold was William's eyes, Isabel thought. 'Do not worry about me. When I was in Salisbury, one of the other girls at the school challenged me to see who could stand longest in the snow barefoot. I won.'

'A school?' the Duke asked. 'You attended a school?'

The damp air suddenly penetrated Isabel's clothing. She didn't want to embarrass William because of her training to be a governess. 'Yes,' she admitted. 'I am not from London. But my parents wished me to have some education.'

'How wonderful,' the Duke said. 'I am always pleased when I meet women who have had the opportunity to learn. Balfour knows I have long been concerned with education and feel that it is vital to our country's progress.'

'I agree,' Isabel said. 'Although I do not know how the school is faring as I received a letter from one of the teachers, Miss Fanworth, that the owner, Madame Dubois, is ill. She has never been sick before and now she can't seem to leave her bed.'

'Dubois?' The Duke's eyes widened. 'You attended Constance Dubois's school?'

Lord Robert's gaze switched from boredom to an intent perusal of his brother.

'Yes. I attended Madame Dubois's School for Young Ladies. In Salisbury.' Isabel answered.

The Duke reached into his waistcoat pocket and dotted a handkerchief to his forehead, but no moisture shone. 'I once knew the woman you spoke of. In my youth. A fascinating woman.'

'Madame Dubois?' Isabel asked.

'Quite fascinating.' The reprimand in the ducal tone couldn't be missed. 'All these years…' His words faded away. He shut his eyes. 'All these years I have not heard of her.' When his eyes opened, he didn't seem to see his surroundings. 'She… Everything about her was delightful. Full of optimism even when she'd lost so much. Full of laughter.'

'I think you might have mistaken our Madame Dubois for someone else. Our Madame was not—I never saw her laugh.'

He took in a breath.

'She did smile, though. If our lessons were perfect or if we did something well,' Isabel added, not knowing why she felt she must reassure him that Madame was not melancholy. 'But she was quite serious with us.'

'Constance Dubois was one of the most spirted women in the world.' His eyes sparked and his voice commanded. Then the Duke's eyes misted and his tone softened. 'All these years…I have guarded against learning the location of her school. I had made certain

I was never informed. And now I have heard without even asking.' He shut his eyes and shook his head. He reached out, intent on Isabel's answer. 'She will recover?'

'It's said she is coughing constantly and her chest is in pain. The letter said her heart is beating fast and she is chilled, and cannot stop shaking.'

His face paled. Isabel had to give him some respite from the strain in his eyes.

'They have called in a skilled surgeon who will bleed her,' she said, 'so there is hope.'

'My Constance.' Wakefield dotted the handkerchief to his head again and backed away. 'At least she is under a physician's care.' He paused, eyes seeing a long-ago memory. 'The school is in Salisbury, you say? I must beg forgiveness for my abrupt departure, but I must see her again. I must.' He turned to his brother. 'You understand. I have to know.'

He turned, darting down the street.

Lord Robert watched his brother leave. 'My brother has carried the memory of the Dubois woman in his heart since his youth. She was a governess to my sisters. Wakefield is considerably older than us, so he and Dubois were closer in age.'

'The whispers were true,' Isabel murmured. 'It was thought Madame Dubois had had an attachment.'

'I would not have been so noble as he was,' Robert said. He adjusted the patch at his eye. 'My brother tossed aside his own desires and wed for fortune's sake. He didn't care for the funds—only that he might provide for his dukedom and his family. The tenants' houses needed so much.'

Lord Robert chuckled, but it lacked humour. 'Love. I dare say when my brother finds this woman he adored in his youth, it will be too late. Or he will discover she has no memory of him.'

He turned to leave. 'I will find my own way home. Good day.'

Standing silent for a moment, Isabel kept her eyes on the direction the men had gone.

'Madame had warned us that when we were in fine households, never to forget our place,' Isabel said. She studied William and repeated, 'In fine households, we were never to forget our place.'

'Your place is in a fine household, Isabel.'

'I am sure. Of course. You are right.'

'Don't be like Wakefield is.' William guided her to the carriage. 'Rushing off. He has just escaped a mire of grief and now he is rushing back to find it again. I cannot understand someone's wish to touch a fire to see how hot it is.'

The driver spotted them and jumped from the perch to open the door.

'But he has his brother for solace,' Isabel said as she settled and snuggled into her coat.

William snorted. The carriage wheels creaked as they began to roll. 'His brother is a worthless rake.' William brushed the moisture from the window, his leather gloves squeaking against the pane.

'But the two of you are friends.'

'We are,' William agreed. 'That does not mean we

do not know each other, but that we do and tolerate each other.'

'And you wish for us to be friends?' Copper tendrils of hair escaped her bonnet and blended with the chocolate colour of her coat.

He ducked so low that he could look at her eyes. 'Isabel. We will have a completely different type of friendship.'

Doeskin touched his face as she pushed him away. 'I might decide not to be friends with you.'

'I will accept that.' He brushed a kiss at her hand before she slid her glove from him.

She bundled back into the seat, huddling. The sun was lost behind a cloud and the temperature had dropped as the day progressed.

He put an arm around her, pulling layers of coat into his clasp and getting feathers in his nose. He huffed them away from his face. 'You might as well be wearing a suit of armour,' he muttered.

Bright eyes again. 'You do.'

'Where has my sweet bride gone?' He dodged feathers again.

'I don't know who you are speaking of,' she said and straightened. Reaching up, she thumped the carriage top. 'But I am going for a walk.'

The carriage stopped and she darted out. He followed. She shouldn't walk alone and he could not let her. But she'd not liked him holding her tight.

They walked, the carriage wheels rolling behind them, snowflakes beginning their flurry. 'The butler told me it would be bad weather,' he said. 'Claimed his bones were trumpeting it to him.'

She kept her pace, her coat hem kicking up.

'You cannot outrun me, Isabel.'

'I would not try. I am merely keeping my blood flowing in the cold.'

A ragamuffin darted from a shop, shoulders hunched, hands in tattered pockets.

'Boy!' she called. 'Boy.'

He turned, soot on his cheek.

'Can you direct us to Somerset House?'

He nodded, and quickly spoke the directions.

'Thank him.' She nudged William with her elbow.

He reached into his frock coat and pulled out a coin. She coughed. He reached again, pulled out another and gave them to the lad, who took them both, grinned from ear to ear and bowed before scampering away.

'Now it is beginning to feel like Christmas.' She walked again, her pace slower. 'I have never strolled in the streets like this. So different than the Christmases at the school past, and the ones before at my parents' home.'

They walked along, not speaking. An older woman pushed a cart along their direction, followed by a shuffling man.

Isabel almost blocked their path. 'Can you direct us to Somerset House?' she asked.

William reached into his coat before she finished speaking.

As they walked on, he spoke. 'You can only ask direction three more times before my pockets are let.'

She laughed. 'You do have enough for three times?'

'Yes.'

She clasped his arm. 'Is not this more fun than losing the coin at a game of cards?'

'I do not play to lose. But, yes, I am enjoying the pace. You do realise the woman sent us in the wrong direction.'

'Yes. And I think she knew it. But we didn't turn either and she surely noticed. So, it is a game we both played.' She paused. 'If both know the rules, it is a game, not a ruse.'

'Don't let the game trip you up,' he said. 'But one must never forget if the opponent is playing, too. We could have easily turned in the wrong direction there, had we not known.'

'We would have found our way again.'

Neither moved until a burst of wind pelted them with snow, mixed with just enough frozen water to sting the cheeks. He stopped. Putting his gloved hand over her fingers clasped on his arm, he waited until the coachman caught up. 'We need to get the horses to the mews,' he said.

This time in the carriage, the feathers didn't brush against him, but he held her close, letting their body heat melt into one. If not for the horses and servants, he would have kept the carriage going for hours.

He wanted this moment to last because he knew this path would not continue. He'd already discovered another property for sale and it would meet his needs. He had not seen it, but that didn't matter.

'After Christmas, I will be moving,' he said.

The clop of the horses' hooves, the sound of someone shouting for dinner and wind buffeting the world sounded before she spoke.

'Why wait?' Her voice had the coldness of the icicles hanging from the eaves.

'The property won't be available until then.'

She turned in his arms, but he kept her firm.

'Why are you telling me now?'

'The game is too serious. We will work out an arrangement that will suit us both. We'll not be tripping over each other, however, and if you wish to see me not at all, I will agree. Perhaps a few soirées here and there but that, of course, is up to you.'

He could feel nothing except his heart beating.

'I think…' The carriage rolled over a bump, and he cushioned her. 'I think that as you are leaving soon, it will be no rush to decide on the particulars. Perhaps we can meet in the summer some time to decide. Or perhaps it would be best after the weather cools again, as people are returning to town and the soirées begin anew.'

He hugged her tight. He would make this a wonderful Christmas for her and let her know that even if he could not love, she would always be able to count on him in the ways that were most important.

She patted his chest.

He closed his eyes. Relieved. She understood.

And he wished wild flowers truly bloomed from

graves and the sun only shone in Isabel's life. He realised something else. He would have allowed someone else to marry her had the man been able to treat her well and love her as she wished.

Chapter Fifteen

Isabel patted his chest. Warm. Deceptive.

He must have a heart and it must be beating. But that was all the good it did.

She rested her hand against his coat. 'I think when the weather begins to warm, I will visit my parents.'

'Have you written your mother that you didn't trap me into marriage?'

'Did I not trap you? Although it was not my goal.' She paused. 'But, yes, she knows there is not a little one on the way.'

'She should realise that her precious, and only, daughter *is* quite accomplished enough even for a duke and not only a viscount's son.'

'She didn't truly intend that in the letter. It's just the way she writes—and speaks. I resemble my father's family in height and looks, and she still thinks me the gangling little creature who cannot keep from tripping over her own feet. She was uncertain I would be able to secure a post as a governess, so the information that I wed someone of the peerage was a shock to her.'

'Has she ever truly seen the Isabel that you are?'

Isabel didn't answer. She put her arm tight and hugged him close. 'I do thank you so much for rescuing me. Both from Mr Wren and from being a governess.' She took her time with the next words because tiny blades had got loose inside her body and were ripping along from one point to the next, puncturing everything that could cause any pleasure inside her.

'And I don't understand why you cannot stay in the house. I can grasp that you're not in love with me. I can understand that you may never be and I can accept that.'

'I am not meant to live with anyone. To feel trapped—confined—smothers me.'

'Love could be pleasant. In only a few days I fell in love with Rambler and he was underfed, yowled and had a bent tail. It was my good fortune to be able to have a cat of my own. Had I been a governess, I could have loved the family pets, but not my own if the mistress of the house had spoken so.'

'You've only had the cat a short time. How could you love him so quickly?'

'He was shivering and had a crooked tail. He needed me. And perhaps I needed him.'

'I think you're mistaking compassion for love. Compassion and love are not the same. And even if I could feel love, then I don't know that it is always a good thing except for a mother and children.'

'I love Rambler. I looked into his eyes and I saw the sad moments and my heart just wrapped around him.'

His voice rose in tone. 'He's a cat. And you cannot just love instantly.'

She looped her fingers around a button of his coat. 'You are not an expert on love. You are an expert on not loving. I can tell you that I fell in love when I looked into his eyes. It might have been a small little seed of love. But then he walks into my sight again and the little seed grows and grows, until it becomes a full-sized love.'

She pulled at the button and then released it. 'It is his loss if he does not care for me and sometimes I'm sure he doesn't and is just there for the food.' She brushed at his coat. 'He just does not quite understand what it is to love someone.'

His kiss dissolved the chill in her body into sunshine. 'Let us enjoy these precious moments we have together today and not worry about a stray cat who has no home.'

He reached up and pulled at a tiny feather in her hat. Her hand locked on the hat, keeping it in place. He pulled a small wisp of a feather from it and tickled her nose.

She tried to snatch the feather, but he held it away from her.

'The cat has a home,' she said. 'With me.' She swatted for the feather again.

He tucked it at his ear and she laughed to see the wisp sticking from his locks.

'Perhaps the cat is fortunate to have found shelter and your heart. But no cats or dogs will be at my new residence.'

'You are so alone that you cannot make a home with me?'

'I doubt I will even stay in the house where I'm moving very long. It's meant to be temporary.'

'Some things should be permanent.'

'I thought the town house was to be.'

'How long had you lived there before I moved in?'

He spoke the words gently. 'Four years, or thereabouts.'

'Then I started putting furniture and pictures and things to make it a home.' Reaching out, she removed the feather he'd lodged in his hair, but his hand clasped over hers, and with his free hand he took the tuft of feather and tucked it in his waistcoat pocket.

She wanted to pull away, but something deep, deep inside her told her she mustn't. And something else told her it might not be just his feelings for her that he moved from, but from the furniture and fripperies she'd added in hopes of making the town house feel like a home to him.

William saw the downward tilt of Isabel's chin as she moved to the carriage door to alight at the town house. He gave a quick pull to her hand and she stumbled at the last steps, right into his arms.

'My pardon,' he said, giving her a squeeze before righting her to her feet. 'I am fortunate I was able to catch you.'

He leaned forward and sniffed. 'Are you…have you been drinking strong spirits? What will the neighbours think?' He swooped an arm at her waist, causing her to stumble against him. 'Do not worry, I will reassure anyone watching that we are most proper folk.' At the gate, he reached to snap an icicle from its clasp on the iron fence.

Then he crunched the tip of it into his mouth.

'William,' she whispered. 'The coachman is watching.'

His lips almost touched her ear. 'This will not impress him as much as the morning after my fourteenth birthday.' He crunched the icicle again and blew a cold breath at her. 'He stopped the carriage to push my boots back into the door so he could close it again—which I didn't find out about until the night I turned fifteen.'

'Four years younger than I am,' she said.

He nodded, their eyes catching. He saw the moment she realised their true differences in age. She was but five years younger and yet perhaps two lifetimes.

He tossed the icicle aside. Before she could think any more he lifted her into his arms and moved to the door, thumping his boot against the base. The butler opened it.

William spoke in tones suitable to Drury Lane. 'I fear my dear Lady Wife has fainted from the cold.' He whisked her inside. In a low tone, he said, 'Close your eyes, Isabel…'

In two quick strides he was at the base of the stairs. His voice still rang to the rafters. 'I must deposit her by a warm fire.'

'No,' she screeched and clasped her arms at his neck. 'You can't take me up the stairs. You'll kill us both'

'Perhaps you are right.' He put her to her feet. His

tone became formal. 'My pardon.' He bowed and in a flash he'd removed his coat and tossed it to the butler.

Before she could ascend the stairs, he stopped her, twirled her around and bent to grasp her legs and hoist her over his left shoulder. 'This will be safer.'

'No,' she yelped out.

But he trundled her up the stairs and was at the top almost before her protest finished. He didn't set her down, but called down the steps, still performing. 'Wine. My Lady Wife must have wine to be revived.' The acting ceased, but the strength of his voice didn't as he continued speaking to the butler at the foot of the stairs. 'Leave it in the parlour, then see that everyone else in the staff who wishes is also revived with the same spirits. We cannot have anyone expiring from this cold.'

She pounded his back. 'Put me down.'

'But I so like carrying you.' He could not see her head. 'Your bonnet is still attached, is it not?'

'Yes. It is hanging by pins.'

He hefted her a few times. 'I can tell. The feathers are making you light as thistledown. But I will find a place where you can recover.'

He spoke for her ears only. 'And I will help you get warm.' His boots sounded as he took her into his bed-chamber.

He put her feet on the floor. Before she fully righted herself, his hands rested atop her shoulders.

'I didn't want to tell you earlier, but you're about to lose that concoction on your head.'

'No wonder. You have shaken it—'

At the same instant, their hands reached to the hat, but his captured hers and lowered them aside as he took out the remaining pins and slid the bonnet free. He put it on the table at his bedside.

Taking her chin in both his hands, he held her face.

Lips covered hers, tasting. Every sensation but his lips fluttered away from her and she waited, savouring the clasp of his hands and their kiss.

His retreat left her chilled, in a way she'd never noticed before. A sort of aloneness that made her want to follow his lips.

'I liked the hat, though. It suited you, and—' he leaned back into her realm '—it gave me an excuse to touch your hair.'

He pulled a pin free—just the right pin—and her hair fell about her shoulders.

'Even the littlest curl peeking out...' he tossed the pin with the bonnet '...distracts me. And when I sat at the table near you at your friends', everyone kept speaking and talking and I thought, how can they be so absorbed in things so unimportant? Can they not see Isabel has removed her bonnet? Are they not aware of those sparkling eyes?' He untangled more pins from her hair. 'I suppose we ate.'

'You said— You said later it was the best meal of your life.'

The merest nod. 'I told the truth.'

He unbuttoned the coat and pulled it from her shoulders, leaving her feeling lighter. He tossed it to the side, then took her gloves from her hands. 'I'll never forget the dinner. Your laughter.' He brushed the leather against her cheek. 'Innocent eyes. Innocent gaze. And laughter so husky I could not stop trying to bring it to your lips again. You laughed three times.'

Her heartbeats changed. Her whole body insisted she get closer to him.

Her fingertips ran the outline of him, over muscled arms, the curve of his neck and the strength of his jaw. Soft skin at his ear contrasted with the roughness where the day's growth of his beard stopped.

With the precise care of savouring each moment, he reached behind her, unfastening her dress and letting it drop to the floor.

His little finger traced her jaw, swelling the feelings inside her. He trailed down her throat and over her breast, swirling against her peaks.

Tendrils of his hair fell forward, brushing against her cheek, caressing like feather-tips. His lips covered hers again, pulling back enough to whisper her name. When he closed his lips after speaking, he trailed them about her neck, sending shivers deep inside her, melting away all thoughts of any world other than the one in the confines of their fingertips.

Through the darkened room, she could see without using her eyes, aware of each contour where their bodies touched. Aware of his breath, his pulse and his thoughts, because in that moment, they were all the same, combined in a way that only the touch of lovemaking could intertwine two people.

Isabel woke, aware instantly that she lay in William's bed and the space beside her was empty. The room had completely darkened except for the fire. A scraping sound had awakened her. She raised her head.

William stood at the fireplace, holding the poker, pushing the coals, moving them about this way and that, flaring sparks, causing the flames to rise or fall as he moved the fuel around. He held his hand too close to the fire and jerked back. The scent of burned hair confirmed his error.

'That is what happens when one plays with fire,' she said.

He chuckled. 'Thank you for informing me. But I had already realised it.'

'William. You could not be more naked.'

'You could,' he said. He moved to the bed, dashing into the cocoon, his body warm and feet cold. He pulled her close, sliding a leg to hook hers and pull her against him.

'You do not think you will miss this when you move away?' she asked.

'I know I will.' He put a kiss on her lips.

She pulled back. 'You do that to silence me.'

He kissed her again. Soft pulses dragged her words away, but a small bit of thought remained.

She pushed and he rumbled a fake growl into her ear and rained kisses at her cheek and down the curve of her neck into the valley at her collar bone.

'I should go back to my bed or you will get no sleep tonight,' she said. She could not go from the room.

'I want none. Besides…' his chuckle poked humour at himself '…it is not first light, so it is hours until my bedtime. And I have a Christmas surprise I have been waiting to tell you about.'

'What?' she asked.

'I wish for you to sing. For everyone,' he said.

She shook her head.

'Others must hear you. I would like to hear you sing.'

'No.'

'Isabel, you must sing again. For others.' He slipped from the bed and reached for his dressing gown. 'Think about it while I am getting the wine,' he said, after tying the sash. Before he left, he placed a showering of kisses about her face.

She didn't have to think about it. She already knew.

He returned. 'Remember how you enjoyed it, Isabel. When you were at the governess school.'

'Yes, it was fun. To sing for the other girls. Perhaps, only for Sophia and your sisters I might not mind. But not with other people around. I can't.'

He slid into bed beside her.

Thinking back to the governess school, she'd done whatever she could to capture the ears and eyes when she sang. She'd moved about the stage, brought herself to tears with emotion, fell in love with the wall behind the audience's heads and suffered whatever the words spoke of. She supposed she would have jumped to the top of the pianoforte and plunged to her knees and slid headfirst to the floor while continuing the song if it would have kept the listeners' attention. She had tried that on a sofa and the girls had loved it. Once, she had taken the hairpins from Miss Fanworth's hair during a performance and looped and looped the hair into a most towering knot and sang. If an asp had slithered into the room, she would have stepped over it to continue, or sang for it.

She had, in the sense of singing for Mr Wren. She had just not realised it. Now when she thought back to his eyes watching as she sang, she shivered. She'd thought he listened to the song, but instead he'd planned her downfall.

How many other times had she misjudged the eyes on her?

Now she remembered an uneasy feeling when one of the other fathers had spoken to her afterwards. He'd suggested he would have liked to have had a governess like her. Her skin had chilled and she had responded quickly and walked away.

She'd forgotten it in the praise of the next person. Not really believed he'd meant anything unpleasant to her. Had taken it as flattery.

The next time she sang for a group, she'd examined everyone's faces and been certain all was well. But Wren had been in that audience, she remembered. The man who'd spoken to her the first time could have invited him.

Singing was more than just words to her and she could not pour her heart, and show all the emotions she experienced, if a pair of watching eyes devoured her.

When her song began it was not merely being in the centre of the viewers' attention—at that moment her very life rested in their power. Sometimes she didn't recognise the Isabel on stage. Sometimes she could not believe the performance herself. The moments filled her in a way nothing else did, but now she had no wish to ever sing for an audience again. The knife to her neck had cut that part of her life away for ever and she didn't wish for it back.

Before touching the wine, William returned a second time to the windows. Isabel. She did remind him of a bird. She should soar, only returning to earth to enjoy the best of the nature's bounty. He'd purchased some earrings to give her after the Christmas soirée surprise and they matched the sky colour in her eyes. They were nothing like the ring his mother had worn. The ring his father had insisted William take from his mother's hand after she had passed.

He imagined the jewellery on Isabel's hand. The unusual ring with the primitive look of irregular stones would fit the performer's spirit of Isabel.

But he could not give the ring to Isabel.

He remembered the mouldering scent of death. Costly candles, more ornate than any he'd ever seen, had been purchased, filling the house with what he thought myrrh or spices from the past would smell like. Mirrors covered with musty cloths that had been packed away from his grandmother's death—a woman who'd died before William could remember her.

His father had insisted that only the best would do for the day of the funeral, and had had token gold rings quickly made in the style of his wife's so he could present them to the others who mourned. William would have expected his father to have had one ring made for each daughter, but he had not.

The first sign of his father's plunge into the past and unawareness of the world left standing.

He was glad he'd left the ring behind. In fact, he wasn't quite sure where he'd left it, but it wasn't in the town house.

The jewellery wasn't elaborate. The stones could be easily mistaken for glass. The design of it was unpolished. A baroque ring with one central stone and nine of different colours set around it. A family heirloom. Oldest son's wife to oldest son's wife. Only now there would be no child and he just didn't want a son of Sylvester's giving it to someone. Better to be lost in the world, than to be on some bit of frippery Sylvester's offspring would wed.

He couldn't give it to Isabel. The ring had not been on anyone's hand since it had been on the hand of a dying woman. His sisters had never even asked about it. He'd seen Sophia wear a necklace that had been in the family for generations and later his Aunt Emilia had insisted his father give heirlooms to William's other sisters as well. But the ring had been the one piece his mother wore every day. It wasn't even pretty. The jewels were a bit misshapen and he didn't even know what they were.

He poured himself a glass of the wine, wishing his mother could have met Isabel. They would have liked each other, he was certain. His mother would have thought her beautiful enough for a viscount and intelligent enough as well.

Chapter Sixteen

When he returned to the bedchamber, he brought not only the wine, but a lamp.

She sat in the middle of the bed, covers pulled high. He handed her the wine and moved to the chair where he usually sat to don his boots. He observed her in the same way he had once watched the morning dawn and felt it the only brightness in the world.

After she'd finished the drink, he said. 'You once left the school and were willing to risk everything to walk into a disreputable place like Wren's. You already had employment as a governess and you walked from that, and you moved about alone in a town you were unfamiliar with in order to find a stage.'

'I was not thinking. I let my vanity override sense. My mother was right.'

'No. She was not. Many times I have heard others sing. I have heard choirs. I have heard operas. But even as you talk, I can hear the husky siren's voice you have. I am not surprised Wren wanted you to sing in his establishment. I am just surprised he was not sensible enough to help promote you to reputable places.'

'I didn't say I have no skill. I just said I have no wish to perform. It is dead inside me. Just the same as your heart is dead inside you.'

'Don't let Wren take that from you.'

'He hasn't. Before I merely sang because—'

'Because you enjoyed it. It is your gift.'

'Because I knew no better.'

'How many times did you sing for others assembled at the school?'

'I do not remember. I didn't count them.'

'More than a dozen?'

'I am sure, but that means nothing. We didn't have a lot of entertainment. It was either that or embroidery, or watercolours or reading.'

'You bought a pianoforte.'

'Just because of the wood and the way a home feels alive with—'

'With music in it?'

'With a pianoforte.'

One arm folded across himself, he rested an elbow on it and propped his chin on his fist. 'Fair enough. But performance is not dead within you. I know it is not. You walk up the stairs as if you are making a grand entrance.'

'I traipse stairs as I always have.'

'Which proves my point. You were born to sing, Isabel.'

'It doesn't matter. Now I am a wife. This may not be a marriage of the heart, but it is still a marriage and

I have no wish to be anything but a governess now. It will just be one for my own children, as you said. I am quite pleased with the thought. Everything…' she straightened the covers '…has worked out for the best.' She crossed her arms. 'We are both happy in the forward path we have chosen.'

He had stayed home, planning, enjoying the last moments he was to live with her, but he'd already sent a trunk ahead to the new residence and given a few instructions on preparation.

He listened for her humming. But it didn't carry through the walls so he didn't know if she hummed or not.

He'd told Sophia his plans for Isabel to sing at the soirée and he'd asked that it be a surprise.

Tomorrow's performance would give society a chance to see the true talent of Isabel and the true woman she was. In just the short time he had been gone she had transformed herself, although really it wasn't herself she had changed. The woman she was blossomed out even the first night when she wore the ripped and dirty dress. An ache spiralled into him at the memory of what could have happened that night. But Isabel never need be in danger again. And she'd never have to wear torn clothing again.

He was thankful he had enough funds so she could purchase so much. The artwork had been a bit ill advised, but she'd even recognised that later. In truth, his house had never looked better. *Her* home had never looked better.

The songbird had a gilded cage, but she would not be confined into the role of a hidden wife. She would be perhaps the best songstress in the world if she wanted. He would make certain to hire older, burly footmen to accompany her on her travels.

He'd already sent a note to his man-of-affairs explaining the new turn of things, telling him to hire someone well versed in the nature of procuring respectable theatrical venues for a singer. Only at the most refined places would Isabel sing. Any obstacles to Isabel's success would be moved aside.

Isabel would have her dreams. He would place them at her slippers.

But she didn't understand. Rising, he moved down the hallway to her room.

He knocked three times, waited, then heard her call out enter. He walked into the room and she sat at the desk, gazing out the window. One paper, blank, sat atop a stack of others on her desk. The cap was still off the bottle of ink. He walked to the bottle and put the stopper back in place.

'Sophia sent a note that said you have no plans to attend her Christmas Eve soirée.' He picked up the pen from the blotter and touched the tip to his forefinger, leaving a mark.

'I know. We have discussed it.' She reached out and took the pen from his grasp, took the stopper from the bottle and wrote another salutation to her friend Grace at the top of the page.

'It will only stir memories of Christmases past when

I was at my parents or with my friends at the governess school. I wish to start anew, but not that way.'

'She said you almost convinced her.'

She paused, pen in mid-air, and looked up at him. 'But she was polite enough to pretend to accept it. I do like that about her.'

'So do I, Songbird.'

She flicked the pen on to the blotter. 'I do not want to be in a crowd of people.'

He watched as she drew a line over the words she'd written on the page.

'Just a brief song at the soirée.'

'You apparently have not heard the term *no* many times in your life.'

He paused, frowning. 'Now that I think of it, I can hardly ever remember hearing it.' He ran a thumb along the firm jawline pointed in his direction. 'And for good reason. I'm nearly always right.'

She looked heavenward. 'Well, not in this instance.'

'Fair enough.' One hand on the desk, he bent his knees and crouched directly in front of her. 'Songbird. My sister, who thinks the world of you, is having a soirée and it would mean very much to her if we would attend. I've even invited the Duke.'

'William. You're not being fair.'

'No. I have a surprise for you and also I thought you might just try a short song.'

The jaw firmed. 'I will not sing.'

'I wasn't going to tell you and let you discover it yourself, but the surprise is that I have arranged for your friend Joanna and her husband Luke to be there.'

'You…did?'

'Yes. I want this to be a special Christmas for you, Isabel. I know you're sad that your parents were not able to come to London to be with you. But you can still have family about.'

'Are you and I family?'

He stood erect. He'd seen the wistfulness in her eyes. He had to escape that look. 'We took vows of for ever. We are wed.' His voice softened. 'Songbird. Do not set yourself up for unhappiness.'

'I fear it is too late.'

William sat with his man-of-affairs, finishing the plans for opening the new residence, when he heard the door on the lower floor crash open.

He put his hand to his forehead for a second, listening to the stairs take a pounding from boots. Then he stood and met the glare of his father.

One look and William stood. A glance dismissed the man-of-affairs. The man bundled his papers, tucked them under his arm and left.

William's father clasped a small box in his hands.

'I found it. I found what you left behind.' He thrust the box on to the table. The lacquered box that held Will's mother's wedding ring. 'You promised your mother. That Christmas Day.'

'Yes. I did. I said I would give it to a wife some day.'

'I thought when you didn't bring Isabel to my house that she didn't want to visit. I thought there might be a babe on the way and she might not wish to travel. And then when you left, I started thinking about it.

You didn't seem to care enough about your wife or our family to honour your dead mother's last wishes. How could you disgrace your mother's memory?'

'I have done no such thing.'

He picked up the lacquered box and held it in both hands. 'This morning, I thought to look. I don't know why. But I searched your old room and I found this. Just tossed in a drawer as if it were a comb.'

Isabel appeared in the doorway. She didn't speak.

'Why is it not on Isabel's hand?' The Viscount's words blared.

William stared at this father.

'You've never honoured her memory as you should,' his father said.

'You have done so enough for all of us.' William met the red-rimmed eyes of his father. 'Take it back or it goes in the refuse.'

'You will have to be the one to put it there, just as you've put your mother's memory into the dust bin.'

'Father,' William spoke. 'Did you not think that her blood runs through each of your children?'

'I don't want it,' Isabel interrupted from the doorway, her voice whip-crack sharp.

'What?' The Viscount whirled, facing Isabel.

'I prefer this one.' She held up her ring finger. 'That one is too large.'

The Viscount turned back, shooting a glare at William. 'She jumps to your defence.' Keeping his eyes locked with his son's, he said, 'Describe the ring, Isabel.'

'I do not wish to. It is enough that I have said I do

not want it. It is an old ring and I wished for something new.'

'Bah.' One spindly finger pointed at William's chest. 'You didn't have it in your house. You have not shown it to her and I cannot believe you even offered it to her. She would have kept it with the women's trinkets she owns. That is what women do.'

He turned to Isabel. 'A thousand pardons. I didn't make him honour his mother as he should have. I let him carouse about all night, thinking him a youth who needed revelry. Instead, I let him become a man who thinks of nothing but himself. I tried to force him into marriage, thinking he would become the son I wanted. But nothing's changed. Even when he visited the country, he didn't stay at my home.'

'I spent much time at Aunt Emilia's.' William's words slapped the air.

'With that wastrel nephew of mine.' His voice rose. 'The two of you are of the same cloth. But him I can take none of the blame for.'

He turned, walking to Isabel. 'Toss the ring, for all I care. My lineage is dead, except for what my daughters might provide. His son may inherit the title—' his head indicated William '—but I hope he inherits nothing of his own father.'

Isabel shrugged one shoulder and interlaced her fingers. She tightened the fingers of her left hand, the band visible to him. 'If this is the concern you've shown your son all these years, then I want nothing to do with you as well.'

She turned and left.

'So this is the way it is.' He kicked the table legs flying and the box flew to the wall and bounced off. Storming from the room, he slapped the door facing and stomped down the stairs.

William moved to the box and picked it up, but he couldn't open it. The death and the drink. His father had changed so much.

The light of the family had rested in one person's hands and she'd died.

The last Christmas with his mother wasn't just his best memory of Christmas; it was his only memory.

And it was the first time he knew she was ill. Very ill.

His mother had awoken them before dawn, rushing them to get ready, and they'd all bustled into the cold, frosted darkness and travelled to Aunt Emilia's. Their morning meal had been taken in Aunt Emilia's ballroom with small tables spread about and the sideboard covered in platters of food. Children and adults together in a room decorated floor to ceiling in evergreen. The windows faced the sunrise and the sun had bathed them all in gold.

William and Sylvester had trudged outside afterwards, wanting to get away from the conversation of the adults and the bob-apple game the children played. William had found a spear tip while he and Sylvester explored ruins.

Then on the way home from his Aunt Emilia's, his family had bundled together in the carriage and his mother had laughed that there were almost too many children to fit inside, as she held Harriet and brushed the strands of her youngest child's hair from her face.

William had shown them the spear tip and they'd all made up stories about the ferocious knight who'd carried it. Her knight had been named William and he'd given the spear tip to his mother as a token. She'd taken it and said she'd keep it always.

They'd returned home to another feast. His mother had had a coughing spell at Christmas dinner, right after sitting down. She'd said she wasn't hungry and left, insisting they stay. His father had followed her and William and his sisters had eaten, never raising their eyes from the food.

No knight could save her.

William picked up the ring and slipped it on the second knuckle of his smallest finger. It wasn't a pretty ring. Not at all. He'd seen so many more that were more elegant. A daisy shape, and each petal held a small gemstone and the centre a larger one. The biggest gem wasn't perfectly cut and it was more obvious than on the others, almost like a lop-sided face. Even the precious metal holding the gems had a primitive feel, except for the leaves which led around the band.

A seventeenth-century baroque ring worn by his mother. The one his father had asked him to take from her hand after death. William, at thirteen, had wanted it buried with her, because how could his mother be his mother without the ring she'd worn every day of his life.

But it had been his grandmother's and the Viscount insisted it would be for William's wife some day.

He examined the ring, and then touched the stones to his cheek.

Isabel stepped into Sophia's house, lamps shining to make the room bright as day. Taper candles burned, adding a festive air. A red velvet cloth draped at the table beside them. Someone took her pelisse and William's frock coat. Since the night before, he'd not said one word to her other than the most basic of pleasantries on the way. He didn't seem angry, but as if he'd pulled away. Already she'd got used to having him in her life and the distance ate away at her. She pushed the ache in her chest from her body. She would not acknowledge how bleak she felt inside at the thought of spending the rest of her life unloved. Even the thought of seeing her good friend Joanna didn't fill her with the pleasure she'd expected, but increased the emptiness of her heart when she realised she would never have the bond Joanna had with Luke.

They walked past another draped swag of fabric and on a table she noted the bough of evergreen resting on a wooden platter with dried berries and twigs around it, giving the room a holiday scent.

A smiling Sophia, dressed in a yellow-silk gown, and wearing jewels to match, rushed to greet them. 'I am so happy you decided to come. It will be so nice to—it will be glorious to hear you sing, Isabel.'

Isabel instantly stopped. 'But I am not going to perform.'

Disappointment flicked in Sophia's eyes, causing a similar pang in Isabel.

'You're not?' Sophia's eyes took in her brother. 'But I have planned—'

'Leave it, Sophia.' William's voice spoke a gentle command. The warmth of his hand rested at Isabel's back. 'Let's enjoy the evening.'

'Very well.' Sophia smiled. 'It is enough having good friends here. But I was certain you would sing for us. I thought that was why...' Her words faded. First her eyes searched her brother's face, then she gave Isabel a smile.

'I think I hear another carriage,' Sophia said. 'My husband is with the other guests. Pardon me while I greet the newcomers.' She moved away.

Isabel turned, clasping her hand over William's arm so she could pull him close and whisper, 'You told her I would sing.'

'Yes.'

'How could you?'

'I wanted you to have a chance to reach to the skies.'

'You wished to force me into it.'

'No. Well, perhaps. But only because it is right for you.'

'How could you think you know what is right for me?'

One side of his lips quirked up. 'Do you not believe you know what is best for me?'

She paused. 'Well, of course. But I do.'

He took her gloved hand, pulled it to his lips and placed a kiss at the back. 'Sophia gave you a safe place to stay on the night you were attacked. Would it not be a wonderful gift for her to introduce your voice to London, on the night before Christmas?'

'Isabel,' a feminine voice called out.

Upon hearing her name, Isabel turned to see her friend Joanna rushing towards them, with her husband Luke following, adoration for his wife in his eyes.

After a quick greeting, Sophia ushered them into the ballroom.

Isabel clasped her friend Joanna's hands. The chatter of voices rose so loud at the soirée the women had to be close to hear each other.

'William told me last night that you and Luke planned to be here.' Isabel said. 'I am so happy to see you.'

'This Christmas is even more meaningful to me than the last one where we four were together at the school. I can imagine Rachel in Huria living in a palace. It suits her so. The more exotic something was, the more it interested her,' Joanna spoke. 'I hope she is as happy as we are. We have both found love matches.'

Isabel dared not turn to William and see the look on his face when the word love was used. Her smile hurt, but she refused to acknowledge the pain she felt. She would have time for that later.

'Have you heard anything of Madame Dubois's illness?' Isabel asked Joanna.

'No. I haven't.'

Isabel quickly told Joanna of the conversation with the Duke of Wakefield. 'It would be so sad if they are never reunited, but I cannot see Madame falling in love with anyone.'

'But we did. Now we are spending Christmas with our true loves.' She turned. 'Did you imagine we would be so fortunate, Isabel?'

'No. I rather thought I would end up like Madame.' She smiled, but didn't look into anyone's eyes. 'But without the school.'

William's smile took in Lady Howell. He had insisted Sophia visit her house and invite her to the soirée.

His plan on whom to invite had been simple, but was not going as planned. He'd invited Luke and Joanna to give Isabel support, but when Joanna had spoken of love—Isabel's face had paled. He'd invited the Duke of Wakefield—who'd not attended—because the Duke's approval carried a lot of sway. He'd invited Lady Howell and a few of her friends, whose voices just carried. But now that didn't seem to have been a grand idea.

He could not disinvite Lady Howell and he couldn't force Isabel to sing.

William looked at Isabel. 'Please come with me for a moment.'

Before she could respond, he led her out the doorway, securing privacy for them. 'Isabel. Do not let one instance destroy the confidence you should have.'

'How do you know? You have never seen me perform.'

He leaned forward, letting her know with his face that he was not believing her words. 'As we were leaving, Isabel, I told the butler to send the maid to your sitting room and find your music and select songs to send ahead.'

'You cannot—'

He touched her arms. 'One song. Just one. Prove to me you cannot. Or prove to yourself that you can.'

Her eyes fluttered and matching pangs hit his midsection. He didn't want to hurt her. He wanted to give her the dreams she had.

'Never mind,' he said. 'I shouldn't have planned this.' He spoke the truth. He did want her to shine and he wished for her to have her glory, but part of the reason was a salve to his conscience. He wanted to give her something because he could not give her himself and that was what she wanted most.

'I cannot tonight. Not tonight,' she said. 'Lady Howell and her pack of friends are here. And it was not right of you to arrange this without my permission. I will not.'

'Is—'

'You more than anyone else should understand what it is like for something to die within yourself.'

'You're right.' He let his fingers brush hers. 'If it no longer means anything to you, then I agree that you shouldn't sing.'

William stood patiently. She didn't answer. He held out his arm and she grasped it. They walked back into the soirée, moving to Sophia's ballroom, but his sister wasn't visible among the milling people.

Luke called out to William and the two men moved away as they talked.

Isabel heard a voice that could haunt a ghost.

Lady Howell appeared at Isabel's side. 'Good to see you. I was afraid your duties would keep you away.' She cackled. 'I'm Lady Howell, in case you've forgotten. And you're looking quite lovely tonight. This must be quite a treat for you to be among society as you were raised to be a governess.'

'A noble occupation.'

'I'm sure,' Lady Howell said. 'And a good governess is so hard to select as they can be so full of airs.'

'But the important thing is to have someone trustworthy for the children.'

'Yes. Not some upstart who might want to catch the eye of one of the servants or a visiting relative and cause disarray.' She leaned towards Isabel, breathing out the odour of soured milk. 'And how did you and Balfour meet?'

'I was singing at the school.'

'Oh, yes.' Her eyelids half-closed. 'And why was William Balfour at a governess school?'

'He'd heard of my voice and thought to see for himself.' She raised her head straight.

'So, your voice carries? I mean, tales of your voice?' She patted her gloved hands together. 'I'm sure you sing quite well.'

'Well enough.' The milky scent surrounding Isabel made her own stomach feel curdled.

'So why don't you gift us all with a song? I'm sure your husband's sister would be pleased to let you sing at her soirée. I noticed she has the ballroom arranged so that people might sit around the pianoforte.'

'I don't wish to.'

'Well, I can certainly understand that.' She tapped her fan against her cheek. 'But I would think a woman who might have a talent good enough to cause a man to search her out at a school might not be so reserved about it. Of course, Balfour wouldn't have wanted to miss someone like you. Young men get trapped by their affections all the time.'

When Lady Howell said the word *trapped* her eyes glistened with a touch of glee.

And William was going to move from his town house and Lady Howell would hear of it, and it would become quite the chortling contest when Lady Howell talked about it with her friends.

'I think I shall tell Sophia I'd like to sing.' Isabel looked at Lady Howell. 'I have quite the repertoire of songs.'

She just could not remember a single one.

Chapter Seventeen

The instant the people assembled in the chairs, Isabel shut her eyes. Not one word from one song could she remember. At the school, she could not have forgotten them if she'd tried. They bubbled from her.

But never had she felt the eyes on her in such a way. Now it was as if every blink batted her. It was not just the ones who wanted her to fail that caused the clench in her stomach, but the ones who wanted her to succeed as well.

Every time she had performed in the past, she'd been at the school, or in her parents' house. She didn't know why she thought she could sing on a stage when she'd dreamed of singing for others. Nothing felt the same.

William stood at the side, watching. She could feel his wish for her to succeed and that added to her fear that she could not.

Joanna and Luke were sitting front and centre. Sophia sat at the pianoforte.

Isabel looked at the music propped at the piano. She'd

forgotten how to read the words even. She leaned over the piano, concentrating on the words, but it didn't stop the feeling that she needed to run.

'Are you familiar with this one?' Isabel asked Sophia.

'Very much.' The puzzlement on Sophia's face was obvious.

Isabel looked at the song and could finally read the words.

Then Isabel fluttered, adjusting her gloves, taking in a breath and trying to calm herself. One could not sing well when the voice quivered in fear. Sophia stared with concern. Joanna watched with a whisper to her husband and confusion on her face.

Isabel turned, and reached to the music, switching out the songs. The notes wavered so she could hardly read them. She took one and put it on top, then put the others behind, one at a time.

Her breathing would not slow.

She handed the music to Sophia and indicated the first sheet. 'Play this. Over and over.' She had to get alone, away from the eyes.

Then she held her palm up to the audience. 'One moment.' She rushed by William and left the room.

She ran to the red cloth Sophia had put behind the evergreens at the entrance.

Dashing the cloth around her, like a shawl that covered the hair, Isabel let the covering conceal her, drooping over her face and body. Then she began to sing softly to herself.

She heard her voice, heard the quaver dissolve and felt the strength returning. Then she walked into the room as the verse began again, singing, sashaying to the front of the room, not looking at anyone. Just her own too-tight slippers.

She stood front and centre, and didn't move, the upper half of her face concealed except for her lips, as she sang about the loss of her love.

William watched. A spirit began singing. The audience could see her mouth clearly and the words fell into the room, adorned with the same velvet of the covering.

No one moved. William wondered how he breathed. His chest felt too taut to let his heart beat.

She continued and, near the end of the song, thrust the cloth back, letting it fall to the floor, and the volume increased with the sight of her face.

She sang for thousands, not just for the few in the room, and the listeners knew they sat near a woman singing for crowds.

As the notes ended, she didn't wait to begin the next, but turned to the pianoforte, pulled out the music she wanted, and then thrust herself into the rowdy tune, swaggering to and fro, stopping a moment here and there as she walked to William.

William's eyes met hers and he saw the uncertainty. He raised his chin, locking his gaze with hers, silently telling her that she controlled the room.

Her eyes changed and her voice became stronger.

She marched to William and he didn't see Isabel, but an older, wiser version of her self. One who'd lived the words to the song. She reached out gloved hands and while she didn't grasp him, her fists clasped as if she had and her head tilted back, but her eyes roved over the audience and she followed the words of the song, and when she moved aside, her hand flicked and she didn't appear to know he existed any more.

Then she did a song about a country miss who'd lost her beloved and was standing above his grave, only to admit it wasn't truly his grave because she was forbidden to even visit the last vestiges of the only person who had ever cared for her.

Handkerchiefs covered half the faces of the women in the room.

Perhaps, he thought, when one plans an event with an explosive one shouldn't use too much gunpowder.

The song stopped. Isabel turned to Sophia and gave a forceful wave of the head. Sophia slid another sheaf of music into place and her eyes were transfixed on the notes.

A joyous tune erupted, perhaps more suitable to a tavern, but Isabel stood immobile. He could see the governess in her smile. A lady singing a tune not meant to be imbued with polish, but Isabel corrected that, adding a strictness, but making the song a private joke shared with the audience.

Oh, we are oh, so proper now, but some of us have perhaps known where I have substituted very proper words in exchange for less suitable ones, have we not?

If one got the jest, one was a part of it.

Then she sang her last song of the night. For William.

His face became immobile. His arms were crossed. Eyes unfathomable. But she had seen that look before. When men listened to her sing and didn't want their emotion to show on their face. It didn't look valiant to be weeping as a woman sang.

The song ended.

Silence. Perfect silence. She curtsied.

Then gloved hands patted with a vengeance and words of praise erupted. Handkerchiefs flourished, dotting eyes.

'My wife,' William's voice broke through the other sounds and passed through Isabel's ears and wedged in her heart stronger than any words of any song.

She rushed to him, and threw her arms around him.

'Is…' He grasped her elbows and pulled her back. She met his gaze and, for one brown flickering instance, saw black before the smile took hold. Her knees locked in place.

He stepped behind enough to pull her gloved hand out for a kiss above.

'They love each other,' Lady Howell grumbled to the woman at her side. 'But who can blame them? He's got funds and she's spirited. I was sure he'd plucked her out of a brothel, but I found out she's a country squire's daughter and been her whole life at some governess school—' Lady Howell grimaced. 'Bah. Life doesn't know what it's doing half the time, but I'd say you can't beat funds nor beauty with a stick.' She paused. 'Well, you can beat beauty with a stick and if you got coin, it can be a gold stick.' She chuckled, turning her head to search the room. 'Any more of that punch left?'

Isabel turned as her hand slipped from William's grasp. 'Yes. Lady Howell,' she said. 'I believe I could have a drink as well. What more could I ask for as all my dreams have come true?'

'Thank you for gifting us with a song, Isabel.' William spoke and then tucked her hand over his arm.

He retrieved a glass for her and moved them to Joanna, Luke and Sophia.

'Now you know what she was like at the school,' Joanna said. 'She read Mrs Radcliffe's novels and claimed them inspiration for her songs. Madame Dubois despaired of her, but Isabel could sing her way out of reprimands.' She looked at William. 'I must warn you, she can make herself cry when she sings if she wishes, so do not be surprised if you anger her and she returns later with tears in her eyes. It could be a trick.'

'I will keep that in mind.' William's voice rolled over them. 'My Songbird is truly a gift to the world. I fear the performance might have tired her. We should be leaving.' He turned to Isabel. 'Please make your goodbyes to your friends, Isabel. Tomorrow will be Christmas and I imagine you'll wish to spend the entire day with them.'

'I thought we…' Isabel saw the flicker of blackness again. The square of the jaw just beyond the smile.

She turned and bade her farewells to her friends, their happiness bouncing over her like sun's rays.

She had created the exact performance she'd wanted. She had been a success and William's gloved hand over hers kept her close at his side as they made their farewells. William helped her into her coat and she collected the new velvet cape and draped it over her arm.

In the carriage, he shook his head, in wonder. 'You're an excellent singer, Isabel, and an even better actress.'

'I've been performing for the students since shortly after I attended the school,' she said. 'First they were surprised I could sing. But when the new wore off, they might yawn or speak to someone else. I determined to make them take notice while I sang and if their gazes moved I darted about, or swaggered or changed to a different song.' She leaned into the coach seat. 'I could not let them ignore me. I could not. Not in those moments. The moments were mine.'

She crossed her arms over her chest. 'When I sing for people, sometimes my heart beats so fast and afterwards I feel as if I have been running the whole time I was standing, but still, it is delicious.'

'I swear, when you looked at me, I could have believed you were the woman in the song.' He shook his head. 'You'll have people sending you hothouse flowers by the crate, but do not fall for such blather.' He looked out the window, frowning. 'The streets are near frozen. This will not help with my moving.'

'But you'll not want to move now? Surely not? It's almost Christmas. I saw your face while I sang. I saw—'

'Isabel. You saw the same as you gave,' he said.

The words hit her harder than anything Lady Howell had ever spoken.

'Oh.' She huffed at herself. She'd been taken in again during a performance.

'I've paid extra to have the home now,' he said. 'I had the servants begin moving my things while we were out. They were to take the majority of things I need, but leave enough for tonight and we can finish tomorrow.'

'On the eve of Christmas? And Christmas Day.' Her

fingers tightened. 'The servants are working…you could not wait?'

She pressed herself against the opposing side of the carriage and turned to him. 'I thought you cared much more for them than that. They have been with you for years.'

'I do care for them, but it is their employment. We were working tonight as well. This was not all frivolity, Isabel. It may seem like it to you, but your voice will open your way in this town. Lady Howell and her friends will spread the news at their Christmas meals tomorrow as this will give them an *event* to share. The next time I go to the clubs, I will be questioned about it. More will hear of it. Within the space of a few days, everyone who knows of us will know of your voice.'

'Open my way into what?'

'All of what you wish. I've put it at your feet.'

'You have?' The chilled air seeped into her clothing.

'Yes. You wished to move to London to have a stage. I've provided you with one.'

Exerting strength to calm her fears, she said, 'I was the one singing the song. I knew what I was doing. My voice would find a way to be heard once I am at a soirée no matter what. It didn't matter that it was your sister's home. I promise you that I can innocently lean against a pianoforte, trail my hand along the keys and start absently singing to myself and have others listening in a heartbeat.'

'I have speeded the process.'

'You speeded the process so you can tramp out the door of your house and make a sham of a marriage.' She spoke the words, and heard them, and felt them. 'And you have chosen to have a disagreement with me to make the process of your leaving seem more justified.'

'This has been a sham of a marriage since before the vows.' Quiet words, barely stabbing the air. 'We agreed to a marriage with no heart involved. I did so because I knew I had no heart to give.'

She matched her control to his.

'Marriage.' She tapped her chin. 'Tell me, what does that word mean?'

'Nothing to us.'

'Well, you put that more clearly than the signature on your wedding paper. I noticed the grimace on your face when you signed. It was not a death proclamation.'

'It very much felt like one. You cannot know what love does to a person. You have been too secluded with the girls in the school and the countryside. I have seen it first-hand. I have seen it from women who have caught the pox from their husbands and who are dying as the husband is visiting a young mistress. I have seen it in the eyes of the men who look at tarts who are fighting for the men's coins. And I have seen what it does to innocent children and people who are merely standing at the side and must suffer because love has grappled someone by the throat and chewed out their minds.'

'Even Mr and Mrs Grebbins knew more about love than you.'

'I don't care who knows more about love than me. I know enough.'

'No. You know nothing about it.' Again she heard her words. They pushed her back into the carriage seat as she struggled with them. It was true. He didn't. If he did, he would not be thrusting hers back into her face. He didn't know of the devotion and the happiness two people could share when looking at the world together.

He spoke to the night. 'Do not care for me, Isabel.'

'Loving you would be the same as loving a gold chamber pot. Rather nice on the outside, but one mustn't get too close or the stink sets in.'

'Thank you. You see, the stink is what happens when one thinks to love.'

'I would quite agree. I am so fortunate we will have a marriage where we are not tripping over each other. But I am very upset that you would expect the servants to work tonight. I will help them crate up your things so you may move sooner. I hope you're taking that hideously arrogant bed with you. I might put something smaller there for guests, or move into it myself.'

'You're completely welcome to do as you wish.'

'I will. Perhaps some dried flowers will give it a fresher smell.'

'You're too kind.'

'Well, it does reek of shaving soap and boot black and leather. Scents that I am quite certain—' She put a hand to her throat. 'They do not do well for me.'

'I agree that they do not. And I quite like them.'

'I hope you are not planning to stay the night at the town house,' she said. 'After all, there is much work to be done moving the things out of the…room. And I can easily direct the servants to send things your way later.'

'I was quite planning to spend the night there as it is still my home for the moment.'

'Please do not forget to leave any instructions you might have for me in the future in such a way as to reach my housekeeper. She will give me all posts and make certain I am kept up to date. Although I do not know how I will make it up to the servants that they are having to work in this season. I will think of something though, no matter how much it costs.'

The carriage rumbled along and Isabel was at the door before the carriage's movement stopped in front of the house.

'If this,' she said, blocking the door and not wanting the coachman to hear, 'is a better state to you than love, then I would wish you a whole lifetime of such bliss.'

She left him behind. He could follow her or not. She didn't care.

When they walked into the house, she said over her shoulder, 'One word with you upstairs, please.'

As quickly as she walked, she could not outpace him. She walked into the windowed sitting room, noting the shutters closed against the cold. She'd seen a crate in the hallway, but no servants in the family chambers. Perhaps they were not too dedicated to be working at the moment either, but she was certain confectionery scents lingered in the air.

'And how are we to handle the addition of children into the house?' she asked.

'I am neither here nor there on the subject. It is not something that must be decided this night or this year for that matter.'

'I wish for them.'

'Then I will do what I can to assist.'

'I somehow knew you would.' She raised her chin. 'I didn't want you to think I would forbid such activities until an heir and a daughter is provided. On the other hand, if a daughter arrives first and second, I will consider myself unable to get the process right and my duty done.'

'We will decide as the time arrives.'

'Very well. Thank you for the wonderful evening.'

'Let us not part on sour feelings. This is for the best, even for you, Isabel. You just do not know it.'

Looking at the floor, she gathered her thoughts. 'You have not dissembled about what you wished for. Not once. I must understand. I suppose I let the dreams I had as a child override the truth.' She raised her face. 'Do not think I am angry at you, William. I am, but I will soon be over it. I am most angry that sunshine does not hide in all dark caves and hungry children do not have fairies to feed them a good meal before night-time. I wish all dreams came true—and simply by writing the words in a song and singing it the world could become clear and all lives be filled with hopes that come true. I have been fortunate because of your intervention. Now I will continue on as planned. I was to remain a spinster for my life and I will always be unwed in my heart. I will not trouble you for a marriage you never wished to have.'

'I wish you pleasant dreams.'

'You as well.' She gave a quick curtsy to him and he left.

She could not quite finish with the untruths. And it had led her into the cave without sunshine.

Chapter Eighteen

A knocking on the door of her bedchamber-turned-into-music-room caused Isabel to sit alert. The lady's maid had already helped her get ready for bed.

William. He simply could not stay away.

Well, he could not stay either, not tonight. She called out to enter. The maid walked in. Isabel's eyes kept trying to make the maid taller and turn her into William, but it didn't work.

'My pardon,' the servant said. 'With the soirée, and the moving and Christmas, I didn't remember to give you this.' She held folded paper in her hand and walked it across to Isabel.

The maid left and Isabel looked at the writing. She knew it was no note from William. It would be from Grace or Rachel, as Isabel had already received a letter from her parents earlier wishing her a joyful Christmas. They would not have time to write again for some time because they would be so caught up in visiting neighbours and sharing the good cheer for the year.

Isabel gazed at the picture she'd had framed. The one Grace had drawn when they were younger. Four smiling faces. Her friends who'd kept her from feeling alone. The other three girls had lifted her spirits even when she'd not mentioned needing a smile. They'd never been further away than a whisper at the school. She'd lost the closeness with them, by distance and circumstance.

She had seen Joanna and Luke, and been able to share in their happiness, but a hollowness had burdened her, until she sang. Then, she'd been enveloped in William's love, but it had been an illusion. A lie. A short-lived lie.

Now the untruths she'd told were settling on her like winter's chill only going deep inside and coating all her feelings in a muck of despair.

She had the servants to keep her company. True, they were paid to be at her home, but surely it was not too terrible to work for her. Or perhaps they simply could not find another post.

Isabel turned the letter to the light and opened it. Rachel had written. The excitement from the words blasted into the room and shot through Isabel's heart. It was all she could do not to stop reading. Rachel was getting married to a prince.

Joanna had Luke.

But not all of them had fared so well.

Isabel didn't know precisely what had happened with Grace and her daughter, except Miss Fanworth said Grace had been satisfied her daughter was cared for. Grace could now continue on, searching out a governess position so she might forget the tragic moments of her past. Isabel imagined Grace keeping the loss deep inside for the rest of her life, the sadness growing greater as the years passed. Much like William's father had mourned.

Nor had Isabel received a post from Miss Fanworth about Madame and she was afraid to write and ask because she might find out something she could not bear. Madame had sounded so ill earlier and Isabel had thought the Duke would return with news, but he'd not attended the soirée.

Isabel continued reading the letter, each swirl of the words dragging like icy drips across the vestiges of her heart. Only, it wasn't vestiges, it was as a big bleeding mess that took up the entire room. She had learned nothing when she caught that bee. Nothing.

Isabel read the words through a blur of moisture. She was invited to the wedding.

She didn't think she should attend. To fall to her knees sobbing as the couple gazed into each other's eyes would not be pleasant. She could imagine the shocked look on faces and herself rolling about the floor in agony.

Looking down at the rug, she sighed. Rolling on the floor would not help. She'd learned to feel things deeply so she could put the emotions into song. That was turning out rather dismally.

A knock again on the door. William. She sniffled. She would forgive him.

But then the door opened slowly and a skirt showed. It would not be him. The maid peeked around. 'I forgot to tell you about Rambler. A boy appeared at the door this morning and was looking for his cat. He'd heard we found one. Rambler ran to him and jumped into his arms.'

Isabel smiled. 'Well, that will make a happy Christmas for the boy.'

She would not cry. She would not. But she did feel all a-sniffle.

'Please tell my husband that I erred when I said I have a cat.'

'I do not believe he is here, but I will see that he is informed when he returns.'

The door shut. Isabel stepped across the room and opened the basket where she kept her sewing. Looking underneath, where she'd hidden them from view, she pulled out the five handkerchiefs. She had not put flowers on them, but simply a strong B with perhaps a few more circles and dots than necessary. For William. She held it to her cheek, and when the soft fabric touched her skin, it was too much.

She took all five and moved to the tiny room and on to the lumpy bed. She sat, her back against the headboard in the small, dark room. She had a whole house, servants, and yet she felt most at home in this room which was the same size as the one at her parent's house.

Even if her mother had been in the same house, Isabel knew she could not have rushed to her and explained. Her mother wouldn't have understood. Her mother had never been anything but the light in the candle in the centre of the room. She'd had six brothers who'd all thought her a gem, then married a man who thought her the whole world of jewels.

Isabel's mother was a good-spirited mother who meant well, but she didn't truly understand tears, or sadness or being alone.

In the darkness, Isabel traced her fingers over the *B*. She was a Balfour now. And probably, in truth, was the perfect wife for her husband. She would learn not to care. She would lock away her feelings in the same way William had. She swallowed. She would find his secret.

If she had daughters, she would teach them to be brave and strong. She would also understand if their hearts were broken and she would give them more comfort than a wadded wet handkerchief.

Singing didn't seem so important now as love. The one thing in the world that she would give up singing for—she could not have.

In the bedchamber, William gave the sleepy-eyed valet the option of waiting to follow until after Christmas Day. The man surely had personal attachments and William didn't wish to disrupt them.

Then the valet examined William's face. That had never happened before. Their eyes had never really met and now the man looked at him as if trying to decipher the back of William's head going straight through from the eyes.

William took the key to the new home. He would not wait until Christmas Day to move. Isabel planned to eat dinner with his sisters, but William would not join the festivities. Spending the day alone would suit him. As soon as Sophia had her own home so she could host his sisters, he'd shut Christmas from his life. He didn't need it.

William marched out the door, letting the cold air blast his face. His fists were at his side and he waited for his carriage. The time seemed eternal until the vehicle approached.

Wind buffeted him. He should have stayed inside to wait for the carriage, but the house had been too warm and the servants not their usual quiet selves. He could hear bustles and taps and hints of disarray. His moving out, along with cooking, had disrupted things.

'Cousin Sylvester's,' William said. He had no desire to go to his new home. He was taking some of the staff to work for him, but they would not begin until the day after Christmas.

'Of course. He will be pleased you're attending his… evening.'

'Wait.' William stopped short, remembering the date. Sylvester always tried to have a particularly ribald dinner party in the late hours and claimed to his friends that it was necessary for them all to attend so they would have something to take the sting out of a pleasant Christmas dinner where one had to sit with elderly relatives and discuss bunions and stuffed gullets and digestive disorders.

But as of late, Sylvester had begun to discuss his own aching head, sorrowful stomach and ingrown toenails more than one would expect. He also discussed hair tonics to excess as he had a deep concern about the thinning spots in his locks.

William would risk the lack of comfort of his body

to protect his ears from a night of Sylvester's slurred words about this remedy or that, and William's necessity of keeping a chamber pot at hand for when Sylvester cast up his accounts.

The moments of solitude would be much better than a night of revelry.

'I wish to inspect my new home and then I will spend the night there.' He didn't wish to speak with anyone.

He placed a boot firmly on the carriage step, aware of the sluggishness and groan of the carriage springs caused by the falling temperatures.

The ride had the spirit of a cortège.

When the carriage stopped, William descended and examined his purchase. A smaller house, further from his club. Further from Sophia's. Closer to Sylvester's. Without the parlour windows and their inside wooden shutters, and the ability to stand at the window looking down over a busy street. The main attraction of this house had been its availability.

He had asked his man-of-affairs to be hasty and, considering all, this was a good selection. He had paid above an expected price to get the residence quickly. Marriage was costly, but he had known it would be so.

William stepped out.

Again the springs in the carriage creaked as the coachman jumped down to give William a lantern. William hurried the man away, knowing he wished to get back to his own family.

When the carriage left, William saw another man, one of his new neighbours, struggling with a wriggling fluff sticking out from where the man held something against his coat. In the other hand, he held a cone of paper wrapped around greenery.

A servant ran out with a lamp and, before the door closed behind him, a little boy, wearing a long-sleeved shirt, rushed from the doorway into the chill.

The father stopped and held out the white barking fluff. The boy took it and hugged. 'Not too tight,' the father said. 'Mustn't squeeze too much or he'll nip your nose.'

The father put a hand on the boy's shoulder, guiding him towards the door while the boy blasted out a selection of names possible for the puppy.

William grimaced. He hoped it would not be a large dog. The barking could quite disturb sleep.

Irritation rumbled through him at the thought he was abandoning his house. Another complication caused by the emotions. The neighbours at the other town house tended to be invisible, but these might not be. The hour was much too late for a little child to be awake.

He raised his eyes higher when a movement at the window caught his eye. The lamps in the house were lit bright as day.

He looked up in time to see a woman, her back to the street, and the man's arm moved into view and held something above her head. Mistletoe. She laughed and moved from view, the mistletoe following.

William turned, trudging into the house, more than ready to put the numbing cold behind him and throw the festivities to the rag-and-bone collectors.

He hated the joyous, wondrous Christmas with all its solitude and bleakness and nonsense.

The cheerful spirit bit into the winter. Each year he looked forward to his favourite day—the day after Christmas. That day he woke up with a smile on his face because normal lives resumed.

The door to the new residence opened without noise. Darkness pressed on each side of him, tomb-like.

The air. The air, instead of seeming warmer from the outside, had captured the chill of the winter and settled into the clasp of the house. Even the scent of lantern oil didn't make it seem warmer.

Above stairs, he saw chairs by a table. Larger pieces of furnishings the owner had left behind as part of the agreement to vacate hurriedly. William kicked a boot heel against the bare floor. No movement. Steady, but not in a comforting way as he'd expected, but in a hard, unforgiving hold.

The fireplace didn't call out to him. The mantel had no engravings, just a wooden structure of average size. He raised the lantern, seeing a pale spot where a picture had once hung on the wall, and at the window, water stains. Shadows flickered like the moments from a bad dream.

He moved through each of the family rooms, seeing the scrapes of life on the walls and the nicks of time about.

Bones, not flesh.

The room with the fireplace and water stains on the wall compelled him to return. William walked to the mantel and put the lantern on it. He found a tinder box and lit the coals in the fireplace, and stood, trying to get the chill from inside himself.

Searching about the house, he found more coals and brought them to the room. The night would be spent sober and he didn't wish to be cold as well.

Again his eyes landed above the fireplace.

The space around the mantel had darkened with the soot and the pale space above indicated a large portrait.

Going to the bedchamber, he saw the trunk he'd instructed sent ahead. On top of it sat a tiny basket, with biscuits, a flask, currants and comfits. Cook didn't want him to starve. He opened the flask and tasted. The water he liked.

He sat the basket aside, opened the trunk and found the box. The box with his mother's ring and the little scrap of feather from Isabel's hat.

He imagined his mother's portrait. The second one. The one started after her death.

His first sight of the completed painting had caused a smothering inside his throat that not even his first bout of drunkenness had cured. His head had ached the next morning—his world had spun, but the picture had remained in the library. Never again had William taken a book from the shelves. The servants had gathered anything from that room he'd wished.

He'd still had to encounter the sight of his father when the Viscount summoned him, shouting out commands that sometimes were nonsense. His father had always been the same—staring at the portrait, an empty glass in his hand. A decanter sat beside him and several others graced the mantel—one container always full.

Above that stone mantel, the picture was not truly of William's mother but a likeness taken from a family portrait completed before her death. The eyes had not been right and yet they had. They'd been dead. He'd never completely erased that image from his mind. Seeing his mother die had not been as hard as seeing the picture of lifeless eyes, staring—every time he entered the room, if he looked in that direction. He learned to keep his eyes from the mantel.

Many times he had contemplated slashing the portrait. But he could not.

Even the room, when he walked by it, door open, and his father inside, had begun to emit some scent of rot.

He'd put a knife into his father's grasp and told him to use it.

His father had stabbed the weapon into the table and sworn to the rafters. William had stood, a brandy bottle in his hand, his cheek cut from a fight he'd been in the night before and his stance defiant.

'Get out of my sight,' his father had shouted.

William had swung the bottle into the door facing as he'd left the room. The shattering crash had resonated. He'd dropped the bottle neck in the hallway on the way to his bedchamber. When the neck hit the rug, he'd looked down the hallway.

Sophia's eyes stared from around her door. Harriet and Rosalind peeped from the other side, all wearing nightdresses. Three wan faces and three sets of eyes looking too large and too old.

He'd begged their pardons, promised them treats for breakfast, suggested a new hair ribbon for Harriet, a book for Rosalind and a new dress for Sophia. He'd said he'd fallen from his horse on the morning ride and was in a foul mood, but his beautiful sisters made his day better.

No one had smiled. At that moment, he had changed. His actions, in his sisters' presence, had become more circumspect. And he'd taken more care when out. He didn't want his sisters losing their only brother and he didn't want to see any more pain in their eyes.

He'd not even realised he must take charge of both the land and the household at first. He'd expected his father to wake any minute and resume the duties to family. Or Aunt Emilia—but her husband had been sick and so had her mother.

He'd waited, but then he'd been able to wait no longer. He'd done the best he could, but he'd not been able to expect everything. One day Harriet had wandered away and he'd been terrified because he'd not planned for it. Not expected it.

William had not wanted to become a parent and particularly not wanted to become a parent for his father. But he'd had no choice.

He raised his head. Nor had his mother had a choice.

His father had, however. William was thankful he'd not realised the tale of him attacking a woman would pull his father from his room or he might have made up the story himself when he was a lad.

Eleven years had passed since his mother had died. He rested his elbow at the mantel and leaned his head on his fingertips, shutting his eyes. His mother had been taken from him and his sisters, and they'd not known what to do. He could understand her being taken from him, but his sisters had needed their mother so much. That made him most angry.

He sat by the coals, watching them as they glowed and then faded away. Several times he moved, raking them around in the same manner he poked about in his head, resurrecting memories of days buried deep in his mind.

Harriet losing her front teeth and thinking they would not grow back. Rosalind stealing a horse from the stables. Sophia and that rakish soldier. Giving up on his father. All before he was Isabel's age.

William knew how differently he'd been at nineteen compared to Isabel.

He stopped, realising that his father had been eighteen when he married. Thirty-two when his wife died. Not much older than William.

William's chest thudded. If Isabel had died at Wren's hands... True, he didn't know her then, but still, the thought took his breath.

Perhaps he understood a bit more now. He didn't even want to think of it, and yet, his father had lost the one true love of his life, for ever.

William thought of Isabel again. Alone. What if something happened to her and he was not with her? Wren was not the only man who might want a song-bird caged.

He could not live with himself if someone hurt Isabel.

He breathed in and it was as if she touched his skin. She would always touch him, whether she was in the room or not. Whether she was in the world or not. And he could not live without touching her.

He could not bear the thought of her being alone. If she wanted someone to love her, she should have it. Isabel should have whatever she wished for.

And he should give all to her that he could.

He had not known what love was about. He had not expected that a person could fall in love with another person when they were not in the same room. But he fell in love with Isabel at that moment because now when thoughts of her surrounded him, he wanted it no other way.

He no longer cared that it might destroy him if something happened to her. He would be destroyed if he didn't spend his life, whatever remained of it, with her.

William stepped into the house, pleased for the warmth after the long walk and thankful for the plum cake he could tell had been baked. Candles added to the early morning light, giving the entryway a glow he'd never seen before.

The butler stepped up, took William's frock coat and gave a grin and a bow of his head. The bow was usual. The smile unexpected.

'Welcome home, sir.'

William's body lightened. For the first time, he felt the house was more than a place to eat, sleep and gaze out the window. Isabel was here.

'Are you not supposed to be having a day to spend with family, today?' William asked.

He nodded. 'I am spending it with family. Just last month I married Cook.'

William's eyes widened. He'd had no idea of the romance. Cook was the mother of the little boy who'd been tiptoeing about for almost a year.

William nodded and moved up the stairway. He didn't want to wake Isabel.

He looked at his little finger, now wearing the heirloom ring. He touched the band, examining the stone. He slipped it to the second knuckle of his left hand and clasped his fingers closed. Vows might have been said, but this ring was the vow of his marriage. Once the band went on Isabel's finger, they would be married for ever, if she would accept the token.

Chapter Nineteen

The aroma of the burning yule log reminded Isabel of Christmases past, and all that had gone before.

She'd risen well before her usual time and still wore the dressing gown because she'd not wanted to wake her maid early.

But soon she'd have to put on a bright dress and an even more festive face to visit William's sister and pretend everything was well, even though Sophia would know the truth. William not being present would tell too much.

She looked at the crumpled handkerchief in her hand, considering whether to burn it or not. The other had flamed briefly, but hadn't given her the joy she'd expected. She'd had trouble not pulling it back from the fire because it felt wrong to destroy something that reminded her so much of William.

The crumpled handkerchief looked exactly like she felt on the inside.

'Is…' The voice at the door caused her to still, afraid her imagination was deciding to torture her.

She turned, suddenly feeling she sat too close to the flames.

William's hair had been pressed into place by the hat he held in his hand, but he thrust his fingers through the locks, causing it to resume its natural state. He still wore the clothes from the night before.

'Isabel. I am doing the same as my father. The same. I am mired in the past of my mother's death just as he was. He could not go on with his life and I could not go on with my life. I could care for my sisters, but I could not trust myself to have a family.'

She longed to reach for him, but didn't. Looking into William's eyes, she could see flickers of the pain from his childhood.

'After Mother died and the roof began leaking, and the house began smelling of rot, I instructed the man-of-affairs to send workmen to check for a leak from the roof. A leak was found and repairs started. My father complained that his solitude was disturbed, but the men kept working on the roof. I realised everyone would listen to me if my father would not speak to save us.'

Isabel didn't move, but waited.

'The house was rotting away,' William said. 'Father had not noticed. Then I turned fourteen and tossed a bottle into the hallway. I couldn't remember what I'd done that night. I wondered how I could protect my sisters and keep them safe, if I was no more aware than my father.'

Stepping forward, he took her hand and looked to the window. 'After my youngest sisters were skilled at taking care of the estate, I moved where I could visit clubs easier and enjoy myself more. I found this house and had every board checked. Every board had to be solid. The windows had to be tight and the sounds of the outside world diminished. Storms kept at bay. The rooms sturdy. The house shut out the world so I could sleep in the day and be alone when I was here. I do not look out the windows to see what is happening. I look out to see that I know none of the people.'

She imagined his father sitting alone in one house, staring at a portrait, and William alone in another, staring out the windows.

'With my sisters, there are three,' he said. 'It is not as if my heart is solely wrapped around one. But with a wife, my heart would solely be wrapped around her. She would be inside me. How fragile that seems to me and yet—' he touched her cheek '—I cannot risk *not* loving you. That would be even worse.'

At the moment he reached out a hand in her direction, she knew he had made a decision.

He made one step forward. 'I was given the gift of a Songbird almost to my window and I would not raise my head enough to hear the music.'

His eyes searched hers and she threw her arms around him and he tugged her so tight and so close he lifted her off the ground.

When he lowered her to her feet, she asked, 'Have you returned to stay?'

'Absolutely. Wherever you are is where I plan to live.'

Then she looked into his eyes and saw what she'd always wanted to see. Love. For her. If he had not held her, she would have grasped him to remain on her feet. But she didn't even have to tighten her hold. He kept her steady.

He held her away so their eyes could meet. 'I had to step in and care for my sisters and manage the estates when my father was mired in grief. I had to. Perhaps Sophia was old enough to manage, but Ros and Harriet were not. Our family's fortunes would have disappeared. And I had to take the place of mother and father when I felt I had lost my own parents as well. I was so angry and buried it so deep. It wasn't my sisters' fault any more than mine and I didn't want them to suffer.'

'But they didn't, because you took care of them.'

'I did. But not for myself. I had no one to turn to and I accepted it. And I decided I didn't need anyone and I became more and more alone. I lingered at Sophia's house, hoping for a feeling of family, but it wasn't there for me. Then you offered it and it was too good to be true. If I love you, I risk the loss again. But I can't be happy without you. Or even content. Or close to it. I want to have you here.' He clasped her hand, closing her fingers, and pulling her fist over his heart.

'I want to spend Christmas with my wife. This year. And every year for the rest of my life.'

Words she had dreamed of from the man she didn't even know to dream of.

She buried herself against him, the wool scent mingling with the warm earthiness of him.

He stepped back and took a ring from his little finger, and took her left hand, their joined hands igniting a glow of love inside her.

'You're not wearing the wedding ring,' he said, rubbing his thumb over the empty spot where the jewellery had been.

'No. I gave it to some children who were singing at the front door.'

His fingers tightened on her left hand. 'Will you keep a different one? It belonged to my mother.'

'Yes. Your sister told me how a grandfather of yours had it made for the woman he loved.'

Slipping the antique ring on her finger, he moved his hand to cover hers.

'I will be your husband, Isabel, for as long as you will have me, and longer. For you will be my wife in my heart, always.'

She stepped back and sniffed, turning to lift the one handkerchief which was embroidered and put aside to stare at it. The one she'd kept pristine. 'William, you must take this quickly before I cry on it as well.'

He tugged at the corner of the linen, taking it from her hand. 'I'm sorry that I gave you cause to need a handkerchief, Isabel. I will always be here to dry your tears should you cry again, but I hope it is never again because of my actions.'

She sniffed and smiled, reaching for the handkerchief. 'Too late.'

He didn't release the cloth, but pulled her back against him, kissing her tears away.

After Christmas dinner, William turned to Sophia. 'Would you play pianoforte for us? I would like to sing something with Isabel.'

Sophia agreed and moved ahead.

Isabel turned to him. 'You sing?'

'I think I do quite well.' He hugged her close. 'My tone is not so fine as yours, but I would like to sing with you. And tonight, when Ros and Harriet arrive, we'll sing again.'

'They're leaving your father alone?'

'Yes.' He smiled. 'In the message Ros sent to let us know to expect them, she said Father wishes to stay behind, but he is in the best spirits she has ever seen. Apparently after he left my home he came to terms with the past when he realised his children were our mother's legacy. But he won't be alone today. Aunt Emilia's friend lost her husband and he has taken it upon himself to become a confidant. And I sent him a message that you had accepted my ring.'

Isabel reached out, her fingers brushing his knuckles. When their eyes met, she saw a man she'd never seen before—a man at peace with the world around him.

Song bubbled inside her and she wanted to sing for everyone—to give sound to the happiness inside her.

They moved to the pianoforte and Sophia waited while Isabel and William chose to sing *Upon Christmas Day in the Morning*.

Isabel could never stop at one song. She was on the third, her heart filled with sound of William's voice blending with hers, when the pianoforte ended abruptly.

She turned, suddenly aware of another presence in the room. Her mother stood at the doorway, beaming. Her father balanced beside her, a cane in his hand and one foot bandaged with enough cloth to make a small bed covering.

Her mother moved forward, clasping Isabel in a hug. 'We could not miss Christmas without you. We could not,' her mother said. 'And when we arrived at your home the butler directed us here as he was not certain how long you might stay.'

Quick introductions were exchanged and William was hugged as well.

'Although you didn't need to introduce him,' Isabel's mother said. 'I could recognise him instantly from your descriptions in your letters. I was so pleased when you wrote after you married that you had found a matching heart.'

'I didn't mean an exact match, but it is near,' Isabel said, laughing and clasping William's arm to pull them close. 'But how could I not love a man who sings as well as he does?'

'I am so pleased you're happy,' her father said, movements slow as he stood beside his wife.

'Are you well, Father?'

'Never better,' he said. 'To see you has been better than any medicinal.'

Isabel introduced her parents to her new family and as the others talked, William pulled her from the room, took her face in his hands, kissed her soundly and stood back. 'Our voices match so well.'

'So do we,' she said.

* * * * *

*If you enjoyed Isabel's story,
you won't want to miss the other three*
THE GOVERNESS TALES *stories*

THE CINDERELLA GOVERNESS
by Georgie Lee
GOVERNESS TO THE SHEIKH
by Laura Martin
THE GOVERNESS'S SECRET BABY
by Janice Preston

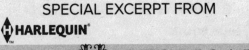
I have come this far... I cannot give up now.

She sucked in a deep breath and reached for the huge
iron knocker. Still she hesitated, her fingers curled around
the cold metal. It felt stiff, as though it was rarely used.
She released it, nerves fluttering.

Before she could gather her courage again, a loud
bark followed by a sudden rush of feet had her spinning
on the spot. A pack of dogs, all colors and sizes, leaped
and woofed and panted around her. Heart in mouth, she
backed against the door, her bag clutched up to her chest
for protection. In desperation, she bent her leg at the knee
and drummed her heel against the door behind her.

After what felt like an hour, she heard the welcome
sound of bolts being drawn and the creak of hinges as the
door was opened.

Grace turned slowly. She looked up...and up. And
swallowed. Hard. A powerfully built man towered over

her, his face averted, only the left side visible. His dark brown hair was unfashionably long, his shoulders and chest broad and his expression—what she could see of it—grim.

"You're late," he growled. "You look too young to be a governess. I expected someone older."

Anticipation spiraled as the implications of the man's words sank in. If Lord Ravenwell was expecting a governess, why should it not be her? She was trained. If his lordship thought her suitable, she could stay. She would see Clara every day and could see for herself that her daughter was happy and loved.

The man's gaze lowered, and lingered. Grace glanced down and saw the muddy streaks upon her gray cloak.

"That was your dogs' fault," she pointed out indignantly.

The man grunted and stood aside, opening the door fully, gesturing to her to come in. Gathering her courage, Grace stepped past him, catching a whiff of fresh air and leather and the tang of shaving soap. She took two steps and froze.

On the left-hand side, a staircase rose to a half landing and then turned to climb across the back wall to a galleried landing that overlooked the hall on three sides. There, halfway up the second flight of stairs, a small face—eyes huge, mouth drooping—peered through the wooden balustrade. Grace's heart lurched.

Clara.

Don't miss
THE GOVERNESS'S SECRET BABY by Janice Preston,
available December 2016 wherever
Harlequin® Historical books and ebooks are sold.

www.Harlequin.com

Love the Harlequin book you just read?

Your opinion matters.

Review this book on your favorite
book site, review site, blog or your own
social media properties and share
your opinion with other readers!

HARLEQUIN®

A *Romance* FOR EVERY MOOD™

JUST CAN'T GET ENOUGH?

Join our social communities
and talk to us online.

You will have access to the latest
news on upcoming titles and special
promotions, but most importantly,
you can talk to other fans about your
favorite Harlequin reads.

Harlequin.com/Community

 Facebook.com/HarlequinBooks

Twitter.com/HarlequinBooks

Pinterest.com/HarlequinBooks

THE WORLD IS BETTER WITH

Romance

Harlequin has everything from contemporary, passionate and heartwarming to suspenseful and inspirational stories.

Whatever your mood,
we have a romance just for you!

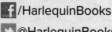

REQUEST YOUR FREE BOOKS!

HARLEQUIN®

HISTORICAL

Where love is timeless

2 FREE NOVELS PLUS 2 FREE GIFTS!

YES! Please send me 2 FREE Harlequin® Historical novels and my 2 FREE gifts (gifts are worth about $10). After receiving them, if I don't wish to receive any more books, I can return the shipping statement marked "cancel." If I don't cancel, I will receive 6 brand-new novels every month and be billed just $5.69 per book in the U.S. or $5.99 per book in Canada. That's a savings of at least 12% off the cover price! It's quite a bargain! Shipping and handling is just 50¢ per book in the U.S. and 75¢ per book in Canada.* I understand that accepting the 2 free books and gifts places me under no obligation to buy anything. I can always return a shipment and cancel at any time. Even if I never buy another book, the two free books and gifts are mine to keep forever.

246/349 HDN GH2Z

Name	(PLEASE PRINT)

Address	Apt. #

City	State/Prov.	Zip/Postal Code

Signature (if under 18, a parent or guardian must sign)

Mail to the **Reader Service:**
IN U.S.A.: P.O. Box 1867, Buffalo, NY 14240-1867
IN CANADA: P.O. Box 609, Fort Erie, Ontario L2A 5X3

Want to try two free books from another line?
Call 1-800-873-8635 or visit www.ReaderService.com.

* Terms and prices subject to change without notice. Prices do not include applicable taxes. Sales tax applicable in N.Y. Canadian residents will be charged applicable taxes. Offer not valid in Quebec. This offer is limited to one order per household. Not valid for current subscribers to Harlequin Historical books. All orders subject to credit approval. Credit or debit balances in a customer's account(s) may be offset by any other outstanding balance owed by or to the customer. Please allow 4 to 6 weeks for delivery. Offer available while quantities last.

Your Privacy—The Reader Service is committed to protecting your privacy. Our Privacy Policy is available online at www.ReaderService.com or upon request from the Reader Service.

We make a portion of our mailing list available to reputable third parties that offer products we believe may interest you. If you prefer that we not exchange your name with third parties, or if you wish to clarify or modify your communication preferences, please visit us at www.ReaderService.com/consumerschoice or write to us at Reader Service Preference Service, P.O. Box 9062, Buffalo, NY 14240-9062. Include your complete name and address.